Dear Manju,
This is my attempt
to capture Punjab
its taste and cul

The
Slim
Punjabi

I would
wait to hear
back from you...

Harmeet Kaur

30th May; 2013
Ph: 9833892753
✉: mail.harmeetk@
gmail.com

Harmeet

The
Slim
Punjabi

AMARYLLIS

AMARYLLIS

This edition first published in 2013

AMARYLLIS

An imprint of Manjul Publishing House Pvt. Ltd.
7/32, Ground Floor,
Ansari Road, Daryaganj, New Delhi - 110 002
Tel: +91 11 2325 8319 / 2325 5558
Fax: +91 11 2325 5557
Email: amaryllis@amaryllis.co.in
Website: www.amaryllis.co.in

Registered Office:
10 Nishant Colony, Bhopal - 462 003

ISBN: 978-93-81506-27-1

Design: seema sethi {design}

Printed and Bound in India by
Thomson Press (India) Ltd.

Bulleh nālon chulhā changā

Jis par tām pakāi dā,

Ral faqeerān majlas keetee,

Bhora bhora khāee dā

❋

The stove is better than you, O' Bulleh Shah,

the one on which food is cooked.

It brings together the holy and the wise

to share their foods and wisdom

A Patiala peg-sized thanks

To Mummy and Papa, for in the whole of this alluring world,
refuge lies where you are

•

To Shunty, for I look forward to a time when we would stay
together again, and play 'Mario' and 'Islander' all day long

•

To Anuj Bahri, my agent, for he made me believe that
I could make it to the bookshelves

•

To everyone at Amaryllis,
for trusting this debut writer

•

And to Dev, for the lovely gift of Bulleh Shah's book. There's a
world out there that we should see

Introduction
Bengaluru: 12 July 2012

It was just a matter of chance. Late one night, while surfing YouTube, I stumbled upon a song that is sung at every wedding in my family:

Madhaniyan...
Hai O' mere daddeya rabba
Kinna jamiya, kinna ne le jaaniya
Loie... Babul tere mehlan vichon teri lado
Pardesan hoi...

I came across many versions of this classic song – one by Musarrat Nazir (a Pakistani actor and singer, who is known for singing wedding songs. Her voice made the song 'Mera Laung Gawacha' a superhit in 1980s); another one by Surinder Kaur (one of the most-prominent Punjabi folk singers, also known as the Nightingale of Punjab. She was the sister of Prakash Kaur, who's also a popular Punjabi folk singer); a different lounge version called 'Punjab'; and numerous others.

So, what hooked me on to this song? Well, I could cite several reasons: it brought alive memories of various family weddings where I had been a part of the traditional ritual of *doli* or *vidai*, a ceremony immediately following nuptials, when the bride's family bids her farewell and she leaves for her husband's home; the mellow tune of the song; the poignant lyrics; and certain other feelings, which you can only experience when you listen to the song in the stillness of the night. Often, that is the time when its meaning becomes more apparent.

Other than the warmth that the tune induced, my mind remained stuck on one word – *madhaniyan*. It took me down memory lane – into my childhood, memories of which don't even cross my mind now.

Coming back to madhaniyan: A *madhani* is a traditional butter churner, still used in many Punjabi homes to make butter from cream. It's a wooden stick attached to a broad circular wooden piece at one end, which has seven to eight equidistant wedges cut out from its circumference. The wedged end is dipped into cream, and the stick is rotated between the palms to churn out the butter. This time-consuming activity is typically called *makkhan ridakna*.

That single word took me back almost twenty years, when I was about six years old and my brother just two. Often in the afternoon my mom would sit on the floor with the *pateela* or *degchi* (pot) of cream and the madhani, churning out white butter that all of us loved. My dad would put it in his dals and on paranthas. My brother, who had just about started walking and didn't know what he ate, was fed with the legendary Punjabi *chitta* (white) makkhan. My mom loved it in her sandwich – fresh white butter spread on a soft slice of bread, sprinkled with sugar.

After churning out the white butter from the cream, my mom would use the residual lassi (literally, buttermilk) to make delicious *kadhi* (a dish prepared using buttermilk, or curd, and gram flour, simmered for long and tempered with spices), which I can only make futile attempts at cooking (that too with set curd that I buy from supermarkets). She would keep aside some butter for fresh consumption, and would make ghee of the remaining, and with the residual of ghee, (little brown lumps called *chhiddi* in Punjabi), she would prepare delicious *panjeeri* (a sweet dish made by dry roasting wheat flour and mixing sugar and chhiddi), which I can't make because I don't get fresh ghee at my home in Bengaluru. Though all this didn't amaze me at that time, but today, I look back and think that hers was, and is, one of the kitchens that have kept Punjabi cuisine alive and kicking. That old madhani still lies in the kitchen of my home in Delhi.

During those growing-up years in Delhi, I failed to take notice of the glamour of food that I was fed daily: It was normal, because eating was an activity that I had to tick off on my 'to-do' list everyday. I used to love eating Chinese, Italian, continental and other western cuisines. During my college years (2003–05), I had even stopped carrying lunch from home; now, in retrospect, I think it must have hurt my mom. I wanted to eat out all the time and failed to realise that whatever I was eating in the canteens of Delhi University colleges was nothing but a Punjabified version of every cuisine.

This reminds me of my visit to the Delhi University campus a few months back to collect a certificate. I cannot even begin to describe my nostalgia, when thirty bucks was still all I spent to relive my food memories of the campus. I visited many college canteens after collecting my certificate just to see what they served. All the famous canteens had started selling Punjabified Chinese and continental food. But the popular items still remained Punjabi and their prices inexpensive – the Irfan and Usman kiosk in the Sri Ram College of Commerce campus sold Masala Maggi for twenty, tea for five, and bread pakora for seven rupees each. The Hindu College canteen sold shahi paneer and naan for thirty-five rupees. The Ramjas College canteen sold tantalisingly spicy rajma chawal, kadhi chawal and chhole chawal. The Gargi College canteen sold rajma chawal and aloo chaat for twenty rupees each. The Lady Sriram College café sold shahi paneer with lachcha parantha for thirty rupees and bread pakora for seven bucks! Kamla Nehru College sold rajma chawal for seventeen rupees. You still don't need a credit card to enjoy some lip-smacking food in college canteens.

The first time my homesick soul cried out was when I was twenty-one. I had recently shifted to Pune to pursue an MBA degree, and my hostel had a fixed time slot for meals in the mess: If you missed that, you stayed hungry. Gosh! Mom wasn't like that. The second time I wept was when I failed to feel that touch of love in my food – and I don't mean the food was terrible. It was better than what an average mess would serve, but it clearly tasted of urgency. Mom wasn't like that either!

Thus began my desperation for *ghar ka khana* or homemade food. It has been more than five years since I have been living away from home. I miss my folks and the uncomplicated ways of life back home. Surprisingly, I have discovered that it is more than just ghar ka khana that I crave for: food for this Punjabi actually transcended beyond her thali. There was another part of my appetite that was not being fed the way it craved for; food that I can just binge on – like phulkas that would be served to me straight from the tawa, kheer that I would desperately wait for to cool in the fridge.... This craving was a new beginning, a newly found realisation of who I am, how simple are the things that gave me pleasure, and how my mom had so much concern for every little thing that I ate.

By the time I completed my MBA and got my first job in Bengaluru in 2008, food was not just a thing that satiated my hunger. It was something that kept me connected to the real me. It kept me connected to my culture, my roots. Till date, whenever I eat dal makhani or butter chicken somewhere other than home, it always takes me back to all the dal makhanis and butter chickens I have eaten at home or at family dinners. I distinctly remember the flavours and textures, just like photographs.

Usually music gets me thinking. A particular song reminds me of my first date, another one of my break-up, yet another one that made me let my hair down, one that fills me with intrigue to know the story behind its lyrics, and one that led me to write this book... But during that time, food had started connecting to me just as much, if not more. It had become more like a tangible asset to my inner self.

Of course, my desire to try new kinds of cuisines would never die.

 I love to taste new dishes, as different tastes seem to touch different parts of my mind. But if you ask me whether they comfort me – my answer is no, they don't. The only food that gives me a refuge-like feeling from hunger pangs is the food that I grew up with – the classic Punjabi cuisine.

As the madhaniyan song still continues to play in a loop on my laptop, myriad memories transport me to the days spent at my ancestral home in Jind, where on seeing buffaloes for the first time, I stood next to them – wearing a pink frilly dress, sporting two long plaits and a smile so big it almost reached my ears – to be photographed.

I remember my grandparents' place in Mohali, where bade papa, my grandfather, had planted a grape vine above the *jhoola* (swing) on iron rods, and the lemon tree in his garden that bears huge, seedless lemons, which he couriers to me in Bengaluru.

I remember my dad teasing and alleging me of being more of a surgeon than a cook, as I used to spend hours cutting vegetables into almost equal-sized cubes. He would then come and tuck a little mustard flower from the *saag* bundle into my hair (In Punjabi 'saag' refers to any leafy bunch of vegetables, e.g., spinach, radish leaves, mustard, etc.) I really do miss the innocence of those times.

I remember the aimless shopping sprees, the *baraats*, the boisterous family get-togethers, eavesdropping on the ladies' conversations on topics that, like the ball in a game of pin-ball, would keep bouncing from their clothes and jewellery, to their husbands and mothers-in-law, their take on local corrupt politicians and sometimes to their collections of cosmetics and lingerie.

I remember my teenage years, when my mother and I used to do *langar sewa* in gurdwara Bangla Sahib in Delhi, where I used to cut onions and sometimes roll chapattis (my highest record being thirty-four, mostly shapeless) amongst a group of other women.

I remember the evening walks in the neighbourhood park, in Rajouri Garden where I stay in Delhi, when I called my mom's friend 'aunty' and she playfully snapped back saying, 'Call me Mrs Ahluwalia and not aunty...!'

I remember my grandfather telling me stories that spoke of the valour and martyrdom of Sikh gurus in a way that had filled me with both pain and pride.

I remember the wintery nights of Delhi, when my friends and I threw barbecue parties on the terrace, where we cooked everything we came across in the kitchen.

Thinking of all this makes me miss home, but it makes me smile too. Behind this midnight veil of homesickness is hidden the Pandora's Box of my memories: that are sunny... robust... and oh so Punjabi!

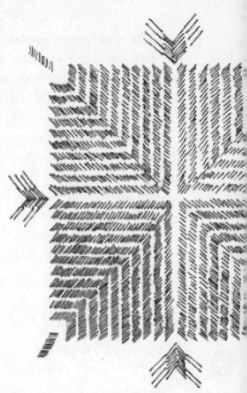

The Slim Punjabi

Let me start by stating a few common myths that surround Punjabis:

1. Punjabi women are bound to become fat after they get married.

2. All Punjabis eventually migrate to either Canada or the UK.

3. Young Punjabi boys join their rich dad's business immediately after school.

4. Chicken and alcohol are Punjabi staples.

5. Punjabis can do bhangra to any song, even *Macarena* and *Coco Jumbo*.

I am sure reading the above so-called myths brought a smile to your face, just as they made me smile while writing them. I won't deny that the word 'Punjab' conjures up images of vast green fields, *sarson da saag te makki di roti* and *dhol* in your mind, because that's what the word conjures up in my mind too. But I would like to differ slightly. Most people would define a Punjabi as somebody who just eats chicken, drinks scotch, works hard, laughs loudly, and flashes his expensive watch and phone. There is much more to a Punjabi than what he may project, or what an onlooker may perceive. There has to be some logic behind why a Punjabi, an upholder of one of the most spoken about and flamboyant culture groups, doesn't attempt to break an onlooker's perception.

Colonel Antoine-Louis-Henri de Polier (1741–95), the first-known European to write about Sikhs, in his manuscript *The Siques* describes them as follows:

> The Siques are in general strong and well made; accustomed from their infancy to the most laborious life and hardest fare; they make marches and undergo fatigues that really appear astonishing. The food of the Siques is of the coarsest kind, and such as the poorest people in Hindustan use from necessity. Bread baked in ashes, and soaked in a mash made of different sorts of pulse, is the best dish, and such as they never indulge in but when at full leisure; otherwise vetches and tares, hastily parched, is all they care for. They abhor smoking tobacco, for what reasons I cannot discover, but intoxicate themselves freely with spirits of their own country manufacture; a cup of the last they never fail taking after a fatigue at night.

Being a Sikh girl born and brought up in Delhi, more than 200 years after Polier wrote *The Siques*, I have seen a very refined and cosmopolitan side of this culture. Though I would be lying if I say that I haven't felt awkward at times. When I used to go for morning walks in track pants, Punjabi aunties wearing crepe salwar-kameezes, diamond bangles and Reebok shoes would look at me with sympathy! At weddings, the women would be decked up in crystal-sequin-loaded saris so densely embroidered that they would almost bedazzle an onlooker. Till date, my elders at home are worried, for they think I am too thin to be healthy. They often tell me, *'Kinni kamzor ho gayi hai!'* ('You've become so weak!') when my BM Index is perfect; but for them no amount of weight is

enough! It is only later that I realised how much I miss this verve when I am away from it.

This book is an outcome of the longing I feel to come back home, of the warmth of sitting on the kitchen slab while my mom cooked, the love of being served food and the slivers of laughter that still tickle me, so much so that I chose to stay alone, only because I wanted a kitchen of my own. Except for my mom's food, I don't think I can relish food cooked by anyone else for days together; I somehow don't feel I belong to that food. Hence, began my love affair with cooking and food.

Since I was sure that I wouldn't hire a cook, and would handle my cooking myself, I wanted my own space where I could experiment, play around, and give shape to my epicurean fantasies. My kitchen is more like an artist's studio, with the reds of apples and blacks of grapes; and it has everything to satiate each and every one of my moods – chocolates for days when I am low; pickles/chutneys for days when I feel numb; sugar-coated cornflakes and popcorn for the phases when I don't feel like doing any cooking; red wine for my celebratory days, juices for times when I am low on energy;

and the aromas of the most exotic spices to challenge my spirit for experimentation.

This book is not about gourmet cooking or fine dining, since I am not an expert in that. Neither is it on diet cooking or about calorie-counted methods to cook, nor one that preaches some secret aspects of Punjabi culture, because neither am I a dietician nor a person knowledgeable enough to comment on culture. This is a practical account of a Punjabi's way of life. By sheer statistical frequency, cuisine takes precedence here because I used to cook everyday, hence gaining some hands-on experience in the art. The recipes featured in the book are for people like me, in their mid-twenties, working and staying away from their homes and somehow *managing* food. The book takes cooking a step ahead in terms of simplicity – almost making it a de-stressing activity. It's a sincere attempt to make bachelors cook, and unwind, and enjoy wholesome Punjabi meals.

My best experiences with Punjabi cuisine have been in the dhabas with my gang of friends. The food that we order is nothing extraordinary; just that it's overdone with ghee and *tadka* (tempering), that gives it a tantalising effect. Dhabas don't use microwaves or hot plates, so the fire of the tandoor gives the food that extra zing. The smoke of charcoal wrapped in the aroma of the food being prepared, the glossy vegetables, the bonhomie in the atmosphere, and the warmth in the eyes of the cook while serving the food that almost blankets the chill of the night…well, all this is never on the menu and is definitely extraordinary!

Like any other cultural group, Punjabi culture too is influenced deeply by its primary occupation, geography and religious beliefs. That's what gives bhangra its typical moves (which actually replicate farming activities), phulkari its original colours (yellow, white, green and red), and the cuisine its richness (to have a fulfilling diet for a day's work in the fields). Leaving the exotic flavour of the spices aside, another critical element that gives this cuisine a character of its own is the way fire is used. The use of tandoors, charcoal fires, *kadhais* and *tawas* impart a flavour to the dishes, which goes beyond the ingredients used.

So what if Punjabis are usually plump (I love to call them 'prosperous' in health!)? It's almost impossible to match the *nakhra* (playful fussiness) and the *tor* (swagger) of a *mutiyar* (a young Punjabi girl), as well as the *josh* (enthusiasm) and the joie de vivre of a *gabru* (a young robust Punjabi guy).

Let me end by stating a few *realities* about Punjabis:

1. Punjabis love to nick name their children 'Goldy' and 'Pinky'.

2. They have a *chak de phatte* attitude towards everything – shopping, eating, drinking, partying, and even lovemaking.

3. At any given time, a sardar knows more sardar jokes than anyone else.

4. Punjabis can definitely do bhangra to any song, even *Macarena* and *Coco Jumbo*.

This book is a love story of a Punjabi and her food, when the food not only satiated her tummy but also pampered her senses.

Cheers,

The Slim Punjabi

Contents

One

Jhelum (Sanskrit: Vitastā)

The staple foods; Punjabi music and dance

The *Rig Veda* is replete with the mention of *Sapta-Sindhu*, the seven transcendental rivers, with Vitastā being one of them. Locally known as Veth, this river embraces Punjab in the Jhelum district, though under the Indus Waters Treaty (1960), the waters of Jhelum belong to Pakistan.

Of the many mythical stories that surround this river, the most well-known is the one that dates back to the days when Kashmir was called *Sati-Desh* (*sati* – truth, *desh* – country or land), after *Sati* (or Uma or Dakshayani), the first consort of Lord Shiva.

Within a lake in the valley called Satisaras (Lake of Sati), lived a demon named Jalodbhava. To destroy him Lord Vishnu struck the mountain at Varamahula (present day Baramulla), thus making a hole through the hills to drain the lake thereby killing Jalodbhava. It is said that Uma entered the lake, bringing its water out through the holes to flow down as streams. Three such streams, namely, Arapath, Brengi and Sandran, confluenced together to give birth to River Veth (Jhelum).

Mughal folklore reflects the fondness of Emperor Jahangir for this river. In his memoirs *Tuzk-e-Jahagiri,* he calls this river 'Behat', and mentions its source to be Verinag in Kashmir. He mentions its water to be so limpid that even a grain of *khus* (poppy) could be seen through it. The spring was originally circular in shape, which he later got changed into an octagon, a characteristic of Mughal architecture.

The river holds a prominent place in Greek folklore as well. God Hydaspes, born to Thaumas (the god of the sea) and Electra (the sea nymph) was brother to Iris (the goddess of rainbows) and the three harpies – Aello, Celaeno and Ocypete. Whether the god was named after the river or vice versa remains an issue of debate. The battle fought in 326 BC between Alexander the Great and Pururava (Greek: Porus), king of the ancient state of Paurava situated between the rivers Jhelum and Chenab (Hydaspes and Acesines), has been recorded in history as the Battle of Hydaspes.

The recipes in this section comprise the staple dishes in Punjabi cuisine. Being the most frequently made dishes, they hold a certain legacy in Punjabi kitchens, a legacy that is lived through every day. The fondness for these dishes is evident by the fact that a Punjabi will travel the world over, eat the most interesting of international cuisines and drink the most exotic of wines, but would feel satisfied only after having *aloo ka parantha* and *dahi* for breakfast, and *baigan ka bharta* or *aloo gobhi* for dinner.

Apart from cuisine, there is another facet of this culture which is a staple: music and dance. Punjabis love to celebrate, not just the traditional ceremonies and festivals but also smaller occasions. I have seen my cousins celebrate weird days: the day one of them returned home after a dressing down he received at school; the day someone spotlessly cleaned up his room; or the day someone made a high score while playing a video game. In my neighbourhood in Rajouri Garden, whenever India won a cricket match, a dhol-wala was especially called so that residents could celebrate the victory with some bhangra. The vivaciousness of celebration was so infectious … the entire street would come alive.

Punjabis love to sing and dance together; it's their way of showing warmth and camaraderie. Punjabi music has penetrated way beyond geographies and demographics of music lovers. I am surprised (and proud) when I hear Punjabi music being played in stores selling international designer labels and food. Many of us might laugh at its flamboyance, but we cannot deny the fact that it does give us a sense of belonging.

The fine arts of Punjab largely include music, painting, literature and architecture. The minor arts include handiwork of master craftsmen and skilled workers, which include designs on cloth, wood, ivory, bone and metal. Art forms an essential pillar of any culture because of a very simple reason: It appeals to the aesthetic sensibilities.

On the one hand, Punjabi music is boisterous and foot-tapping, while on the other, it has a lot of spiritual connect blended with mysticism. Where it creates the magic of camaraderie, it also creates an enigma of escape from the materialistic world and creates a liberating aura of enchantment. Sufism has a considerable influence on Punjabi music. Sufi mystic poets like Bulleh Shah, Waris Shah, Baba Farid and several others have written poetry and literature that has been sung by legendary singers like Alam

Lohar, Kuldeep Manak, Reshma, Shazia Manzoor to name just a few, giving Punjabi music a rich heritage of melody.

Both food and music are outcomes of emotions, both are meant to be tasted; both can be served to others, as well as enjoyed in solitude. When the heart is saturated with some emotions like love, longing, pain or desire, a song is created. And sometimes, a dish in the kitchen...!

Rajma Chawal

Rajma Chawal (red kidney beans and rice) is the ubiquitous Sunday lunch for Punjabis. The dish is also called *motthi chawal*. What is interesting about this dish is that no two households can ever end up preparing rajma with identical taste – everybody has a different style, which is what makes this dish simply brilliant. Having said that, below is my recipe for this dish: my claim to fame amongst my friends!

Ingredients (serves 2)

Oil: 2 tsps
Zeera (whole): ½ tsp
Cinnamon: 1" stick
Bay leaves: 3 nos.
Onion, chopped: 1 medium
Green chillies, slit: 2 nos.
Ginger-garlic paste: 1 tbsp
Tomato, chopped: 1 medium
Salt: as per taste
Red chilli powder: as per taste
Haldi (turmeric) powder: ½ tsp
Zeera (cumin) powder: ½ tsp

Dhania (coriander) powder: ½ tsp
Rajma, soaked overnight: 1 cup (soak the rajma in double the amount of water as the beans swell up)
Water: 6 cups
Coriander leaves, chopped: a few sprigs for garnish

Cooking

In a pressure cooker, heat oil on medium flame. Once heated, add whole zeera, cinnamon and bay leaves. After they sputter, add onions, green chillies and ginger-garlic paste. Stir fry till onions turn golden brown. Then add tomatoes and stir fry till they soften a bit. Add salt, red chilli powder, haldi powder, zeera powder and dhania powder and stir fry for a minute. Now add the soaked rajma, six cups of water, and fasten the lid of the pressure cooker. After the first whistle, lower the flame and let it cook for thirty minutes. Open the lid once the steam has been reduced. Slightly mash some of the rajma against the walls of the pressure cooker, to thicken the consistency of the gravy. However, you can add more water if you like it a bit watery; and for a thicker gravy, let it simmer for some time.

Garnish with coriander leaves. And serve hot with either steamed or zeera rice!

Bhangra & Gidda

My colleague from South India claps his hands, shouts an energetic *'Oye Hoye!'* and tops it with a quick bhangra move whenever he finishes a task at hand. He would instantly turn towards me to know if he is doing it right. Sometimes he would ask me the meaning of the lyrics of random Punjabi songs. Both music and dance have found an enthusiast in my colleague; language and culture take the back seat here. Bhangra, the key dancing style of Punjab, needs no introduction. Almost everybody can manage to perform a step or two. It's a dance that is performed at nearly all Indian weddings.

At a typical Punjabi wedding, bhangra is more than the leg-shaking that people do to the music played by the DJ. It's an emotion, and expression of energy and vivaciousness of Punjabis. Often, the dhol-wala takes centre stage. Forming a large circle, the people start dancing around, so that during the performance others can join in the circle from time to time. The elderly and the shy ones are dragged in jovially. As the dhol-wala plays the rhythmic beats, every now and then he gives signals to the dancers to fasten their steps. (As I write this, there is *chaukdi* playing in my mind... a chaukdi is a particular sequence of dhol beats, which one can dance energetically to. Its popularity reflects in the fact that it's the first sequence every dhol-wala learns, because he knows he's got to play that at every wedding!) The dancers whirl around with energetic steps – stomping and clapping in a synchronised manner. A short pause in the dancing, and a *boli* (a couplet from a traditional Punjabi folk song) is recited in fine rhythm after brief pauses in the dance:

Bari barsi khatan gaya si, khat ke le āndā ghyo,
Bhangra tān sajdā je nache munde dā pyo...

(Whatever you have earned in exchange for your crop,
buy some ghee from it,
The bhangra will be more vivacious,
if the groom's father joins in and dances.)

Following this, the dance resumes once again, and the mentioned family member (here, the father of the groom) joins in or is playfully pulled in, if he resists.

Bhangra lyrics sometimes compromise on meaning just to accommodate rhythm and humour; but usually they comprise various hues of relationships, such as youth and marriage. There are numerous songs dedicated to heroes, pride and philosophy as well. More frothy topics include beautiful girls, their swaying walk, and colourful dupattas, and handsome, robust men, who are intoxicated with love as well as alcohol.

Traditionally, bhangra was performed by the farmers of Punjab to celebrate the harvest, and at times also to describe village life while working in the fields. It commenced with the sowing of wheat and concluded with Baisakhi (the harvest festival of Punjab, celebrated on 13 April every year). The energy and vigour of this dance also reflects the feelings that were a result of seeing a healthy crop. A lot of energetic stunts have been incorporated in the dance; the most popular stunt being the *mor* (peacock), in which one dancer sits on another's shoulders, while the third person hangs from his torso by his legs. Two-person towers, pyramids, and various spinning stunts are also performed.

The female version of bhangra is called *gidda*. Punjabi women love to sing and dance, and they perform this lively dance on festive and social occasions, especially weddings. In Malwa, the gidda performed during weddings is called *viyahula gidda*.

It is customary in Punjab to celebrate the festival of Teeyan in the month of sawan (spring). This festival starts on the third lunar day in the month and lasts till full moon day. Fairs are held at many places, *jhoolas* (swings) are hung from the trees, and girls dance to their heart's content. At such times, gidda is performed under a peepal or a banyan tree, and is known as *teeyan gidda.* The following lines from a song depict the scene beautifully:

Dhan bhag mera, peepal akhe;
Kurian ne pingan paaian.
Sawan vich kurian ne
Pinghan asman charahian.

('How blessed am I,' says the peepal tree
that the girls have hung swings from my branches
on which, in the month of spring,
girls go as high as the sky.)

The rainy season too, in a way, is the season of gidda because the rain and the dark clouds inspire the girls to dance out their pent-up feelings and desires. Gidda is not performed according to any cut-and-dry rule, but the harmony of beats is like a disciplinary essence in its movements. Girls performing this dance indicate through gestures the various activities in the life of a Punjabi woman in a village like spinning cotton, fetching water from the well, grinding, etc. Whatever they portray, they sing it with an appropriate boli. Mimicry is also very popular in this dance. Women love to dramatise and mimic their relatives, like *saas* (mother-in-law), *nanad* (sister-in-law), *devar* (younger brother-in-law), *jeth-jethani* (jeth–elder brother-in-law, jethani–his wife), etc. All this gives women a chance to express themselves without any inhibitions.

Like bhangra, gidda too is performed in a circle, with girls dancing in circles and waving their arms and wrists. Every now and then, one girl comes forward and recites a boli, while the others clap, which forms an essential part of the rhythm. The subject of the boli can vary from an argument with the mother-in-law to any social affair, and the lyrics are usually satirical. Towards the end of the boli, the other girls pick up and join in the singing, with two girls dancing in the centre of the circle (called *ghera*). Their heavily embroidered dupattas and ornate jewellery makes this dance a visual delight; whereas the dholki beats, the active dance moves, and the clapping create a mesmerising atmosphere.

Bhangra is not just a dance form; it is a genre in itself, which not only includes Punjabi pop, rap, hip-hop, reggae and drum-n-bass, but also the dance, which has, acquired various styles from different regions of Punjab, such as Luddi, Jhumar, Dankārā and Dhamāl (described later, under 'Some more Folk Dances'). All these styles are now collectively known as bhangra. Over the years, bhangra has become an international rage, popularised mainly by Sikhs living in England and Canada. Artists like Jazzy B, Punjabi MC, Lehmber Hussainpuri and others have given it a facelift by marketing this genre in a glitzy manner.

Baigan ka Bharta

There's a very interesting description of baigan (aubergine) in colloquial Punjabi:

Bahron aaye malang, harian topian udde rang!

'Some happy-go-luckies came from outside, wearing green caps but purpled faces.'

It took me almost six months to get this one right; I even ended up burning my finger once. And one day my perseverance paid off – I could finally roast the baigan perfectly enough to get that typical smoky flavour. I used to savour baigan ka bharta in dhabas; I loved its silky texture, charcoal-smoke flavour and its glossy look. If I have to describe the benchmark for my flavour preference, I would rather have the baigan slowly roasted on an angeethi and then tempered with other ingredients. It's just brilliant, and it inspires me to try getting close to perfection in my kitchen – as this dish only gets better with practice!

Ingredients (serves 2)

Oil: 4 tsps
Zeera (whole): 1 tsp
Bay leaves: 2 to 3 nos.
Onion, coarsely chopped: 1 large
Green chillies, chopped: 2 nos.
Ginger: 1" piece, pounded
Garlic: 4 to 5 flakes, pounded
Tomato, coarsely chopped: 1 large
Brinjal, roasted: 1 medium sized
Salt: as per taste

Haldi powder: a pinch
Red chilli powder: as per taste
Dhania powder: ¼ tsp
Zeera powder: ¼ tsp
Coriander leaves, chopped: a few sprigs for garnishing

Roasting the brinjal

The biggest hurdle for a beginner, and a challenge for even the most-seasoned cooks is roasting the brinjal – you might just end up burning the vegetable or your fingers. So here is the trick: lightly grease the brinjal with cooking oil before roasting it (this is to make peeling easier; the amount of oil should be as little as two to three drops). Then with a knife dig inside the brinjal from top, reaching four to five inches inside the vegetable. This way, you would have a firm grip on it, and you can rotate it easily over the gas flame. Roast it until the skin cracks from many places. To check if it's done, gently move the knife; you should be able to feel the soft pulp inside and a distinct smoky aroma flooding your kitchen.

(Once you master the art of roasting the brinjal, you can even go a step ahead and insert garlic flakes and cloves inside the raw vegetable, and then roast it.)

Once roasted, DO NOT dip it in water to peel off the skin. This just takes all the juices and flavours away. Instead, keep the brinjal on a plate, remove the knife, and keep a bowl of water ready. Dip your fingers in the water, and peel off the skin gently, which would come off easily. Keep cleaning your fingers by dipping them in water every now and then. Once completely peeled, keep it aside.

Cooking

Place a kadhai on medium flame, and put four teaspoons of

oil into it. When heated, add whole zeera and bay leaves. Once they start sputtering, add chopped onions, chopped green chillies, pounded ginger and garlic, and stir fry till the onions become light golden. Add the chopped tomatoes and the roasted brinjal together. Stir fry the whole mixture until the tomatoes and brinjal are mashed. Then add salt, haldi powder, red chilli powder, dhania powder and zeera powder and mix well. Cover the kadhai and simmer for five minutes. Keep it covered till the time you eat or serve.

Garnish with coriander leaves and serve with phulkas or paranthas.

TWIST: At the time you add the brinjal, you can also add some parboiled peas. Not only does that give a lovely colour to the dish, but also enhances the taste.

As a teenager, I often used to hear my *nanaji* (maternal grandfather) quote Bulleh Shah while talking to my parents. It never made any sense to me, until the day I developed some interest in knowing about the mystic and philosophical side of Punjabi culture.

Abdullah Shah (1680–1758), popularly called Sāin or Baba Bulleh Shah, the greatest mystic poet of this region, was born in Uch, Bahawalpur, Punjab (now in Pakistan). He was a contemporary of Guru Gobind Singh, the tenth guru of the Sikhs, and paid a great tribute to the guru thus:

'I neither speak of the past; nor do I speak of the future; but I talk of the time of Guru Gobind Singh and declare openly: "That but for him all the Hindus would have been converted to a foreign culture and religion".'

As a child he mastered just 'Alif', the first letter in Arabic, whereas his classmates advanced in classes. After being taken out of school, he left home to discover the manifestation of 'Alif' in everything around him: trees, flowers, insects, mountains, himself and others. He thought of only one. The following song written by him, called 'Ek Alif', communicates the same philosophy – of true knowledge being lost by pursuing the false.

Parh parh ilm te faazil hoya
Te kaday apnay aap nu parhya naee
Bhaj bhaj wadna ay mandir maseeti
Te kaday mann apnay wich wadya naee
Larna ay roz shaitaan de naal
Te kadi nafs apnay naal larya naee
Bulleh Shah asmaani ud-deya pharonda ay
Te jera ghar betha unoon pharya naee
Bas kareen o yaar
Ilm-oun bas kareen o yaar
Ek Alif teray darkaar

(You studied books to become a scholar,
But you never attempted to read or study yourself.
You run to enter the places of worship, the temples and the mosques,
But you haven't stepped inside your own heart.
You are prompt to fight with Satan,
But you haven't yet won your own pride.
Bulleh Shah, you try to hold the high skies
But you don't attempt to hold the thing that resides within you.
Stop the race, my friend
Quit seeking all this knowledge, my friend,
It's only an Alif that you need)

Chholiye ki Sabzi

Chholiya is green in colour – a smaller version of black chhole. The *asli* (real) chholiya is sold in a bush-like bunch, where you have to pluck open the pods one by one, and take out the chholiya. It's so fresh and juicy when had raw, and can be mixed in salads too. Nowadays, chholiya is sold in markets; even grocery stores sell it in packets (already plucked out). For many of us it proves to be a time saver – however, plucking fresh chholiya from the bunch is a different experience altogether!

Ingredients (serves 2)

Oil: 2 tsps
Zeera (whole): ½ tsp
Cinnamon: 1" stick
Bay leaves: 3 nos.
Onion, chopped: 1 medium
Green chillies, slit: 2 nos.
Ginger-garlic paste: 1 tbsp
Tomato, chopped: 1 medium
Salt: as per taste
Red chilli powder: as per taste
Haldi powder: ½ tsp
Zeera powder: ½ tsp
Dhania powder: ½ tsp
Chholiya, washed: 250 gms
Water: ¾ cup
Coriander leaves, chopped: a few sprigs for garnishing
Ginger, julienned: a few for garnishing

Cooking

In a pressure cooker, heat the oil on medium flame. Once heated, add whole zeera, cinnamon and bay leaves. After they begin to sputter, add the onions, green chillies and ginger-garlic paste. Stir fry till the onions turn golden brown. Then add the tomatoes and stir fry till they soften. Add salt, red chilli powder, haldi powder, zeera powder and dhania powder and stir fry for a minute. Now add the chholiya, and ¾ cup of water. After the first whistle, simmer and cook for five to six minutes.

Open the lid of the cooker once the steam escapes, and stir fry the chholiya for a bit. Let some of the water evaporate; it tastes best when kept slightly juicy.

Garnish with coriander and julienned ginger. Serve hot with phulkas, paranthas or steamed rice.

Aloo Gobhi

Back home, I used to wait for winters so that *phoolgobhi* (cauliflower) would be available in the markets. Now all vegetables are available throughout the year – frozen and packed. I hate to see cauliflower cut and cling-wrapped in hypermarkets, because for me half the fun lay in cutting a big flower into florets, munching a little in the process, and sometimes finding a big fat green worm within. This dish is very dear to me, as it was one of the most frequently prepared dishes at home.

Ingredients (serves 2-3)

Potato, diced into half-inch pieces: 1 large
Cauliflower, cut into florets: 1 medium
Oil: 2 tsps
Zeera (whole): 1 tsp
Dhania seeds (slightly pounded to break them): 1 tsp
Onion, chopped: 1 large
Green Chillies, chopped: 2 nos.
Ginger-garlic paste: 1 tbsp
Tomato, chopped: 2 medium
Ginger, julienned: 1" stick
Salt: as per taste
Red chilli powder: as per taste
Haldi powder: ½ tsp
Dhania powder: ½ tsp
Zeera powder: ½ tsp
Coriander leaves, chopped: a few sprigs for garnishing
Ginger, julienned: a few for garnishing

Cooking

In a deep vessel, parboil the potatoes for five minutes. Add the cauliflower and boil for another two minutes. Drain the vegetables and keep aside.

In a kadhai, heat the oil on a medium flame. When heated, add whole zeera and pounded dhania seeds. Once they start sputtering, add chopped onions, green chillies, ginger-garlic paste and stir fry till onions turn brown. Add the chopped tomatoes and stir fry the whole mixture till the tomatoes are mashed. Then add the boiled vegetables, julienned ginger and salt, red chilli powder, haldi powder, dhania powder and zeera powder, and mix well. Cover the kadhai and cook for fifteen minutes with the gas on low flame. Leave it covered till the time you eat or serve.

Garnish with coriander leaves and some julienned ginger. Serve hot with phulkas or paranthas.

I think I am the only woman in my huge family who can't perform a *kirtan*. My grandmother fears this may become a hurdle in marrying me off, as more often than not, a young girl is expected to know this art. All the girls who have become a part of my family as daughters-in-law have proved their mettle in this art and further reinforced her fear. To top it, the pitiable singer that I am, I don't think I can ever sit down and please the *sangat* (congregation). However, this doesn't take away the fact that I enjoy being a part of the audience. I love to listen to the *shabad kirtan* in gurdwaras. I often get carried away by the voices and the aura of peace and *sahaj* (bliss) that the *rāgis* (musicians who perform the kirtan) create.

Well, for those who haven't been part of a kirtan, it is the sacred music of the Sikhs, which involves melodious singing of praises of the god. The Sikh gurus used the Indian classical ragas in their sacred compositions; these are known as shabads. In addition to thirty-one classical ragas, they also used *dhunis* (tunes) of Punjabi folk music, which were popular in those times. They also popularised instruments like rabāb and sārangi, along with percussions of dholak, mridang, dhādh and khartāl.

As per Sikh *rahat maryādā* (mannerisms or code of conduct), this performance of singing hymns is called shabad kirtan. The *chowkies* (music sessions) at the Golden Temple in Amritsar in Punjab set the model of kirtan at *takhts* (thrones). A typical shabad kirtan is done in a trio, where one rāgi plays the harmonium, another plays the tabla and the third one generally plays a string instrument.

My favourite shabad is *mitti dhund jag chānan hoya* (literally, the fog disappears to reveal a brighter world), for its perennial relevance to all my moods.

Kale (Black) Chhole

Kale chhole (black gram) remind me of the last day of Navratris (a Hindu festival of nine nights that celebrates and worships the nine forms of Shakti or Devi), when my neighbours used to invite me home and give me prasad, that comprised poori, halwa and kale chhole. (On the eighth day of the Navratris, known as Ashtami, young girls traditionally called 'kanjaks' are worshipped. The ladies typically invite eight to nine young girls from the neighbourhood to their homes, wash their feet, tie *mouli* or the red holy thread on their wrists, put a vermillion mark on their foreheads, and offer prasad.) They also remind me of my regular gurdwara visits as a kid with my parents, where on Saturdays dry kale chhole are distributed as prasad by many families. In my kitchen, I make them dry or as a chaat or salad, though with gravy, they make a lovely main course dish too.

Common Ingredients for all versions (serves 2):
Kale chhole: 1 cup (soaked overnight)
Water: 6 cups
Salt as per taste

Common cooking step for all versions:

Boil the kale chhole in a pressure cooker, with six cups of water and a little salt for forty minutes (post the first whistle, when the flame is simmered). Don't throw away the dark brown water, you can use it for the gravy, and in case you are making the dry version, you can have it like a broth (with a little salt, black pepper and a dash of lemon juice). It's extremely nutritious due to its high iron content.

GRAVY VERSION

Ingredients

Oil: 2 tsps
Zeera (whole): 1 tsp
Onion, finely chopped: 1 medium
Green chillies, slit: as per taste
Ginger-garlic paste: 1 tbsp
Tomato, finely chopped: 1 large
Turmeric: ½ tsp
Zeera powder: ¼ tsp
Dhania powder: ¼ tsp
Salt: as per taste
Coriander leaves, chopped: a few sprigs for garnishing

Cooking

Heat oil in a kadhai placed on a medium flame. When heated, add whole zeera. Then add chopped onions and slit green chillies and stir fry till onions become light golden. To this add the ginger-garlic paste and stir fry for a minute. Now add chopped tomatoes, haldi powder, zeera powder and dhania powder, and stir fry the whole mixture until the tomatoes are mashed. Add the boiled kale chhole, and the drained broth. Add salt, cover and let it cook for ten minutes on simmer. Leave it covered till the time you eat or serve, so that the flavours seep into the chhole.

Garnish with coriander leaves. Tastes best with either steamed rice or zeera rice.

DRY VERSION

Ingredients

Oil: 2 tsps
Zeera (whole): 1 tsp

Water: ½ cup
Amchoor: ¼ tsp
Zeera powder: 1 tsp
Dhania powder: 1 tsp
Salt: as per taste
Coriander leaves, chopped: a few sprigs for garnishing
Juice of 1 lemon to squeeze in just before serving

Cooking

Strain the boiled chhole from the dark brown water. Keep aside.

Heat oil in a kadhai placed on medium flame. When heated, add zeera. Once they sputter, add chhole and about half a cup of water. Add all the spices and mix well. Stir fry till the water evaporates. Don't overdo the cooking as this would make the chhole hard. Again, leave it covered till the time you eat or serve, so that the flavours seep into the chhole and the chhole remain soft.

Garnish with coriander leaves, add a dash of lemon juice, and serve with phulkas or paranthas.

CHAAT VERSION

Ingredients

Oil: 2 tsps
Zeera (whole): 1 tsp
Zeera powder: 1 tsp
Dhania powder: 1 tsp
Salt: as per taste
Onion, finely chopped:1 medium
Tomato, finely chopped: 1 large
Green chillies, chopped: as per taste
Chaat masala: 1 tsp

Juice of 1 lemon to squeeze in before serving
Coriander leaves, chopped: a few sprigs for garnish

Cooking

Cook the chhole as per the dry version (without the amchoor and water). Once done, add chopped onions, tomatoes and chillies. Add chaat masala and lemon juice, and mix well. Garnish with chopped coriander.

Matar Paneer

Punjabis love paneer (cottage cheese)! They consider it to be a substitute for chicken. Can't blame them, paneer is quite rich in protein, a source for vegetarian Punjabis (however sparse they may be!). I know of a shop in Karol Bagh in Delhi that sells masala paneer, which is prepared by adding chopped ginger, coriander and zeera to the paneer before setting it – needless to say, I am extremely fond of it. Coming back to the dish, it is pretty simple to make. You can't experiment much with it, because the ingredients are simple, yet you can do a lot with it by experimenting with the flavours of spices you use, or with the consistency of its gravy.

Ingredients (serves 2)

Oil: 2 tsps
Zeera (whole): 1 tsp
Onion, finely chopped: 1 large
Green chillies, finely chopped: 2 nos.
Ginger-garlic paste: 1 tbsp
Peas: 1 cup
Tomato: 100 ml puree (for gravy), or 1 medium chopped (for dry)

Salt: as per taste
Red chilli powder: as per taste
Haldi powder: ¼ tsp
Dhania powder: ½ tsp
Zeera powder: ½ tsp
Paneer, cut in half inch cubes: 200 gms
Fresh cream: for garnishing (gravy version)
Coriander leaves, chopped: a few sprigs for garnishing

GRAVY VERSION

Cooking

Heat oil in a kadhai placed on medium flame. When heated, add whole zeera. To this add chopped onions, chopped green chillies, ginger-garlic paste and stir fry till onions become brown. Add the peas, and stir fry for two minutes, i.e., till their skins swell. Add the tomato puree and salt, red chilli powder, haldi powder, dhania powder and zeera powder, and stir fry the mixture for fifteen minutes or till the oil separates. Now add the paneer and mix gently. Cook for five to seven minutes. Cover the kadhai and cook for two minutes on low flame. Leave it covered till the time you decide to eat or serve.

While serving, spoon in some cream along with chopped coriander. Serve hot with phulkas, paranthas, or rice.

DRY VERSION

Cooking

Same as above, just add chopped tomatoes instead of puree, and stir fry till they mash.

Garnish with coriander and serve hot with phulkas or paranthas.

The Instruments

Every musical instrument has a specific emotion attached to it, and it sounds best when used to express that particular emotion. Such is the case with Punjabi music, where certain instruments are used for hymns, some for ballads, others for dance and some for folk songs.

Technically, there are five categories of Punjabi musical instruments:

1. Stringed instruments like rabab, tumba and sārangi
2. Metal instruments like cymbals and chimta
3. Wind instruments like flute, harmonium and algoza
4. Leather instruments like tabla, dholak, dhol and dhādh
5. Earthen instruments like matka

Usually young boys in a Punjabi family are adept at playing the dhol. A dhol is in fact a primary instrument, which is extensively used to set the mood for dancing at festivals and celebrations.

The *dhol* is a high bass, huge barrel-shaped wooden drum with skin mounted and tightened at a different pitch on both sides. The width of this drum is typically fifteen inches. It is played with two different types of wooden sticks – the 'bass' stick, which is called *daggah* (stick made of heavier wood, bent at the playing end), and the 'treble' stick called *tilli* (thinner, made with a flexible material like cane). The drummer is called *dholi* or *bharaj*, and the dhol is strung over his neck using a thick strap.

A *gharah* or *matka* is a simple earthen pitcher and is a key instrument in many folk songs and ballads like *Heer*. To play the gharah, the sides are struck with rings worn on fingers of one hand, and its open mouth is played with the other hand. Since it is hollow, it produces a distinct rhythmic beat.

Another interesting instrument is the *dhādh*, a small percussion instrument of the *damru* style. (A damru is an hourglass-shaped, two-headed drum with two brass resonators tied to its centre with a thread. When shaken, the resonators strike the membrane on either side to produce beats. The damru is strongly associated with Lord Shiva and his performance of the cosmic dance of Tandava.) However, the dhādh differs slightly from the damru as it is a hand drum, played by beating on the mounted skins on either side, each skin tightened at a different pitch.

In olden times, singers used to sing *vārs* (Punjabi ballads) accompanied by beats on the *dhādh*. Such people were called dhādhis (bards). Guru Nanak and Guru Ramdas (the first and fourth of the Sikh gurus, respectively) called themselves dhādhis of god, who were chosen to sing divine praises and make others do the same. The dhādhi musicians were encouraged by Guru Hargobind, the sixth Sikh guru, because they sang vārs recounting the heroic deeds of old warriors to inspire Sikhs with courage. Even today dhādh-sārangi players are very popular in Punjab.

A *chimtā* is a tong-like instrument that consists of two long, flat pieces of iron with pointed ends, and seven pairs of metallic jingles mounted on it. The joint is held in one hand, while the two parts are struck against each other to produce a chiming sound. Arif Lohar, the famous Punjabi folk singer from Pakistan, accompanies his songs with this instrument.

The tradition of chimtā goes back to the *nāths* or *jogis*. The nāths were considered to be wizards who had complete mastery over respiration and other bodily functions; they were believed to have the ability to cause rain or drought, control wild animals, serpents, scorpions, ants and insects, ride tigers and transform themselves into any shape at will.

Guru Nanak's Muslim companion, Mardana was an expert at playing the *rabāb*. Guru Nanak would sing, while Mardana would play the instrument. Being one of the oldest and first stringed instruments used in Central Asia, the rabāb is suited for devotional music and is very popular with the *mirasis* or professional kirtan singers.

The rabāb has a piece of hollow wood at the top and a hollow, circular wooden belly covered with sheepskin at the bottom. It has two bridges, one in the middle and the other at the tip. Usually it has six strings, which are manipulated by six pegs at the top. Some rabābs have four or five frets made of gut tied around the finger board, while others have a wooden *tumba* (gourd) at the top. It is played with a *mizrab* (a wooden plectrum), and produces a pleasing effect.

A difficult instrument to master, the tumba is an *iktara*, a single-string instrument, made famous by Punjabi folk singers like Chamkila and Kuldip Manak. The string is struck with the forefinger or sometimes with the mizrab, and the *swaras* (notes) are made by pressing the string to the stick. Many legendary songs have been characterised by the tumba's typical high note sound.

Another instrument popularised mainly by folk singers is the *algoza,* which consists of a pair of wooden flutes, also called *jodi* (a pair), and is played by using only three fingers on each side. Folk artistes use this in their traditional singing of folk songs like 'Mirza', 'Chhalla', 'Jugni', etc. The instrument is also used as an accompaniment with folk dances.

An extremely popular wind instrument, used especially for kirtans, is the *harmonium*. It is also called 'sound box' as it is a reed-blown instrument like a big harmonica with leather bellows and a keyboard. When the keys are touched and bellows inflated, the air passes through the inner reeds and produces twelve tempered swaras. It is used for both vocal and instrumental music, though many classical singers shun its use because its sound does not exactly match with the human voice, since the notes are fixed.

A stringed instrument like the *sārangi* is considered a better accompaniment.

The word sārangi is derived from the Hindi words *sau* meaning hundred and *rang* meaning colour, thus implying that the music produced by the instrument has the exuberance of a hundred colours. One of the most famous players of the sārangi was Abdulla, a Muslim musician who played in the company of Nātha (a dhādh player) in the court of Guru Hargobind.

Sārangi is a multi-string instrument, played either by itself or as an accompaniment to vocal music. It is held in a vertical position and played with a bow. It can almost replicate the vocal nuances of *gamaka* (shakes) and *meend* (sliding movements). The body of the sārangi is cut from a single log of teak wood, and the lower part is covered with skin. Generally there are three strings made of cat gut, which are controlled by an equal number of pegs on the upper parts of the instrument. Some sārangis also have a few subsidiary strings under the main three strings.

Bhatts and dhādhis, the roving spiritual minstrels, are usually accompanied by instrumentalists, who carry folk instruments such as algoza, iktārā and dhādh sārangi. These instruments add a lot of charm to their ballad recitals.

Usually things we cannot do, or we are not good at, intrigue us all the more. Similar is the case with musical instruments and me. In spite of my ardent love for music, I cannot play even a single instrument. I was initiated into learning the violin some time back, but I don't seem to have made any substantial progress.

Aloo Matar

I hold this dish very close to my heart because it is my younger brother's favourite. This is one thing he can eat thrice a day. Whenever I make aloo matar, it reminds me of the simplicity, the innocence and the mischief of the close bond I share with him. Whenever he visits me, this is a definite presence on our menu!

Ingredients (serves 2)

Oil: 2 tsps
Zeera (whole): 1 tsp
Onion, finely chopped: 1 large
Green chillies, finely chopped: 2 nos.
Ginger-garlic paste: 1 tbsp
Peas: 1 cup
Tomato: 100 ml puree (for gravy) or 1 medium chopped (for dry)
Salt: as per taste
Red chilli powder: as per taste
Haldi powder: ¼ tsp
Dhania powder: ½ tsp
Zeera powder: ½ tsp
Potatoes, diced and parboiled for five minutes: 2 medium
Coriander, chopped: a few sprigs for garnishing

GRAVY VERSION

Cooking

Place a kadhai on medium flame. Add the oil and when heated, add whole zeera. When it begins to sputter, add chopped onions, chopped green chillies, ginger-garlic paste and stir fry till onions become brown. Add the peas, and stir fry for two minutes, till the skin of the peas swell. Add the tomato puree salt, red chilli powder, haldi powder, dhania powder and zeera powder and stir fry the mixture for fifteen minutes or till the oil separates. Then add the potatoes and cook for five to ten minutes. Cover the kadhai and cook on simmer for a couple of minutes.

Garnish with coriander and serve hot with phulkas, paranthas, steamed or zeera rice.

DRY VERSION

Cooking

Same as above, just add chopped tomatoes instead of puree, and stir fry till the tomatoes soften.

Garnish with coriander and serve hot with phulkas or paranthas.

Masala Bhindi

So far, I haven't met anyone who dislikes bhindi (lady's fingers). As a kid, my mom used to give me the job of cutting it into roundels. It beautifully blends with dry masalas. It goes extremely well with curd. For a quick snack after office, I mix a little of the prepared dish into a bowl of curd and eat it. Give it your own touch, and if you hate bhindi, let's meet sometime!

Ingredients (Serves 2)

Oil: 4 tsps
Zeera (whole): 1 tsp
Onion, sliced lengthwise: 1 medium (optional)

Green chillies, slit: 2 nos.

Bhindi: 250 gms

Salt: as per taste

Saunf (fennel), roasted and coarsely crushed with a rolling pin: 1 tbsp

Red chilli powder: as per taste

Dhania powder: 1 tsp

Zeera powder: 1 tsp

Amchoor: 1 tsp

Preparing the bhindi

While picking the vegetable make sure you pick the slim and the *kachcha* (perfectly ripened) ones. You can check by breaking off the tip a little – if it breaks off easily, it is perfect; else it is *pakka* (over ripened). Wash the bhindi (before chopping it) in running water two to three times. Once washed, place the bhindi on a newspaper or kitchen cloth to dry completely. Once dry, remove the top and the bottom, and cut the bhindi in 1-cm broad rings, or slit them length wise. Remember to always handle it post washing, when it is dry, otherwise while cooking it will become sticky.

Cooking

Place a kadhai on medium flame. Add oil and when heated add whole zeera, followed by sliced onions. Stir fry till the onions become translucent. Then add green chillies and bhindi, and stir fry till bhindi becomes soft. Add all the masalas – salt, crushed saunf, red chilli powder, dhania powder, zeera powder and amchoor in the end, as they will soak away the stickiness. Do not cover the dish, as the vegetable will lose colour and will become soggy.

Serve hot with phulkas or paranthas.

A couple of months back while cleaning the house, my parents finally decided to discard all their old music cassettes. Their collection comprised some old Bollywood movies, a lot of Punjabi singers like Reshma, Surinder Kaur, etc., and to my surprise – even Boney M! I tried to collate as much of their favourite music as I could on a CD, and couriered it home. Most of all, they were very excited to get their Reshma back!

Reshma was born in a family of gypsies in Rajasthan, India, in 1947 (though she has often said that she doesn't remember the year in which she was born). Soon afterwards, Partition took her to Pakistan. Her voice was discovered by a Pakistani radio channel and it got her a lot of popularity. Despite not having received any training in classical music, some of her songs have acquired an almost legendary status, like 'Hai O rabba naio lagda dil mera', 'Akhian nu rehn de akhian de kol kol', 'Sun charke di mithi mithi cook mahiya mainu yaad aunda', 'Dama dum mast kalandar', and many others. She sang the song 'Lambi Judai' for the Hindi film Hero (1983).

One of her songs – 'Chori Chori' – is immortalised as one of the greatest love songs ever produced.

Wey main chori chori tere naal laa laiyyan akkhaan wey
Duniya tou jakhaan te main duniya tou
Duniya tou jakhan tay mein pyar tera rakhan
Wey main chori chori teray naal laa laiyyan akkhaan wey
Maa-paiyan di laj tere layee main gawayi wey
Tu harjai sadi kadar na pai wey
Phir vi main jhallee ho ke
Raah tera takkan . . .
Wey main chori chori tere naal laa laiyyan akkhaan wey

(Secretly, I have fallen in love with you
I shy away from the world and the people;

But my shyness doesn't let me love you less,
Secretly, I have fallen in love with you
I have put my parents' honour at stake for you
You, being unaware, don't value me;
But still, being as innocent as I am
I wait for you to come to me . . .
Secretly, I have fallen in love with you)

Lobia Masala

Like rajma, lobia (black-eyed beans) is another superhit dish in Punjabi homes. The key to make superb lobia is to keep the gravy chunky. This helps in not just making the flavours come alive with each bite, but also in keeping them distinct – I love the tanginess of this dish. No one can beat my mom at this one.

Ingredients (serves 2)

Oil: 2 tsps
Zeera (whole): 1 tsp
Hing (asafoetida): a pinch
Onion, chopped: 1 medium
Green chillies, chopped: 2 nos.
Ginger-garlic paste: 1 tbsp
Tomato, chopped: 1 large
Lobia, soaked (for about four hours): 1 cup
Water: 4 cups
Salt: as per taste
Haldi powder: ½ tsp
Dhania powder: ½ tsp
Amchoor: ¼ tsp
Coriander leaves, chopped: a few sprigs for garnishing

Cooking

Place a pressure cooker on medium flame. Pour in the oil. When heated, add whole zeera and hing. To this add chopped onions, chopped green chillies and ginger-garlic paste, and stir fry till onions become light golden. Add the chopped tomatoes. Stir fry the whole mixture until the tomatoes mash. Then add lobia and four cups of water, including the water in which the lobia was soaked. Add the salt, haldi powder, dhania powder and amchoor, and lock the pressure cooker lid in its place, keeping the flame high. After the first whistle, lower the flame and let it cook for fifteen minutes.

Garnish with coriander leaves. Tastes best with steamed rice, but can be served hot with phulkas or paranthas as well.

Egg Curry

Always remember, if you have eggs in your refrigerator, you will never go to sleep hungry. Eggs are simple to cook, and extremely nutritious. They have always come to my rescue whenever I have been too tired to cook. All my friends prefer this curry with the yolk, since it naturally makes the gravy thicker, but I prefer it without, because it makes the dish lighter.

Ingredients (serves 2)

Oil: 2 tsps
Zeera (whole): 1 tsp
Onion, finely chopped: 1 large
Green chillies, finely chopped: 2 nos.
Ginger-garlic paste: 1 tbsp

Tomato: 100 ml puree (for gravy) or 1 medium chopped (for dry)
Salt: as per taste
Red chilli powder: as per taste
Haldi powder: ¼ tsp
Dhania powder: ½ tsp
Zeera powder: ½ tsp
Eggs, hardboiled and cut half lengthwise: 4 nos.
Coriander leaves, chopped: a few sprigs for garnishing
Fresh cream for garnishing (in gravy, optional)

GRAVY VERSION

Cooking

In a kadhai, put oil to heat on a medium flame. When heated, add whole zeera, chopped onions, chopped green chillies, ginger-garlic paste and stir fry till onions become brown. Add tomato puree and stir fry the mixture for fifteen minutes or till the oil separates. Add salt, red chilli powder, haldi powder, dhania powder, zeera powder and stir fry for a minute. Then add the egg halves, stir the gravy gently, and cook for five to seven minutes. Cover the kadhai and cook for two minutes, the flame being simmered. Leave it covered till the time you eat or serve.

You can avoid the yolks if you don't like them. Garnish with coriander. While serving, you can add some cream. Serve hot with phulkas, paranthas or rice.

DRY VERSION

Cooking

Cut the eggs into smaller parts, the yolks again being optional. The cooking method remains same as above, just add chopped tomatoes instead of puree, and stir fry till they mash.

Garnish with coriander. Serve hot with phulkas or paranthas.

Some more folk dances

Bhangra and gidda, of course, take the spotlight when it comes to dancing. There are some other forms of Punjabi dancing, which are equally rich in heritage. They are not as popularised as bhangra is, maybe because they are not a part of every household, or because artistes have not used them in their popular performances, hence their lack of international exposure. This fact doesn't take away the cultural heritage that these styles hold, all of which collectively fall under bhangra's category.

One popular dance style is called *naqal* (this is a Persian word, which means imitation). This is not exactly a form of dance, but a performance which represents the sordid details of relationships, in a satirical way. For example, a dialogue between a master and his slave makes a popular naqal performance – like the one given below:

Servant: Shahji, will you have something to drink?

Shah: Not now, I don't feel like it…

Servant: Have something, Shahji, it is already quite late in the day, and you have not had anything at all.

Shah: Very well then, bring something if you must!

Servant: (Brings a bowl full of milk) Here, Shahji, have a bowl of milk.

Shah: No, I must have 'something' and not milk, because you wanted me to have 'something' only.

Servant: Then what shall I bring?

Shah: Bring 'something' as you said, otherwise I am going to fine you. Don't forget that I appointed you on the clear understanding that for every mistake you make, you will forfeit one month's pay.

Servant: (Puzzled, brings a glass of buttermilk) Here, Shahji, take this…

Shah: (Takes a good look) I am telling you I don't want buttermilk. I'll have only 'something'!

Servant: (Remains lost in thought for sometime) Very well, wait for a while Shahji, I'll bring 'something' for you.

After a while Shahji feels thirsty.

Shah: O Ruldoo! Bring me a glass of water!

The servant suddenly brightens up, snaps his finger, fills a glass with water and puts a dead fly in it.

Servant: Here, Shahji, take this…

Shah: (Looks into the glass) You fool! Look! There is something in the water. Go and throw this away and get me some clean water!

Servant: (Beaming) Shahji, this is that 'something' which you have been demanding…!

(Shahji looks at the dead fly in the glass and grimaces.)

Naqal is a very subtle form of entertainment, and is very popular in the villages of Punjab. A naqal troupe comprises, besides dancers and singers, clowns and musicians. The leader of the troupe is generally called ustad. As jesters, they represent the common man and issues of politics, relationships, modernisation, etc., in a frivolous yet incisive manner. They also perform legends and semi-historical tales like those of *Dulla Bhatti*, *Sohni Mahiwal*, etc.

Kikli is quite popular amongst young girls, and is usually performed in pairs: two girls cross their arms, and interlock their hands with each other. They then swirl together in this fashion, with the upper part of the body bent a little backward, and arms fully stretched. The swirling motion creates a sense of ecstasy, making it difficult to break the kikli in the middle. Therefore, the girls go on and on till their arms are exhausted! It can be performed by any number of participants, but typically the number remains between two and four.

Another style, almost similar to bhangra is *jhumar*, derived from '*jhum*', which means to sway. Jhumar and bhangra have similar features, but the former is a slower and more thematic representation of bhangra. The most common step of jhumar is the one in which the dancer places the left hand below his rib and gesticulates with his right hand.

Jhumar characterises itself on a story or imitations of field activities. Essentially a dance for the harvest season, men perform the gait of animals, agricultural activities like ploughing, sowing and harvesting. For example, two men become bullocks, a third a plough and the fourth a farmer. After the harvest step, the group joins in and dances in slow, collective bhangra, as jhumar is devoid of acrobatics. A dance style of western Punjab, it is seldom performed now.

Luddi is a dance performed on auspicious occasions, usually to celebrate a victory. Dancers lift both arms, hop on one foot, and move in a circle, swinging their bodies and shaking their shoulders. Though no songs are sung with luddi, it's a dance bursting with enthusiasm.

The most active form of bhangra is called *dhamāl*, which is accompanied by leaps in the air, fast steps and occasional shouting. A more artistic form is *dankara*, which is derived from '*dan*' meaning stick. As the name suggests, it is performed with decorated sticks.

Sammi is another popular dance. It belongs to Sandal Bar, which is now in Pakistan. After Partition, most of the Sikhs and Hindus residing in the western part of Punjab migrated to the eastern region, or to other parts of the country. They brought with them their culture and thus, Sammi became popular in the eastern half of Punjab too.

This dance is performed by women and like gidda, is performed in a circle. The dancers stand in a ring formation and swing their hands, they bring their hands from the sides up to the chest and clap, and then take their hands down according to the rhythm and clap again. Repeating this gesture, they bend forward and clap again, and go round and round in a circle. As the rhythm is maintained with the beat of the feet, various kinds of swinging movements are performed with the arms. This is a very simple dance. Most of the gestures are confined to the movements of the arms, clicking and clapping. No instrument is required as an accompaniment to this dance. Rhythm is kept up with the beating of feet and clapping.

Aloo Methi

Aloo Methi (potato and fenugreek leaves) is one preparation that tastes different to me in every city ... possibly due to the variance in methi leaves. The leaves taste divine! In fact, that's the trick: the amount of flavour of methi you can retain determines how well you can make this dish (a simple method is to not chop the leaves – just use the plucked leaves as they are – to retain the maximum flavour and iron content. In case you want to chop them, wash the leaves before chopping, rather than after, because chopped leaves lose colour and flavour in water). For the sake of the flavour, I keep this dish very basic – I don't even add ginger-garlic paste, so that it only tastes of methi, and nothing else.

Ingredients (serves 2)

Oil: 2 tsps
Zeera (whole): 1 tsp
Potato, diced: 1 large (or even the small round ones – halved)
Green chillies, chopped: 2 nos.
Methi leaves, chopped: 1 big bundle
Salt: as per taste
Haldi powder: a pinch
Red chilli powder: as per taste
Dhania powder: ½ tsp
Zeera powder: ½ tsp

Cooking

Pluck out just the methi leaves from the bundle. Wash the leaves in running water three to four times – this would help remove all sediments. Keep aside.

Place a kadhai on medium flame. Pour in the oil. When heated, add whole zeera, and diced potatoes. Cover with a lid, and let them cook for ten minutes on low flame. Then add the chopped green chillies, and the methi leaves. Add the salt, haldi powder, red chilli powder, dhania powder and zeera powder and mix well. Cover the kadhai with a lid again, and cook till the potatoes are done. Leave it covered till the time you decide to eat or serve.

Just before serving, cook for five minutes on high flame so that the excess water evaporates. Serve hot with phulkas or paranthas.

Chitte Chhole

Literally, *chitta* (in Punjabi) means white, and chitte chhole, thus refer to its key ingredient – chick peas. However, colloquially, sometimes this dish is also called 'Chikkad Chhole', owing to its thick black-brown gravy that resembles *chikkad* (wet mud). The colouration is produced by boiling the chhole in tea water. This dish centres on that perfect proportion of spices, which would need some trials to achieve. Although variants of readymade chhole masala are easily available, I personally avoid pre-packaged spice mixtures, as they lead to the same taste everytime. I love to try and give my own touch to make it taste better!

Ingredients (serves 2-3)

Tea leaves: 2 tsps
Water: 5 cups
Chitte chhole (chick peas), soaked overnight: 1 cup
Cloves: 6 nos.

Cinnamon: 1" stick

Oil: 4 tsps

Zeera (whole): ½ tsp

Dhania seeds, slightly pounded to break them: ½ tsp

Bay leaves: 3 nos.

Onion, chopped: 2 medium

Green chillies, slit: 2 nos.

Ginger, pounded: 1" piece

Garlic, pounded: 6 flakes

Tomato, chopped: 2 medium

Salt: as per taste

Red chilli powder: as per taste

Haldi powder: ½ tsp

Zeera powder: ½ tsp

Dhania powder: ½ tsp

Imli ka pani (tamarind water): ½ cup

(Soak a small chunk of tamarind in a cup of lukewarm water for two to three hours. Then in the same cup, gently mash the tamarind with your fingers to get the pulp off the seeds. Strain this thin paste. You can store the leftover paste in the refrigerator.)

Coriander leaves, chopped: a few sprigs for garnishing

Onion, finely chopped: 1 small for garnishing

Juice of 1 lemon: to squeeze in just before serving

Cooking

To ensure that the chhole look rich in colour, boil two teaspoons of tea leaves in a cup of water. Strain the leaves, and keep aside the decoction for boiling the chhole.

In a pressure cooker, put the chhole, four cups of water, one cup of tea decoction, cloves and cinnamon. Lock in the lid of the pressure cooker. After the first whistle, simmer and cook for thirty minutes. Keep aside.

In a kadhai, heat oil and add whole zeera, dhania seeds and bay leaves. After they begin to sputter, add onions, green chillies and pounded ginger and garlic. Stir fry till the onions turn golden brown. Then add tomatoes and stir fry till they mash a little. Add salt, red chilli powder, haldi, zeera powder and dhania powder and stir fry for a minute. Then add imli ka pani and the boiled chhole, along with the water.

After it comes to a boil, simmer and cook for fifteen to twenty minutes, gently mash some chhole against the base of the kadhai.

Garnish with coriander and chopped onions and add a dash of lemon juice. Serve hot with phulkas, paranthas, or with steamed or zeera rice.

Folk Songs

In any language or culture, folk songs usually borrow their metaphorical nature and imagery from the most common things in life. Their lyrics are simple, and reflect their respective culture. Folk songs have come of age, and do not lend themselves to imitation. Therefore, it's a little unfair to translate the folk songs, as translation can be easily done for textual compositions, but not for their emotional import and situational rhythms.

Punjabi folk music is primarily vocal in character, and is seldom accompanied by instruments. Its nature is as simple as a villager singing a song while ploughing or digging his fields, driving his cart, or walking home. Or, a group of women, plying the charkha and singing in twos or threes. But for songs which are sung on special occasions, the use of instruments is essential particularly the dhol and the tumba. The rhythmic patterns of Punjabi folk songs are determined by the day-to-day activities of the villagers, like the sound of the grinding stone, the drone of the spinning wheel, the creaking of the Persian wheel, the beat of the horse's hooves, etc.

The subjects of folk songs in Punjabi culture are innumerable. Extolling the virtues of nature is common – there is a song for a woman when she sees the new moon, one for the peepal tree, and another for the blossoming fields, and so on.

The ceremonial songs, especially the ones sung at weddings, are most popular. For example, the song given below is sung at the time of the doli, i.e., when the bride is leaving her parental home after the completion of all wedding ceremonies. My grandmother, (and even my mom) irrespective of whose marriage she is attending, always has tears in her eyes during the doli.

Sada chirian da chamba ve, babal assan ud jana
Sadi lammi udari ve, babal kehre des jana
Tere mehlan de vich ve, babal dola nahin langda
Ik it puta devan, dhiye ghar ja apne
Tera baghan de vich ve, babal charkha kaun katte?
Merian kattan potrian, dhiye ghar ja apne
Mera chhuta kasida ve, babal das kaun kade?
Merian kadhan potrian, dhiye ghar ja apne

(Ours is a flock of sparrows, dear father, we'll fly away
On a long, long flight, we don't know to which land we shall go.
Through your mansion's door, dear father, the doli won't pass.
I'll have some bricks removed from the wall; you go to your home, O daughter.
In your mansion, dear father, who will spin the wheel?
My granddaughters will spin; you go to your home, O daughter.
There is my unfinished embroidery; who will complete it, father?
My granddaughters will do it; you go to your home, O daughter.)

There is a wide variation in the melodies and tunes that were prevalent in different regions of undivided Punjab. In the west, especially in the plains of Singh Sagar Doab, certain folk forms like mahiya and dhola were, and still are very popular. Boli is popular all over Punjab; however, the style of performing is different in eastern and western Punjab.

Mahiya, which originated in the area that is now part of western Pakistan, especially Pothohar, is sung all over Punjab. In almost all parts of Pothohar (before Punjab was divided), one came across people singing mahiya during work, especially while farmers toiled in their fields. 'Mahiya' originates from the word 'mahi', meaning lover, after the legendary lover Ranjha who was called Mahi (tender of buffaloes) as he looked after the herd of cattle owned by his love, Heer's father. Mahiya, in substance, is that form of folk verse in which the lover is addressed in the most touching expressions of love and pathos. A triplet of mahiya is called 'tappa' (literally meaning a hop), in which the first line contains a pen-picture, a description or an illustration, but sometimes it has no special meaning or relevance, since it is used only to maintain rhyme. The second and third lines contain the real substance. These two lines are very expressive and overflow with emotions of longing. Every tappa is an entity in itself.

Do kapre sile hoe ne,
Bahron bhaven rusdhe an,
vichon dil tan mile hoe ne.

(Two pieces of cloth are stitched together,
Though we might sulk and fume at times,
Within our two bodies, the heart is one.)

Dhola, an equally popular form of folk music, is highly lyrical and sentimental in character, love and beauty being its chief contents. Dhola has a variety of forms, those prevalent in Pothohar being quite different from those popular with the tribes of Sandalbar. The Pothohari dhola is rather condensed in form. Each stanza consists of five lines, which can be further divided into two parts of three and two lines, respectively. The first two lines of the first part rhyme with each other, while the third one is left loose. The second part, which is a couplet, intensifies and polishes up the meaning of the first three lines. Although this couplet is a sustained part of the first three lines, in a way it is quite self-contained. The singers of dhola liberally use this couplet even independently. The kind of dhola prevalent in Sandalbar has no fixed form, and its tune and rhythm keeps changing according to the variety of emotions portrayed.

Dhola ve dhola, hai dhola,
Aja doven nachiye, hai dhola
Rut mastani, hai dhola
Badi divani, hai dhola

(Hey lover, listen O lover
Let's dance, O lover
The air's so enchanting, O lover
It's melody in love, O lover)

Boli is the most popular form of folk music of eastern Punjab. It is generally a kind of couplet, and is the most miniature form of folk songs in vogue. However, it is very effective and interesting. It has the brevity of a proverb, the appeal of mahiya and a sweetness of its own. Bhangra and gidda are danced to the accompaniment of this form of folk songs. In form, a boli may, however, vary from one line to four, five or even more lines. A typical boli can be like this:

Sasadiye tere panj puttar, do aibi do sharabi;
Jeda mere haan da, o khideya phul gulabi.

(O mother-in-law, of your five sons, two are indulgent and two are alcoholics;
The one that is suited for me, blossoms like a pink rose.)

There is another category of folk songs called songs of Trinjan. It refers to sessions where Punjabi women would gather to spin cotton/yarn. Spinning for them is a collective activity alongside which they would sing as well. Often on wintery nights all the women would assemble at someone's house and keep spinning and singing throughout the night.

Trinjan songs cover all aspects of life and the long-cherished dreams of a woman, her aspirations, fears, love and longings. These songs, combined with the drone of the spinning wheel, create an enchanting atmosphere. A newlywed who is missing her husband sings:

Har charkhe de gere, yād āwein toon mitrā

(At every spin of the wheel, I am reminded of you, my beloved)

During these spinning sessions, enduring friendships are formed and the girls who get married in far off places remember their trinjan friends with nostalgia;

Nit nit vagde rahn ge pani,
Nit patan te mela,
Bachpan nit jawani bansi,
Te nit katan da mela,
Par jo pani aj patano langda,
Oh pher na aonda bhalke,
Beri da poor Trinjan dian koorian,
Pher na bethan ral ke.

(Streams would flow every day,
 And folks at ferries would meet,

After childhood comes youth
And the spinning continues.
But waters that have gone ahead
Their backward flow restrains,
Like a boat cruises to far off lands,
The trinjan girls,
Shall never meet again.)

There is an abundance of tales of devotional, heroic and romantic nature in Punjabi folklore. Typically, they are in verse form. Tales of Puran Bhagat, Gopi Chand and Hakeekat Rai belong to the devotional type, whereas Raja Rasalu, Sucha Singh Surma and Jeuna Mor belong to the heroic category. The most popular tales of romance are Heer-Ranjha, Sassi-Punnu, Mirza-Sahiban and Sohni-Mahiwal, and many eminent poets such as Waris Shah and Hashim have narrated them in verse form. These tales are sung in typical strains. For example, Mirza-Sahiban is sung in long wistful notes; the singer generally places one hand on his ear, and makes melancholic gestures with the other while he sings. The notes of *Sindhu Bhairava* (a raga in Hindustani classical music) can be traced in Heer-Ranjha, while Puran Bhagat is sung in the musical notes of *Raga Asavari* and *Raga Mand*. Sohni Mahiwal is sung in *Raga Bhairavi*, and so is Yusif Zulaikhan, but the tunes are different.

Further, there are loris or lullabies. A completely different style, they are sung in different tunes with an invariably slow tempo. Every tune, irrespective of its context, tends to create a drone, a dreamy atmosphere which helps put a child to sleep.

There are satirical songs on mothers-in-law and songs of battles which extol the virtues of courage, *shahidi* (martyrdom) and victory. There is a song for everybody, for every mood, and for every day.

Stuffed Paranthas

This is THE breakfast! The most difficult thing to change about a Punjabi is to alter his breakfast: A Punjabi loves his paranthas, and loves to have them with thick dahi or lassi, and dollops of white butter. My mom pokes my parantha with a fork to make little holes so that more butter can seep into it! Only she can trick me into eating food rich in butter. After all, it's about love and not calories! The basic method of making a stuffed parantha remains the same; just the filling changes. So, I'll take the reverse route – I will first explain the cooking method and then go on to the various fillings. I have given the recipes for aloo, paneer, gobhi and mooli (radish) fillings. However, you can also make your own ones using grated carrots, mashed peas, etc. Make sure you stuff as much filling as you can to make those delicious paranthas burst as you dig into them!!!

Cooking

Take a medium-sized ball of plain wheat flour dough, and flatten it into a small, thick roti (diameter four-to-five inches) with a rolling pin. Take one or two heaped spoons of the filling, place it at the centre of the small roti, and fold its sides over it. Dust this ball of filling with wheat flour and flatten it again to a normal-size roti. Flatten it very gently, as the filling, if moist, would burst out. In such a case, dust a little flour over the part that has burst out and flatten gently.

Heat the tawa and slightly grease it with just a touch of oil. Placing the roti on it, cook till golden brown on both sides, delicately frying in the end with a little ghee or salted butter.

Fillings

ALOO KA PARANTHA

Ingredients (makes 4-5 paranthas):

Potatoes, boiled: 3 large
Ginger, chopped or grated: 1" piece
Coriander leaves, chopped: as much preferred
Green chillies, finely chopped: 2 nos.
Red chilli powder: as per taste
Anardana: ½ tsp
Zeera (whole), roasted: ½ tsp
Amchoor: ½ tsp
Zeera powder: ½ tsp
Dhania powder: ½ tsp
Salt: as per taste

Method

Mash the boiled potatoes with your hand. Grating the potatoes is not preferred, since mashed potatoes taste better because of their coarse and chunky texture. Mix all the ingredients together and mash again so that the spices are mixed evenly.

PANEER KA PARANTHA

Ingredients (makes 4-5 paranthas)

Fresh paneer, crumbled: 200 gms
Ginger, chopped or grated: 1" piece
Onion, finely chopped: 1 small
Coriander leaves, chopped: as much preferred
Green chillies, finely chopped: 2 nos.
Red chilli powder: as per taste
Zeera powder: ½ tsp
Dhania powder: ½ tsp

Ajwain (carom seeds): ½ tsp

Salt: as per taste

Method

Crumble the paneer with your hand. Again, preferably, do not grate, as the paneer would taste better due to its coarse and chunky texture. Mix all the ingredients together gently and use immediately else the paneer would start losing water.

GOBHI KA PARANTHA

Ingredients (makes 4-5 paranthas)

Cauliflower, grated: 1 small

Ginger, chopped or grated: 1" piece

Coriander leaves, chopped: as much preferred

Green chillies, finely chopped: 2 nos.

Red chilli powder: as per taste

Zeera powder: ½ tsp

Anardana: ¼ tsp

Ajwain: ½ tsp

Amchoor: ¼ tsp

Dhania powder: ½ tsp

Salt: as per taste

Method

Mix all the ingredients very gently. Add salt just before cooking else the mixture will start losing water.

MOOLI KA PARANTHA

Ingredients (makes 4-5 paranthas)

Mooli (radish), grated: 1 large

Ginger, chopped or grated: 1" piece

Coriander leaves, chopped: as much preferred

Green chillies, finely chopped: 2 nos.
Red chilli powder: as per taste
Zeera powder: ½ tsp
Amchoor: ½ tsp
Dhania powder: ½ tsp
Ajwain: ½ tsp
Salt: as per taste

Method

Using your hands, squeeze out all the juice from the grated radish completely. Then, mix all the ingredients very gently. Add salt just before cooking else the mixture will start losing water.

You can also chop and add some of the softer radish leaves for that extra flavour. Usually the fat, big radishes are most suited for making paranthas.

Music is often regarded as a means to a definite emotional end. Of the many sounds which constitute the domain of music, the human voice is considered the highest form, and therefore intoning, chanting and recitation of mantras, kirtan and singing, are regarded as the most effective means of divine expression. Music is therefore considered a sacred art.

The first five gurus (1469–1606), namely Guru Nanak Dev, Guru Angad Dev, Guru Amar Das, Guru Ram Das and Guru Arjan Dev were great singers and musicologists. In 1604, the sacred hymns of the five gurus, bards and saints, were collected and named the *Adi Granth*. The *Granth* is written in verse and the hymns are not arranged in the Holy Book according to their authors, but according to the thirty-one ragas or musical measures in which they were composed.

The way ragas and music have been used to communicate deeper meanings in the Guru Granth Sahib is very ingenious. For example, in *Raga Sorath*, which is performed late at night (9 p.m. till midnight), Guru Nanak refers to the darkness of superstition and maya, which envelops the individual. In *Raga Maru*, performed in the afternoon (noon to 3 p.m.), Guru Amardas (the third guru) calls that person a warrior who fights against his mind and evil inclinations. Sukhmani Sahib is composed in *Raga Gauri*, again a late afternoon raga (3 to 6 p.m.).

The fact that out of the 1,430 pages of the Guru Granth Sahib, there are about 1,343 pages that are mostly set in ragas, is reflective of the harmony between the gurus and music. Like the ancient seers, the gurus realised the power of music over mind and body, and as such they conveyed their knowledge through the medium of music. The sacred music appeals to all even though the meanings of some of the words may be unintelligible to some. People consider it to be a song, but in fact it is a meditation on divinity.

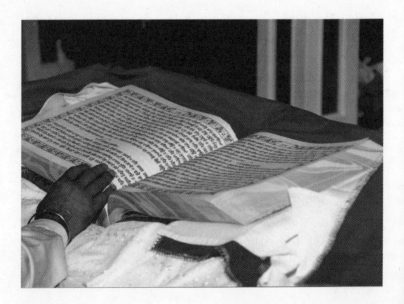

Crispy Chicken

I have always prepared this dish for my friends. As a snack served with drinks, it was quite a hit at our parties at home. Crispy chicken in my life is synonymous with bonhomie and laughter; therefore, I don't think I can ever make this dish 'just' for myself.

Ingredients (serves 2)

Chicken, preferably boneless: 1 kg
Bread crumbs: 1½ cups
Oil: sufficient for deep frying
Chaat masala: to sprinkle on top while serving
Juice of 1 lemon: to squeeze just before serving

For Marination

Ginger-garlic paste: 3 tbsps
Egg, beaten: 1 no.
Curd: 2 tbsps
Red chilli powder: as per taste
Black pepper: ¼ tsp
Dhania powder: ½ tsp
Zeera powder: ½ tsp
Salt: as per taste

Cooking

Wash the chicken thoroughly, cut into one-to-two inch pieces and keep aside.

In a bowl, mix together all the ingredients for marination, add the chicken and leave it in the refrigerator for two to three hours.

On a flat plate, spread the bread crumbs. Gently mix the marinated chicken in its bowl. Then take one piece at a time, and roll it in the bread crumbs. Deep fry in a kadhai till it turns golden brown. Put only one piece at a time; make a batch of six to seven pieces in one go.

Serve with chutney or mayonnaise or curd dip. Add a dash of chaat masala and lemon juice for that extra zing.

Dahi Chicken

I discovered dahi (curd) chicken away from home. A friend of mine taught me how to make this dish, in lieu of the rajma chawal that I cooked for him. It's a very interesting preparation! I like the way dahi is used, and how the chicken slowly cooks in its natural juices. Back in my kitchen, I did fine-tune the recipe in terms of the choice and use of spices. It's simple and extremely flavourful.

Ingredients (serves 2)

Chicken: 1 kg (boneless, cut into bite size pieces or with bones)
Zeera (whole): 1 tsp
Cinnamon whole: 1" stick
Cloves: 4-5 nos.
Dhania seeds (slightly pounded to break them): 1 tsp
Ginger-garlic paste: 3 tbsps
Thick curd (whisked, to remove any lumps): 2 cups
Mint leaves (finely chopped): 8-10 nos.
Green chillies, finely chopped: 3 nos.
Red chilli powder: as per taste
Salt: as per taste

Oil: 1 tbsp
Bay leaves: 2-3 nos.
Coriander leaves, chopped: a few sprigs for garnishing

Cooking

Wash the chicken thoroughly and keep aside.

In a dry pan, roast zeera, cinnamon, cloves and dhania seeds till they release their aroma. Then with a rolling pin, crush the spices over to make a coarse powder. Keep aside.

Put the chicken pieces into a bowl; add the coarse spice powder, ginger-garlic paste, thick curd, chopped mint leaves, chopped green chillies, red chilli powder and salt. Let it marinate for two to three hours.

Place a kadhai on medium flame. Pour in some oil. Once heated, add the bay leaves and stir for a minute. Then empty the bowl of marinated chicken into the kadhai, and mix well. Cook for ten minutes on medium flame, and then simmer till the chicken is done. You need not use more oil as the yoghurt will release its own oils. Keep covered until you decide to serve, for that will help the flavour of spices to seep in.

Garnish with chopped coriander. Serve hot with phulkas or paranthas.

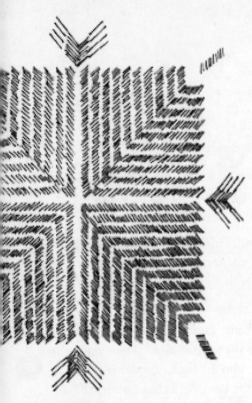

Two

Chenab (Sanskrit: Chandrabhaga)

The exotic foods; legendary love stories of Punjab

Known as *Ashkini* (the dark one) or *Chandrabhagha* (named after its two tributaries *chandra* – moon and *bhaga* – fate) to Indians during the Vedic period, and *Acesines* to ancient Greeks, the waters of the Chenab have been allocated to Pakistan under the Indus Waters Treaty (1960).

The word Chenab is derived from Persian '*chen*' meaning moon, and '*ab*', meaning river. Chenab rises from a height of 16,000 feet, formed from the glacial melt of the snow on the Upper Himalayas.

In some of the passages in *Rig Veda*, the medicinal character of this river is mentioned. According to a local myth, living along the banks of Chenab and bathing in it for seven consecutive days while observing a fast, assures salvation or moksha.

This river is nothing less than an icon in the Punjabi and Sufi histories. The legendary Punjabi tales of Sohni-Mahiwal, Mirza-Sahiban, Sassi-Punnu and Heer-Ranjha have immortalised the sentimental character of this river: it was in its waters that Sassi, when merely a baby, was thrown into by her parents; it was around the region of Chenab and Ravi that the love of Sahiban and Mirza blossomed; Ranjha mesmerisingly played his flute on the banks of this river; and it was in its waters that Sohni drowned one night. All the four love legends of Punjab have a tragic ending, where the lovers died in pursuit of their love, but have been immortalised by generations of story tellers for posterity.

I may sound hyperbolic, but this section contains food for love. Whenever I have indulged in preparing the dishes in this section, I have been filled with loving memories of my home. I often visualise my mom sitting peacefully and preparing for cooking, which would last more than the usual cooking time, like cleaning the spinach leaf by leaf: If only I could be as patient as she is, the food I cook would probably taste as great as hers. Probably that's why they say, food made with love always tastes a little different, and better!

Like food fuels our bodies, love fuels our soul and our conscience. This does not necessarily mean 'being in love with someone'; it goes beyond that … to a feeling of 'being loved'. Again, it all begins from a feeling of being accepted by your parents, society, beloved, spouse, children, friends, and even by one's self. Love is a critical need for survival. We need to have faith in someone, and *we would want* someone to have faith in us, and this essentially does not have to be the same person.

Painting, photography, fashion, music ... love has inspired almost all forms of art. Literature hasn't remained untouched either: Punjabi history has some legendary love stories, which have been recited, sung, enacted and even made into films. There are four pivotal tragic love stories; unfortunately it's the tragedy that makes them iconic: Heer-Ranjha, Mirza-Sahiban, Sassi-Punnu and Sohni-Mahiwal. All these love stories centre on the feeling of longing for the beloved, which has been interpreted on spiritual and mystic grounds as a quest for the beloved: the God or the Alif. Usually, every love story is looked upon from two distinct perspectives: one is moral or societal and the other, personal. The society laden with moral values, on one hand, gave poison to Heer, and on the other, makes offerings with spiritual convictions at her tomb, where vows are taken and blessings are sought for redemption from all unfulfilled desires.

Love was an inspiration for this section as well. Featured are some delicate foods, ideal for a cosy date at home: simple, yet rich in content. They might be a bit time-consuming, but ultimately it's time well spent, time that fed love: Even that tastes better when simmered and savoured.

Dal Makhani

An internationally famous dal preparation, Dal Makhani is a must-have for any Punjabi dinner. The more you simmer this dal, the more heavenly it tastes! The name itself reflects the richness of this dish, where dollops of churned-at-home white butter are mixed into the prepared dal to impart that typical creamy, silky texture. Nowadays, people have switched to using fresh cream as a substitute, due to convenience and availability of the same in grocery stores. I switched too, but back home, it's white butter all the way!

Ingredients (serves 2)

Salted butter: 4 tsps
Zeera (whole): 1 tsp
Dhania seeds, slightly pounded to break them: 1 tsp
Cloves: 6 nos.
Cinnamon: 2" stick
Bay leaves: 3 nos.
Onion, chopped: 1 large
Green chillies, slit: 3 nos.
Ginger, pounded: 1" piece
Garlic, pounded: 6-7 pods
Tomato, chopped: 1 large
Salt: as per taste
Red chilli powder: as per taste
Haldi powder: ½ tsp
Zeera powder: ½ tsp
Dhania powder: ½ tsp
Mah ki Dal, soaked for five to six hours: ¾ cup
Rajma, soaked for five to six hours: ¼ cup

Water: 5 cups
Fresh cream: 1 cup
Coriander leaves, chopped: a few sprigs for garnishing

Cooking

In a pressure cooker, heat the butter. Once heated, add whole zeera, dhania seeds, cloves, cinnamon and bay leaves. After they begin to sputter, add onions, green chillies and pounded ginger and garlic. Stir fry till the onions turn golden brown. Add tomatoes and stir fry till they mash a little. Then add salt, red chilli powder, haldi powder, zeera powder and dhania powder and stir fry for a minute.

Now add the soaked mah ki dal and rajma, and five cups of water. Lock the pressure cooker lid in its place, and after the first whistle, simmer for thirty minutes.

When the dal is done, remove from flame and mix fresh cream into it, stirring continuously. Gently mash the dal against the walls of the cooker; this will help make the dal thicker.

Garnish with coriander. It can be served with almost anything: Phulkas or paranthas, zeera rice or naan.

Punjabi Kadhi

Kadhi as a dish per se has its typical rendition in almost every culture. It's a dish which needs to be simmered too: the more it simmers the creamier and silkier its texture. Punjabis like their kadhi thick. The base of this dish is curd and besan (gram flour), the curd being slightly sour. It doesn't consist of any vegetables; however, sometimes a few chopped leaves of spinach are added (I guess it's more of an attempt to throw in some colour and include greens in one's diet than any significant attempt to impart taste). Another thing which differentiates Punjabi kadhi is the use of pakora – which not only makes it more filling, but also add that extra flavour and zing to each spoonful.

Ingredients (serves 2-3)

For Pakoras
Besan: 1 cup
Onion, chopped: 1 small
Green chillies, chopped: 1 nos.
Salt: as per taste
Red chilli powder: as per taste
Coriander leaves, chopped: a few sprigs
Water: enough to make a thick mixture
Oil: sufficient for deep frying

For Kadhi
Besan (gramflour): ½ cup
Curd: 1 cup
Oil: 2 tsps
Zeera (whole): ½ tsp
Dhania seeds, slightly pounded to break them: ½ tsp
Methidana (fenugreek seeds): ½ tsp
Ajwain: 1 tsp
Cloves: 5 nos.
Cinnamon: 1" stick
Bay leaves: 3 nos.
Ginger, pounded: 1" piece
Garlic, pounded: 5 pods
Green chillies, slit: 2 nos.
Salt: as per taste
Red chilli powder: as per taste
Haldi powder: ¾ tsp

Zeera powder: ½ tsp

Dhania powder: ½ tsp

Water: 5 cups

Cooking

For Pakoras

Heat oil in a kadhai for deep frying. Mix all the remaining ingredients together and gradually add water to make a thickish mixture – thick enough for small dumplings that can be dropped in the oil. This mixture should be of medium consistency as too thick would make the pakoras hard, while too thin will not hold shape and lead to flat pakoras! Now, with a serving spoon (or even with your hand if you feel more comfortable), take small portions and drop dumplings into the heated oil. Fry till their colour becomes rich golden brown. Keep aside.

For Kadhi

To sour the curd a little, mix a pinch of salt in the curd and keep it at ambient temperature for two hours. Then whisk the curd and the besan together till it attains a smooth texture. Keep the mixture aside.

In a kadhai, heat the oil. When heated, add whole zeera, dhania seeds, methi dana, ajwain, cloves, cinnamon and bay leaves. After the zeera sputters, add pounded ginger and garlic, as well as the slit green chillies. Stir fry till the ginger and garlic turn golden. Then add salt, red chilli powder, haldi powder, zeera powder, dhania powder and stir for a minute. Add five cups of water, and stirring continuously, add the besan-curd mixture. If the mixture is not stirred while pouring the besan-curd mixture, lumps will form.

When the kadhi starts boiling, lower the flame. Let it boil for twenty to twenty-five minutes till it attains a homogeneous consistency. Add more water to suit your preference of thickness.

Serve hot with steamed rice or phulkas.

Bharwan Sabziyan

Often many local Punjabi eateries pass off 'spicy' food as 'teekha' (with a lot of chillies) food; spicy food need not necessarily be teekha! This dish is spicy, but it doesn't have copious amounts of chilli powder to make your eyes water! It has a filling of assorted *khada masalas* (whole spices like cloves, cinnamon, saunf, etc.) that are dry roasted and freshly powdered, to give a different character to the vegetable all together. The vegetables used to make the *bharwan* (filled in) style are bhindi, chhote baigan (smaller aubergines), tindas (Indian round guard) and chhote karelas (small bitter gourds). Given below is the method for making all four, so that you can prepare whatever is available…

Ingredients (serves 2-3)

Any of the four vegetables: 250 gms
Oil: 2 tsps or sufficient for deep frying (if using karela)

For the masala (for 250 gms of any vegetable)
Zeera (whole): 1 tsp
Dhania seeds: 2 tsps
Saunf: 2 tsps
Cloves: 4-5 nos.
Cinnamon: 1" stick
Ajwain: ½ tsp
Amchoor: 1 tsp

Red chilli powder: as per taste

Salt: as per taste

Making the masala

In a pan, dry roast whole zeera, dhania seeds, saunf, cloves, cinnamon and ajwain, till they start sputtering rapidly and release their aroma. Don't blacken them: just roast them till they turn dark brownish. Grind into a coarse powder and add amchoor, red chilli powder and salt. Keep aside for filling in the vegetables.

Preparing the vegetables

Bhindi: Wash the bhindi and thoroughly dry on a newspaper. Remove the top and bottom and carefully make a half slit, lengthwise – don't cut it into two pieces – just a shallow slit to fill the masala. With the help of a knife, slide and fill in the masala generously into the slit. Keep aside.

Tindas: Gently scrape the tinda to remove the surface skin. Wash and dry thoroughly. Make a slit in the vegetable twice – like a cross. Again, it should not be split into four pieces – just shallow slits that would be enough to fill in the masala. With the help of a knife, slide and fill in the masala generously along the slits. Keep aside.

Baigan: Wash the baigan with their stalks on. Carefully make a half slit, lengthwise – the baigan shouldn't be cut into two pieces – just a shallow slit. With the help of a knife, slide and fill in the masala generously along the slit. Keep aside.

Karelas: Wash and lightly scrape the karelas. Make a shallow slit lengthwise. Rub salt into the karelas and keep them aside for two hours. Marination in salt helps to reduce their bitterness. Wash them thoroughly and leave them to dry completely. Then fill the masala in the slit with the help of a knife and tie up the karela with a string, so that the masala doesn't spill while frying.

Cooking

For bhindi, chhote baigan, or tindas: In a non-stick kadhai, heat the oil. When heated, carefully place the filled vegetables inside, one by one. Toss gently, just enough to coat them with oil. Cover and cook on low flame, till the vegetables are done. Keep tossing at regular intervals so that the masala doesn't get burnt.

For chhote karelas: Heat oil in a kadhai for deep frying. Once heated, slide the tied up karelas into it one by one. Deep fry till golden brown. Drain on a kitchen tissue and untie them. They should be slightly crispy and brilliantly spiced.

Serve hot with phulkas or paranthas.

Heer Ranjha

Ranjha Ranjha kardi ni main,
Aap hi Ranjha hoyi ...

(Calling out my Beloved's name all the time,
I have lost myself, and have become one with Him ...)

The legendary and tragic love story of Heer and Ranjha has been rewritten by several authors and poets, each with a little twist, the most famous being the one composed by Waris Shah. Some believe that it was he who gave the love story its tragic ending, which is nothing short of a legend. Whether the love story of Heer and Ranjha had a happy ending or a sad one is a topic of debate, but the fact of the matter is that theirs was a love that went beyond; theirs was a quest for the beloved ... the beloved being the God. The *qissa* (tale) is as follows:

In the wilderness, a short distance away from the village of Takht Hazara, Dhido lay on a patch of ground that he had cleared of all twigs and thorns, his head pillowed on his left hand, his right forearm across his eyes to shield him from the speckled sunlight that broke through the leaves. He was fast asleep. His face was soft, delicate, and almost effeminate in the finesse of its features. By his side lay his *wanjhli* (flute), the charmed reed that left not even a single soul unstirred when he played it.

Dhido was not cut out to be a farmer. He liked herding his father's cattle and playing his flute – doing the latter to perfection. He was the youngest of the sons of late Mauju, head of the Ranjha clan, and had been a victim of an unfair division of lands, which entitled him to a stretch of barren fields. He worked harder than his brothers on his fields that would never yield anything beyond an odd year of wheat, no matter how hard he worked.

Many women of the village, including his own *bhabhis* (sisters-in-law), eyed Dhido with desire. With his constant rejection, the attitude of his bhabhis hardened. Initially, they used to cook his favourite dishes to take for him in the fields, but now they delighted in being stingy towards his helpings at meals. His midday meal was soon reduced to a few stale phulkas and a small onion. Earlier they had sought occasions to be alone with him, but now avoided him and answered him in monosyllables.

Their jibes became more bitter and hurtful with each passing day. The women joked about his effeminate looks and vanity; they mocked him at his failure to plough the lands, and even scorned his music which they once loved. No matter how hard he tried to ignore them, Dhido found it increasingly difficult to escape their derisive behaviour. Things reached their nadir one morning while he was tying his turban in front of the small mirror that hung on a wall in the veranda. Nooran, the youngest of his bhabhis, in a voice loud enough for everyone to hear, said: 'Look at him, preening like a peacock! He thinks he is the most handsome of men. But look at his gait, his delicate face, his soft girl-like hands, I doubt if he is a man at all!'

The peals of laughter that met this remark broke Dhido's patience. He left his father's house amongst loud and unbridled mockery. He ran across the fields, impatient to get away from Takht Hazara. He could think of no one in the village who would lament at his departure. Towards dusk, he played his flute to himself, and then slept on the ground with hunger clawing at his stomach, and feet covered with blisters.

Days passed as he wandered aimlessly. On the morning of the fifth day, Dhido saw at a distance a line of trees and knew he was approaching Chenab. Although his journey was without a destination and the river was no landmark, yet the thought of reaching it buoyed his flagging spirits. Across the river, he saw a large and prosperous village and even though he didn't know which village it was, he knew he had reached his destination. With no money in his pocket to pay Luddan, the boatman, to cross the river, Dhido reached for his flute and soon the soft, poignant notes of a mournful melody wafted across the waters and worked the way he knew they would. The other enchanted passengers forced Luddan to take him on-board, towards the village that was called Jhang.

Jhang was home to Heer, who, at sixteen, was already talked about for her beauty. She was the only daughter of Chuchak Khan, the head of the Sayal clan. News of the stranger and his music reached her too, and one day she decided to go to the riverbank to catch a glimpse of him. As she approached the river bank, notes of Dhido's flute wafted to her ears, her steps slowed down and they drew her towards Dhido. Thus, with soft, stealthy steps she came to the riverbank holding her breath, fearing that he would notice her intrusion and stop playing the flute. Dhido raised his eyes just once, and they caught Heer's. They held their glances for a moment; and Heer knew her life would never be the same again.

That evening Malliki, Heer's mother, noticed that her daughter was distracted. When she sat down for her evening meal, she merely picked at her food. Late in the night as she lay awake in her bed, her thoughts turned to Dhido. She could hear his music in her mind. She went back to the moment when he had first looked into her eyes and bewitched her. The memory brought back the desires that she had been suppressing within herself. She buried her face into her pillow and thought of a way to not let him leave Jhang. Her father had a large herd of cows and buffaloes but for a long time they had been without a suitable cowherd. She thought perhaps she could persuade Dhido, (Ranjha) to take on the job.

Ranjha had loved being a cowherd to his father's cattle too, and thus took up the job as Chuchak's cowherd without much ado. Thereafter, a routine set in. Heer used to release the cattle from the pen. Ranjha would play his flute and the cows and buffaloes, enraptured by his music, followed him. Each morning Ranjha brought the herd to the pasture, and Heer and her friends joined him in the forest and dallied with him till the sun reached its zenith. Then they would return home and the girls would bring food for him. Finally, after supervising the milking in the evening, Ranjha would return to Chuchak's home, have his dinner and retire to the hut that had been provided to him.

On the fourth day, when they broke for the midday meal, Ranjha secretly caught Heer by her wrist. She felt her heart race but did not attempt to break free. Her friends saw them, exchanged smiles and hurried away. Ranjha drew Heer down on the mound beside him. He drew her close and started caressing and kissing her passionately. She submitted herself to him without any restraints, as if she had been waiting for this moment all her life.

After this, as if by tacit agreement, Heer's friends left them alone as much as it was safe to do. The world saw the light of their love shine in the changes wrought in both of them: Ranjha, once a carefree, gregarious young boy now held his peace and Heer, once vain now chose to stay in the background.

*

Before her transformation, Heer and her friends often used to play tricks and pranks on the less fortunate inhabitants of the village. A favourite target was Kaidon, a lame kinsman of Chuchak, who lived in a little hut on the outskirts of the village with his two cows and four goats. Because of his handicap and his evil tongue, he had never found a partner to share his frugal life and later had adopted the garb of an ascetic. The girls regularly ridiculed Kaidon's handicap and at times when he snapped back, they went to the extent of snatching away his stick, which he used as his crutch, forcing him to crawl to his hut while the passers-by watched him and laughed.

Heer started bringing him food and often spent time tidying up his simple home and helping him with his household chores. But Kaidon's heart was hardened. He could not bring himself to forgive her, and looked for even the smallest of ways to avenge the humiliation that he had been subjected to in the past.

The village buzzed with curiosity about Heer's transformation. Kaidon listened to all that was being said with great interest, because he knew that in the secret of Heer's transformation lay the key to his revenge. He started keeping an eye on her. One day, he made his way to the pastures, and after finding a place to hide, waited for what the day would bring. The intimate secret of Heer and Ranjha, hence, lay bare in front of his eyes.

Filled with revenge, Kaidon went to Chuchak's place and shouted out everything he saw amidst an audience comprising the entire Chuchak household. At the same time, in an attempt to save Heer,

Sajda, one of her friends who had seen Kaidon spying on the lovers, entered the courtyard with dishevelled hair, torn shirt and scratches on her cheeks, accusing Kaidon for physically abusing her in the pastures. With this, Kaidon's accusation against Heer was forgotten in the face of a greater calamity. Kaidon realised that Heer and her friends had outwitted him once again. The panchayat punished him with a public flogging and a year's banishment from the village.

Meanwhile in an attempt to salvage his daughter's honour, Chuchak and other elders of the household decided to get rid of Ranjha and hire another cowherd. They also decided to find a suitable groom for Heer. On the other side, in Ranjha's hut, the lovers lay in each other's arms and in spite of their impending separation, which they both instinctively knew was inevitable, they managed to steal a few intimate moments. When it was time for Heer to return, she broke down and wept in Ranjha's arms. Holding her tenderly, all he said was, 'Rab rakha' (God shall be our protector).

And so Ranjha was made to leave Chuchak's house. Luddan offered him his house to stay in an attempt to prevent him from leaving Jhang. In the meantime, the health of Chuchak's cattle began to deteriorate. Malliki, Chuchak's wife proposed the idea of getting Ranjha back as their cowherd. Packing a lot of *choori* (a dish made with chapattis broken into tiny bits, and dressed with lots of ghee and sugar – recipe on page 221) while leaving to meet him, she thought of a compelling way to get him back. On being persuaded by her to return to his job, Ranjha asserted that he didn't work for the wages but for Heer, and that's what kept him tied to their house in spite of the insignificant wages. Hearing this, Malliki assured him: 'Come back, my son. Come back and take your place in the household and I promise you that when it is time to look around for a groom for my daughter, yours shall be the first name that we will consider.' Taking it as a promise, Ranjha returned to the Chuchak household.

One afternoon, while in the forest, Heer and Ranjha encountered five *pirs* who, upon seeing the intensity and conviction of their love, solemnised their relationship. However, in the background, the search for a suitable groom for Heer had gained momentum and it could no longer be kept a secret from the lovers. Ranjha accosted Malliki when she was alone: 'You have broken your promise, the promise you made when you persuaded me to come back.' To which Malliki replied: 'I made a promise. And I have kept it. Your name is being considered as the prospective groom. Do not do anything to spoil your chances.'

At last the day came when it was no longer possible to hide the reality. A proposal had come for Heer from Saida, the son of the chief of the Khairas, a powerful and wealthy clan. The proposal had been accepted with joy and pride but Heer had only become aware of it when she had seen the *shagun* – the clothes, the *mithai* and the coins waiting to be carried to Rangpur, the home of the Khairas. In a state of panic, Heer fled to Ranjha and asked him to run away with her. Ranjha assured her that when the *maulvi* came to read the *nikah*, he would step forward and tell him the truth that they were already married.

Finally on the day of marriage, Ranjha was beaten up by Chuchak's kinsman, and was locked up in a little hut on the outskirts of the village. The maulvi, too, was a part of the conspiracy and had promised that no matter what Heer's response to the all-important question was, he would convey her assent. Heer was given an opiate that dulled her senses. Her chin fell upon her chest, her eyes closed and she tried to summon all her strength to scream her refusal. He repeated his question and Malliki said loud enough for all to hear: 'She is too modest, my daughter, she will not speak. But she has nodded!' The maulvi declared that the nikah had been performed.

When the doli was to leave, Heer somewhat regained her senses. She spat at the feet of a weeping Malliki and said: 'May there never be a mother like you!' While sitting in the doli, she looked at the maulvi and cursed him: 'Our bodies are doomed when we die, only to be eaten by worms. May your body be consumed by worms while you live!'

When Ranjha came to his senses, he broke out of the hut and with fear, anger and despair ran after the doli. Heer looked at him and said: 'I know this, that wherever I am, wherever I go, my prayers to God will always be for you.'

In the days that followed, Ranjha lost his senses; he would eat food only when it was placed before him, bathe only when led to the river, and sleep only when someone told him to do so. He left the hut the Sayals had given him and began to wander through the forest, which held so many happy memories for him. One day, he met a yogi who was taken aback by Ranjha's detachment and calm acceptance of life. Ranjha followed him to his hermitage and became his pupil. Soon after his initiation, he wandered from place to place, and people in trouble began to gravitate towards him. Gradually, his fame spread far and wide as a man who had come close to God. Wherever he stopped, people came flocking to him and his reputation as a saint grew. At last, he camped at a place called Rangpur.

Heer had resolutely refused to submit to Saida's physical advances, telling him that she was the lawfully wedded wife of Ranjha. Only Saiti, Saida's sister, understood the sorrow that supped at Heer's heart for she too knew the pain of love. One day, Saiti heard of a fakir who had stopped for a few days outside the village. Thinking that he could help Heer, she went out to see him. When it was her turn to meet the fakir, she told him her sister-in-law's predicament. The fakir agreed to Saiti's request of coming to her home and meeting her: The fakir was Ranjha. So the next morning, Saiti led

Ranjha to the courtyard where Heer sat on a cot. 'You cannot help me,' Heer declared. Ranjha recognised the voice of his beloved. For a moment the world stood still for him. Heer looked sharply into his face and recognised him in the strange garb. She reached out and put her hand on his cheek and they looked into each other's eyes. Heer sobbed loudly and threw herself into her lover's arms.

With the help of Saiti, Heer and Ranjha fled Rangpur and reached the outskirts of the town of Kot Kabula. They were apprehended by some kinsmen of the Khairas, and upon being presented to the chief of Kot Kabula, Heer challenged her marriage to Saida. After a week, upon being presented to the *qazi*, the five pirs were called upon along with the witnesses from Jhang and Rangpur. The pirs confirmed the nikah they had performed in the forest. The chief pronounced Heer and Ranjha innocent of any charges of adultery against them.

Back in Jhang, Chuchak and Malliki appeared to have put the past behind them and welcomed Heer and Ranjha. Ranjha expressed his desire to return to Takht Hazara as he had been away from home for very long. Chuchak and Malliki asked for some time, insisting on departing Heer with preparations befitting a Sayal bride. Ranjha hesitated, not willing to be parted from Heer now that she was at last his. Heer, finding a middle way suggested Ranjha to return to Takht Hazara and prepare for her arrival, and that she would make in a week.

Back in Takht Hazara, Ranjha's return was met with joy by his brothers. In Jhang too, Heer was met with cordiality even by Kaidon who had returned from his exile. What she didn't know was that Kaidon and her brother Sultan were planning to kill her by poisoning her food. They believed that Heer had brought shame to the clan, and thus she should be duly punished.

On the day of her departure, Heer was dressed in her bridal finery and the doli, decorated with flowers waited for her to embrace it. While bidding a tearful farewell to her parents, she heard Kaidon's voice, soft and gentle, over her shoulder. He asked her to eat one morsel, for his sake before leaving. Heer responded to the poignancy of Kaidon's words and ate the laddoo from the platter he held ...

Ranjha sat outside his door when the messenger rode up to him. He got up to his feet excitedly, but as he looked into the man's face, he saw the frown upon his brow. On being told that Heer was dead, Ranjha went inside the house and spread his prayer mat. He knelt down to pray to Allah and the five pirs; and died while praying.

And so they lived, and so they died, leaving behind a legend that inspired innumerable artists, poets and philosophers. In Punjabi qissa literature, this tale enjoys the status of religious poetry.

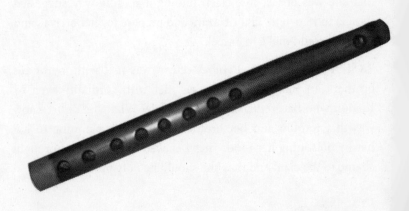

Bhein Ki Sabzi

Disclaimer: This dish is subject to availability of bhein (lotus stem)! When cooked, it gives a superb texture – soft, and yet hard enough to bite. The masala sits very well in between each perforation.

Ingredients (serves 2-3)

Bhein (lotus stems): 2 nos. (combined length should be close to 1 foot)
Water: ½ cup
Oil: 2 tsps
Hing: a pinch
Zeera (whole): ½ tsp
Dhania seeds (slightly pounded to break them): ½ tsp
Cinnamon (Dalchini) whole: 1" stick
Cloves: 5-6 nos.
Onion, chopped: 1 nos.
Green chillies, slit: 2 nos.
Ginger-garlic paste: 1 tbsp
Tomatoes, chopped: 2 large
Salt: as per taste
Haldi powder: ¼ tsp
Red chilli powder: as per taste
Zeera powder: ½ tsp
Dhania powder: ½ tsp
Coriander, chopped: a few sprigs for garnishing

Cooking

A very important step towards making this dish is picking good bhein. Owing to its underwater growth, its holes are usually lined with mud. Therefore, while buying it, make sure you look through each to check that it isn't too muddy!

Peel the lotus roots gently, discarding a slice off from the top and bottom. Cut it into half-cm slices and wash thoroughly to remove any mud inside the holes. In a pressure cooker, pour half a cup of water, put in the sliced bhein and pressure cook for one whistle. Strain and keep aside.

In a kadhai, heat oil. Once heated, add hing. Once it sputters, add whole zeera, pounded dhania, cinnamon and cloves. Then add chopped onions, slit green chillies, ginger-garlic paste and stir fry till the onions become translucent. Add tomatoes and stir fry until mashed. Add salt, haldi powder, red chilli powder, zeera powder and dhania powder and stir fry for a minute.

Now add the boiled bhein and mix well. Cook for ten minutes with the kadhai covered, stirring occasionally. The dish is done when bhein is soft (but not mushy).

Garnish with coriander, and serve with phulkas.

Ajwain Wali Arbi

Arbi (Colocasia) is a very tricky vegetable. DO NOT ATTEMPT to peel raw arbi with dry hands, as you will end up suffering from an itch for the next couple of hours! Always rub some oil on your hands before you attempt peeling it. Well, this method of making the arbi is itch-free, as it is peeled post boiling. It is made only in ajwain and dry masalas, and I love its herby flavour. There is a certain rustic appeal to this dish, coupled with the simplicity of its preparation.

Ingredients (serves 2-3)

Arbi: 250 gms (while picking the vegetable pick big, round pieces)
Oil: 4 tsps
Ajwain: 3 tsps
Salt: as per taste
Red chilli powder: ½ tsp
Dhania powder: ½ tsp
Zeera powder: ½ tsp
Amchoor: 1 tsp
Juice of 1 lemon: to squeeze in just before serving

Cooking

Boil the arbi in a pressure cooker for one whistle. Don't overdo it, as the vegetable would mash up. Peel the arbi, cut into thick roundels and keep aside.

Place a kadhai on medium flame. Pour in the oil. Once heated, put the ajwain. To this add the arbi pieces and salt, red chilli powder, dhania powder, zeera powder and amchoor. Mix well till the pieces are covered with spices evenly. No need to overcook, as the arbi is boiled already.

While serving, add a dash of lemon juice. It is best had with phulkas.

Palak Paneer

There have been innumerable variations to this simple dish. Each variation adds some more tempering – more spices for zing, paneer being fried to avoid breakage, haldi for colouration, etc. However, palak paneer is rendered best when it's kept as simple as it can be, so that the palak is at its flavourful best, with its natural green colour, and the paneer just absorbs the leafy juices and maintains its delicate self that just melts in your mouth.

Ingredients (serves 2-3)

Fresh palak (spinach) leaves: 1 bundle
Tomato, cut into halves: 2 medium
Water: ½ cup
Green chillies: 2 nos.
Oil: 2 tsps
Zeera (whole): ½ tsp
Ginger-garlic paste: 1 tbsp
Salt: as per taste
Red chilli powder: as per taste
Zeera powder: ½ tsp
Dhania powder: ½ tsp
Paneer, cut into cubes: 250 gms
Fresh cream: a little for garnishing

Cooking

Remove stems from the spinach and wash it thoroughly under running water. Make sure that it is absolutely sediment free.

Put the washed spinach and tomatoes in a pressure cooker. Add half a cup of water (only to create steam) and boil for one whistle. Then in a blender, grind the spinach and tomatoes together along with green chillies. Use the water in which the spinach was boiled as well. Keep this puree aside.

In a kadhai, heat the oil and add whole zeera. When the sputtering is over, add the ginger-garlic paste and sauté for two minutes. Then add the spinach puree and stir. Add salt, red chilli powder, zeera powder and dhania powder. Add a little water if needed. When the gravy comes to a boil, simmer and cook for ten minutes. Add the diced paneer just before taking off the gas. Mix gently so the paneer doesn't break, and remove from flame.

Top with some fresh cream before serving. Serve hot with phulkas.

Mirza Sahiban

O jiss din Mirza jamiya, uss din ayi jumay di raat
Unno gutti mil gayi ishq di ...

(The day Mirza was born, it was the night of the *juma*;
the night only fed him with his first dose of love ...)

Sahiban, at sixty-one, looked into the mirror and saw that the once bright eyes had grown dull, the once thick luxuriant black hair was now streaked generously with grey, and the once beautiful skin had turned sallow and wrinkled. She looked back at her life, and felt grateful for what had been her share of it. Although she seldom permitted her mind to dwell upon the memories of her yesteryears, still, they came gushing through the tears in her eyes, and she struggled to keep from drowning in them.

Mirza was eleven when he went to live in Sahiban's village, Jhang. He was her elder cousin, and a skinny, puny boy at that age. They had a daily routine – Sahiban would pass by his door and he would come, take her school bag from her hands and walk her to school. They made

a strange pair – the tiny, snivelling brat, who carried a bagful of books in which he had no interest, and the lovely girl, too tall for her age, who walked with an awkward stoop and obviously enjoyed every moment she spent at school. Then just outside the madarasa he would hand her the bag and run away. At the end of the day, the routine would be repeated in reverse.

During their walks, Sahiban often insisted Mirza to study, and he decided to start attending the madarasa. There, he became an object of mockery as he was too slow and weak in his studies. The maulvi spoke to him with bitter sarcasm, and beat him daily. One day, in an attempt to save him, Sahiban pleaded with the maulvi not to beat him and that she would take on the responsibility of his studies. When she attempted to do so, she realised that he was far slower than what she had expected. However, in matters not connected with books, he was a bright and alert lad. But, he still worked hard in an attempt to please her, and the maulvi took note of that.

The days slipped into weeks and the weeks into months and before they knew it, three years had passed since Sahiban had first tutored Mirza, who had grown into a strong young man. One day, when she went to his aunt Biro's house carrying a book for him, his father, Binjal Jat was sitting in the courtyard. He told her loudly that Mirza no longer needed books. Rather he needed to concentrate on learning the skills of earning a living, as well as horse riding, archery and swordsmanship. He added that he would be taking Mirza along with him back to Danabad. Hearing this, Mirza stepped back, refusing to go with his father. Binjal enticed him by offering him an Arab mare and Mirza immediately agreed to return. From the triumphant smile on Binjal's face, Sahiban sensed that he was keen to take Mirza away from her. Within a week of his departure, she had forgotten Mirza and the only memories that remained were those of a puny boy who carried her books to school.

After a year or two she heard news of Mirza's exceptional skills at horse riding, and his mastery over the bow and arrow. The news stirred nothing in Sahiban – neither admiration for his achievements, nor a desire to meet him again. She had grown up to be an exceptionally beautiful girl, vain and proud of her looks. Being the youngest, her elder brothers showered her with love, expensive clothes and ornaments. Her vanity was further fuelled by the fact that she was engaged to Tahir, the son of Nasir Khan, chief of Chandaran. Not only was his clan the richest and the most powerful in the region, but Tahir was the most eligible bachelor in Punjab, known for his swordsmanship and horse riding skills. Sahiban's pride detached her from most people in the village, who started avoiding her due to her arrogance and vicious tongue.

One day, while sitting below a tree and fantasising about her married life, as her friends frolicked by the banks of Chenab, Sahiban saw a man on a horse, gazing down at them. He was a stranger, yet she felt attracted to him. It was not just his face but also the power he exuded as he sat on the white mare that demanded attention. There was an amused arrogance in the way his head was tilted back as he looked down at the girls who he had startled. When they asked him the reason for his presence there, he replied that he just needed some water to quench his thirst. One by one, Sahiban's friends got him water but he did not drink from their pitchers. Ultimately, when it was Sahiban's turn, she filled her pitcher and walked towards him. He cupped his hand, and she poured out the water for him, but he did not drink; his eyes were fixed upon her face. He requested her to come to Heer's grove at night. Sahiban felt trapped: She had no intention of going to meet him, and yet, strangely, she felt compelled to do so. He then exclaimed, 'Sahiban! Do you not know me, Sahiban? Have the years wrought so much change in me that you cannot recognise your Mirza?' As he put his hand on her cheek, her eyes filled with tears of memories of that little boy who used to carry her books to school.

'Yes,' she said, 'the years indeed have wrought a great change in you. You no longer look the same.' She could hear the whispers of her friends in the background.

'You were not like this either, Sahiban,' Mirza whispered into her ear, following it with a repetition of his earlier request. She nodded.

That night, in Heer's grove, Mirza did not talk about her beauty and sensuousness at all. Instead, he talked about his home and horse and about his sister, Sheebo, whom he loved a lot. Sahiban spoke about her friends and her brothers. Almost an hour later when they rose to leave, Mirza asked her if she would meet him the following night as well. She agreed. The next night, Mirza held her close. Sahiban felt her heart racing, reciprocating to his touch. Sensing this, he caressed her and she too, responded to his passion.

Sahiban's life started to centre around their meetings. All day she would wait for the night to descend so that she could steal away to her lover. It was as if the day was mere existence – she came alive only during the couple of hours she spent in Mirza's arms. She started leaving her home a few minutes earlier each day, and returning a few minutes later. Consequently, it wasn't long before her family took notice.

On the tenth day when she returned late, the household was still and asleep. Only Shamir, her eldest brother, sat in a corner of the courtyard smoking his hookah. His eyes were fixed on Sahiban's face as she entered, and when she passed him to go to her room, he held her wrist. 'Come, Sahiban, come and sit with me for a while. I get to see so little of you these days that you have become quite a stranger,' he said. She knew what was going to follow. She sat down on the small *mooda* kept next to Shamir's. He told her that people had started gossiping about her frequent visits to meet her childhood friend. She replied saying that people would talk, and if one worried about that, one would end up living according to dictates of others. Shamir sat quiet, but she was nervous, and she didn't dare look him in the eye for the fear that he might glimpse the secret in hers. After a long pause, he said if people kept talking about it, the news will reach her fiancé's ears. She pondered over his words. In her moments of ecstasy, she had forgotten about Tahir.

All through that night, she fought the dark foreboding that overwhelmed her heart. If she did not stop meeting Mirza, Shamir would step in and take charge. Her restlessness lasted till the next night, when she met Mirza again. After listening to everything, Mirza advised caution. They kept their meetings in the night to the minimum, and instead took advantage of the evenings when she would go out with her friends to the river bank. He would wait for her in the shadows of the distant trees and she would find an opportunity to steal away from her friends and meet him.

Those blissful days dissolved softly, one into the other, and it seemed they would never end. But Sahiban knew that Mirza would not stay on forever. She knew that he would have to go back to his parents, but she tried not to let her mind dwell upon that. It was enough for her that each day brought the joy of being with him, and with each meeting their relationship reached a higher sense of fulfilment.

One night, as she returned from one of her infrequent visits to Heer's grove, she again found Shamir puffing at his hookah in the courtyard. This time, his tone was stricter than what it had been the last time. He asked her if she would give up on meeting Mirza on her own accord. When she replied in the negative, he said, 'Then I must find another way to end this affair.' After looking at her, he got abruptly to his feet and went inside his room. Sahiban sat alone in the courtyard, fear and anxiety gnawing at her heart. She knew her brother well: He was a man of action. She mused on his words and worried about their import. By the time dawn broke, she was close to panic.

When she met Mirza the next day, he comforted her with strong yet gentle words. He told her that Shamir would not attempt to do him any physical harm, as that would lead to a vendetta between the two families, and earn him the wrath and censure of not only the maulvi but of the entire community. The worst Shamir could do, would be to persuade his parents to call him back. He urged Sahiban to be strong in her belief in their relationship, because nothing could come between them if they decided not to give up on each other.

Meanwhile, Shamir left, only to return five days later. As he entered the courtyard, Sahiban saw their father, Kheeva Khan, look at him with uncertainty on his face. She saw the look that passed between her father and her brother, and noticed the nod that Shamir gave him. She did not worry, as she remembered that if she were sure of her love, no harm would come to them. But, as she had feared, two days later Mirza received an urgent summon from his father to return immediately, and he left with time only for the briefest of reassurances that he would return soon.

Months passed and there was no message or news from Mirza. Sahiban's initial despair and grief turned into silent anger. All day she nurtured that anger, but as night approached, she longed for him. Often she would weep silently in agony and frustration. Slowly, she learnt to curb her hopes and forced herself to think of Tahir.

Unable to free herself of Mirza's thoughts, she went to his aunt Biro's house and threw herself at her feet. The aunt promised her that she would send a message for him. Sahiban replied that if he didn't return within four days, she would give everything up and go to him. Biro looked into her eyes with a conviction that assured Sahiban that Mirza would be in Jhang in the next four days.

As the fourth day drew to a close, Sahiban waited for Mirza by the minute. As the last rays of the sun disappeared, she heard distant sounds of galloping hoof beats. She leapt to her feet and as the sounds became louder, her heart stood still. When she caught the first glimpse of him in the gathering shadows, she burst into tears. 'Forgive me, Sahiban,' he said. In between her sobs, she complained to him for not even sending her a message. He denied that saying he had sent numerous messages but there was no response from her. When she refused to take his word, he lifted her on to the saddle of his horse and rode towards his aunt's house.

At Biro's place, he commanded her to tell Sahiban about all the messages he had sent her. Biro looked at them with guilt and fear, and Sahiban knew that he spoke the truth. She knelt beside Biro and asked her why she hid the messages from her in all these trying months. Biro explained that a lot was at stake – bad blood between Shamir and Mirza, enmity and vendetta between Tahir's family and hers, and that she had sought to avoid all that by keeping Mirza's messages from her. She also added that now that she had understood the intensity of their love, she would herself go to Sahiban's father and beg for her hand for Mirza.

A hush descended on the courtyard as the three of them entered. When Biro asked for Sahiban's hand for Mirza, Shamir just stood still and did not say a word. Kheeva Khan reminded Biro that she was already betrothed to Tahir, whose family had been pressing for an early marriage. Shamir at last lost his patience and started verbally assaulting Mirza, calling him a waster. His father chided him, asking him to be quiet, since Mirza was a guest in their house. Shamir chaffed at his humiliation. Taking advantage, Biro continued that Mirza and Sahiban loved each other deeply and moreover, Mirza was her cousin and in matters like marriage, cousins had the first right. She admitted being a part of Shamir's conspiracy to make Binjal send for Mirza and to keep all his letters and messages from Sahiban. Kheeva Khan, giving in to his daughter's happiness, demanded that the request for her hand should come from Mirza's parents as well. If that happened before the next full moon, he promised, he would break her engagement with Tahir and wed her to Mirza.

Mirza went away the next morning and Sahiban was certain that what her father had asked for was a mere formality and would soon be fulfilled. At last when it was the night of the full moon and Mirza did not return, she knew something terrible had happened. She went to Biro's place, where she lay on her bed, her face turned towards the wall. A worried Sahiban asked her if she were unwell. Turning her face towards Sahiban, she wept and told her that Mirza's mother, Nasibo, had refused for her marriage with Mirza, as she was afraid of the hostility the broken engagement would cause. Sahiban, shocked at first and then deeply pained, said that if Mirza had bowed before his parents' wishes, then she must bow before them too. Saying so, she left for her home.

*

Four days of extended festivity and revelry to celebrate the coming together of two important families were planned. On the appointed day, the music could be heard long before the *baraat* made its way up the village street. Suddenly, Sahiban panicked. She decided on the spur of the moment to make one last effort to reach out to Mirza. If that failed, she would kill herself.

She reached out for Biro to send a message to Mirza, asking him to take her away in the next three days. She added that he must come and do so, else she would kill herself. Biro, making no protest, agreed to send for him.

On the third day, when everybody had retired to bed after the festivities, Sahiban heard a gentle tap on the door. Before opening the door, she removed her bangles and anklets. As she opened the door discreetly, she saw Mirza standing, wrapped in a heavy blanket. Clasping her hand, he led her out into the street. Together they walked away from the village, his horse, Shahzadi, walking behind them. When they were at a safe distance from the village, he swung her on to the saddle and climbing up beside her, galloped away. All through the night and well into the next day, they rode at the same breathless speed.

In the late afternoon, they came to a spreading banyan tree near a small pond. Choosing to rest, Mirza guided Shahzadi to the base of the tree. The strain of the last few days had overtaken Sahiban, and she wanted to rest too, though the anxiety within her would not let her. Comforting her, he said that nobody could catch up with them, as they had had a head start of six hours. An hour or two of rest would not endanger them. Saying this, he sank to the ground, putting his bow and quiver at the base of the tree. He held Sahiban close, and feeling secure in his arms, she too fell asleep.

As she slept, she dreamt that they had been discovered and were surrounded by a ring of horsemen. She dreamt that Mirza had caught hold of his bows and arrows and leapt to the tree. There, hidden behind the thick leaves he aimed his arrows at the horsemen one by one, killing them. In her dream she watched her brothers fall – first Shamir, then the others in succession. As each of them fell, she felt sorrow well up within her. She felt choked. Drenched in perspiration, she awoke with a start. And yet the sorrow did not leave her because she knew that if her brothers did catch up with them, her dream would come true.

Sahiban dwelt on the unstinting kindness her brothers had lavished upon her all those years. She thought of their wives who would be widowed if they were killed. If that were to happen, she realised that she would not find any joy with her lover, under the burden of this guilt.

Her eyes caught Mirza's quiver. She drew out the arrows; two at a time. Holding them across her bent knee, she snapped each into two and threw them as far as she could. There was one arrow left in the quiver when she heard Mirza stir besides her; she turned towards him, afraid that he would wake up and discover her perfidy. She lay besides him, thinking of the enormity of what she had done. Confused and restless, she lay in his arms more lonely and miserable than she had ever been in all the months that he had been away.

Preoccupied with her thoughts, Sahiban did not hear them approaching. All of a sudden when she looked up from the ground where she lay, she saw a horseman standing quietly not even twenty yards away. When she glanced to his left, she saw two more. It was indeed as she had dreamt. Softly, she elbowed Mirza and whispered to him that they had been found. In a move as quick as a flash of lightning, Mirza caught hold of his bow and quiver and leapt into the tree. Shamir, knowing Mirza's skills in archery, ordered the other horsemen to stay back until he had exhausted all his arrows.

Sahiban heard the singing of the bowstring as Mirza fired his arrow. There was a sharp cry and a horseman kneeled forward and fell from the saddle; it was Tahir. Mirza shouted from the tree to her, asking her to hand over his arrows, suspecting that they might have fallen to the ground. She stood still with her back towards the tree trunk, knowing that there were no arrows on the ground. Impatient, he finally jumped down from the tree and searched for them. Finding them in the grass near the pond, he knew what she had done.

'Why, Sahiban?' he shouted, as she looked into his eyes, and saw him defeated and crushed. Immediately he added, 'I understand,' and stepped out from the shadow of the tree. The circle of the horsemen still held back, neither understanding nor believing what they were seeing. Mirza demanded Shamir to give him the honour of a single combat and death, rather than butchering him like an animal. Shamir agreed and drew his sword. Mirza went up to Shahzadi and drew his sword from where it hung beside the saddle.

It was a combat of equals, and at last Mirza thrust his sword deep into Shamir's side and drew it forth again. Shamir clutched at the gaping wound and took a few steps towards Sahiban. His body swayed, his knees buckled under him and he fell to the ground. She ran to him and took his head in her lap. He made an effort to raise his head, but slumped back as life ebbed out of him.

'Get him!' Saif, her youngest brother called. They rode in upon Mirza and slashed at him with their swords. Mirza fought back as best as he could but it was of no use. Saif flung himself off from his horse and with his sword raised high above his head, charged on him.

'Enough! Enough!' Sahiban cried. 'Leave me at least with his body!'

'Leave him!' Aftab, her second brother called. 'Leave him. He will be dead soon enough anyway.'

Seeing Mirza's body slashed with swords, Sahiban was overridden with guilt. She wanted to kill herself. She looked around and saw at Shamir's waist, her grandfather's dagger that Shamir always wore with pride. As she pulled it out from its scabbard, Mirza stopped her. 'If you die now our love will die with us,' he said in gasps. She took him in his arms and when she knew that he was not looking at her, she gently drew the lids down over his lifeless eyes.

Aftab took Sahiban by her arm. The story of the arrows had gone forth and women of her village looked at her with distrust, whispering amongst themselves that she was an inauspicious woman. She had been the cause of the death not only of her brother and her fiancé, but also of her lover. Sahiban was all too numb to pay attention to such comments.

As the sharpness of her grief reduced and became a constant, dull ache, her once malicious and arrogant tone softened. She became content and at peace with herself. She began to live her life as Mirza lived his – a life full of kindness and compassion for all around her. Slowly, she forgot Mirza.

Many people regard Sahiban as a faithless woman, who betrayed her lover's trust the time he needed it the most. But had she killed herself the day Mirza died, posterity would have sung songs in praise of their love. But by choosing to live, she had condemned herself to be remembered as the faithless woman who betrayed her lover. However, in the life that she lived since her lover's death, she became like him herself. She believed that through her, Mirza lived.

Navratan Pulao

The name suggests the body of this pulao (*Nav* – nine; *ratan* – gems) – it contains nine elements of various colours. With every spoonful you experience a different taste and texture. When served with a delicious raita, it is a meal in itself.

Ingredients (serves 2)

Oil: 2 tsps
Hing: a pinch
Zeera (whole): 1 tsp
A few diced pieces of the navratans: baby aubergine (baigan) with skin, cauliflower, wadiyan bits (a typical Punjabi wadi is a sundried lump, made of a thick paste of ground urad dal and spices), soyabean chunks (easily available in grocery stores), peas, beans cut slant-wise, onion slices, carrot, capsicum.
Green chillies, chopped: 2 nos.
Salt: as per taste
Red chilli powder: as per taste
Dhania powder: ½ tsp
Zeera powder: ½ tsp
Water: 2 cups
Rice, soaked for an hour: ¾ cup

Cooking

In an aluminium patila (boiling vessel), heat oil. When heated, add hing and whole zeera. To this add the navratans and chopped green chillies. Stir fry the vegetables on high flame till the onions become translucent. Then add salt, red chilli powder, dhania powder and zeera powder and stir fry for a minute. Keeping the flame high, add two cups of water and bring to a boil. Add the soaked rice, simmer, and place lid partially. Let it cook till the rice is done.

After turning off the gas, leave it covered till the time you are ready to eat. Any kind of a raita is good accompaniment.

Sarson da Saag te Makki di Roti

This is Punjabi cuisine at its rustic best. It brings to life so many memories, which if I start putting down, would be enough to make a novella! Not just the final dish, but even the preparation of this saag is an experience in itself – picking out the weeds from the leaves, peeling the hard stalks (called *gandalān*), the dollop of white butter on the saag while serving, making the roti without using the rolling pin…. If there was one dish I would have to choose to represent 'me' – this would be it.

Since it's an elaborate dish, you can make a slightly larger quantity and store it in the fridge. It has a shelf life of two to three days, if refrigerated.

SARSON DA SAAG

Ingredients (for many servings!)

Sarson (mustard) leaves: 750 gms to 1 kg (depending on the bundle size)
Palak (spinach) leaves: 250 gms
Bathua (pig weed) leaves: 250 gms
Water: 1 cup
Ghee: 2-3 tbsps
Green chillies, chopped: 3 nos.
Ginger, finely chopped: 1" piece

Garlic, finely chopped: 8-10 cloves
Tomato, finely chopped: 1 large
Salt: as per taste
Red chilli powder: as per taste
Makki ka aatta: 2 tbsps

Cooking

Clean all three leaves of any weeds, wash thoroughly and put them in a pressure cooker, along with one cup of water. After the first whistle, simmer and cook for fifteen minutes. When cooled, blend into a coarse paste and keep aside.

In a kadhai, heat the ghee. When heated, add chopped green chillies, ginger and garlic. Stir fry till the garlic becomes translucent. Add tomatoes, and stir fry till they mash a little. Add salt and red chilli powder. Now mix in the saag. Keeping the flame high, let it boil, after which you should lower the gas and cook for thirty to thirty-five minutes, stirring occasionally. While it is boiling, sprinkle the makki ka aatta and mix well (it helps to bind the saag, so that it doesn't leave water while serving). Serve hot topped with a dollop of home-made white butter.

MAKKI DI ROTI

Ingredients

Makki ka aatta: 3 cups
Plain wheat flour: 1 cup
Water, lukewarm: enough to make dough
Ghee: 1 tsp
Salt: a pinch
Ajwain: ½ tsp
(This dough is best kneaded with lukewarm water)

Cooking

Mix all the ingredients and knead into a soft dough, adding lukewarm water bit by bit. Cover it with a moist cloth and let it rest for half an hour. Take a little portion of the dough in your hands, flatten it roughly into a roti in between your palms (if you find it difficult, you can also flatten it on your kitchen slab, spreading a plastic sheet beneath).

Heat the tawa and place the roti on it. Cook on both sides till golden brown. While serving, fork it and brush some ghee on top.

Butter Chicken

This dish is synonymous with Sardar families. When I meet new people, they often ask me if we make butter chicken everyday at home. No! We don't make it everyday, but we make sure we spend enough time on this dish to make a lovely dinner for us! Butter chicken is actually a source of pride for me as a Punjabi. I have broken down the recipe into simpler steps, to help you make this classic dish with ease.

Ingredients (serves 2)

Chicken, cut into pieces: 1 kg

For first marination
Red chilli powder: ½ tsp
Juice of 1 lemon
Salt: as per taste

For second marination
Thick curd: 1 cup
Red chilli powder: ½ tsp

Ginger-garlic paste: 2 tbsps
Juice of 1 lemon
Garam masala powder: ½ tsp
Mustard oil: 2 tbsps

For the gravy
Salted butter: 3 tbsps
Green cardamoms (slightly pounded): 4-5 nos.
Cloves: 5-6 nos.
Cinnamon: 2" sticks
Peppercorns: 10-12 nos.
Ginger-garlic paste: 1 tbsp
Green chillies, chopped: 4-5 nos.
Tomato puree: 400 gms (2 tetrapacks of 200 gms)
Red chilli powder: as per taste
Salt: as per taste
Garam masala powder: ½ tsp
Water: 1 cup
Honey (or white sugar as an alternative): 1 tbsp
Kasoori methi (dry fenugreek leaves), crushed: ½ tbsp
Fresh cream: 1 or less cup (depending on how rich you want it to taste)

Cooking

First Marination

Mix the red chilli powder, lemon juice and salt. Apply to the chicken pieces and keep aside for half an hour.

Second Marination

To the thick curd, add red chilli powder, ginger-garlic paste, lemon juice, garam masala powder and mustard oil. Apply this marinade paste to the chicken pieces and refrigerate for three to four hours.

Roasting the chicken

Traditionally, this is done in a tandoor, after putting the chicken on the *seekhs* (skewers). However, in the absence of the tandoor, we can do it in the kadhai as well. In the kadhai, stir fry the chicken for ten to twelve minutes or until almost done. You don't need oil for this as the second marinade already has mustard oil. Remove and set aside.

Final Makhani Gravy

Heat the butter in a kadhai. Add green cardamoms, cloves, cinnamon and peppercorns. Sauté for two minutes, and add ginger-garlic paste and chopped green chillies. Cook for two minutes. Add tomato puree, red chilli powder, salt, garam masala powder, and one cup of water. Bring to a boil. Reduce heat and simmer for ten minutes. Add sugar or honey and powdered kasoori methi. Add the roasted chicken pieces. Simmer for five minutes, remove from flame and then add fresh cream, as much as your mood allows you to indulge!

Serve hot with any accompaniment of your choice: rice, phulkas, paranthas, or naan.

Sassi Punnu

Maa-pe kadi ais tarah, te doli nein si torde,
Dhian nu wiande si O, enj nein si rorde

(None of the parents ever parted with their daughter like this,
they bid her in a doli after marrying her; they didn't throw her
away like I was thrown.)

Dark clouds had covered the sky during the day. As dusk fell, they
seemed to get darker. Kapil Muni, however, failed to take notice
of the dark clouds as that was the brightest day of his life – after
long, sterile years, he and his wife, Ramba, had been blessed with
a child.

Ramba had delivered a baby girl in the early hours of the night
after being in labour for almost the whole day. Kapil Muni
had wished for a boy, but when he held the infant in his arms,
happiness welled up in his eyes, leaving no room for misgivings.
For a long time, he cuddled the baby in his arms; then, handing
it over to the midwife turned to do what he was most adept at –
casting a horoscope. He quickly drew up his tables. As he started
making deductions, a frown creased his brow – he checked and
rechecked his calculations. The stars were telling him that his
daughter would one day bring him shame and there were no
mantras, no acts of charity, no remedies at all that could thwart
this prophecy.

Where a daughter was concerned, it was easy to foresee what
'shame' would mean, perhaps she would be involved in an illicit
love affair, perhaps bear an illegitimate child, or perhaps fall in
love with a boy from a lower caste, or a different religion; Kapil
Muni shuddered at these thoughts. What had started as the
brightest day of his life had turned out be the darkest, just like

the skies above. Overridden by restlessness, he thought that whatever dishonour she would bring would not be to him alone, but also to ancestors, all worthy men who had lived virtuous lives. Thus, he thought, he could not risk keeping his daughter with him.

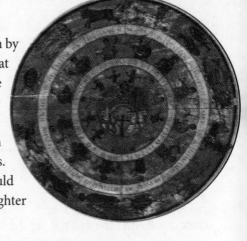

He made a quick, clear decision. Neither would he kill her nor would he keep her. He would set her adrift on the Sind river that flowed close to the village, and let destiny take its course through its waters. If she was destined to live, someone would find her and give her a home and the shame of what she would do in the future would no longer be his.

He looked around for something that would carry his daughter on the waters and his eyes rested on a wooden box, his repository of old horoscopes. He took a few handfuls from the bundle of cotton that his wife had been hoarding for a new quilt, and carefully padded the inside of the box, making a soft warm cushion for the baby. Next, he stole into the room where Ramba slept, tired and exhausted, with the baby sleeping next to her. He quietly went to the cot, picked up the baby and crept out of the room. Once again, while he held her to his chest, he felt the same warm love that had overwhelmed him the first time he had held her. Picking up the box and a length of saffron silk that the zamindar had gifted him for reading his son's horoscope, he started walking towards the river. Once at its bank, he unfolded the silk, wrapped the baby in it and lowered her into the box. Closing the lid while fighting the urge to hold her once more, he let the currents take his daughter away towards her destiny.

*

Mahmood stood knee-deep in cold water, pounding the dirty clothes against a rock. It was not a suitable morning for his work as the sky was laden with clouds. Tired, as he sat down on a rock for a few moments of rest, he saw a neat rectangular box floating down the river towards him. He grabbed it as it floated past, and when he opened it, he could hardly believe what he saw – a beautiful little baby, wrapped in saffron silk, was asleep inside. As if responding to his moment of surprise, she opened her eyes, and her face crinkled into the most heart-melting innocent smile. As she began to wail, he held her to his chest and ran towards his little hut in Bhambhor.

His wife, Nasib, held the baby to her chest as the old *dhobi*, still panting, handed the baby over to her. Appalled, Nasib started preparing a feed for her. At night as she sat down looking at the baby, peacefully asleep, she asked Mahmood to start searching for her parents the next morning, at which he remarked that if her parents wished to find her, they wouldn't have cast her away in the river. Nasib, however, insisted on making an effort; but as she lay in the bed, she imagined how wonderful it would be if the parents were not found and the baby could be theirs.

After ten days of earnest searching, the couple gave up and savoured the joy of this strange and unexpected gift – a child in their lives when they had given up the hope of one. They named her Sassi, and as she grew, each day brought moments of delight to them – the first downy hair on her head, the first gurgling sounds she made, the first time she turned over to her side, the first time she responded to her name, the first step she took. As she blossomed into a young girl, her beauty attracted praise and admiration from far and wide. With devoted parents who instilled values in her since childhood, it was little wonder that she grew up to be an embodiment of decency, content with her lot, serene in her poverty, and ever willing to share the little she had with others. The little town of Bhambhor loved her and took her to its collective heart.

When Sassi was about twelve, there was a wedding in the community and she looked stunning in her bright clothes. When she was called upon to join in the singing and dancing, she instantly became the centre of attention and all eyes turned to her.

'Who is she?' rose the whisper in the babble around her.

'She is Sassi, Mahmood's daughter.'

'Wonderful are the ways of Allah! The child was brought to them by Him in a strange fashion … in a wooden box, carried down by the waters!'

'Hush! Fatima! The girl can hear you …!' said an old lady.

Sassi fled home to avoid the eyes of all women. Her mother, surprised by her early return, asked her if she was fine. When she offered her some *phirni* (a sweet dish made with milk and rice), Sassi drew away and resigned to solitude. As the night drew and she didn't leave her room, Nasib grew worried and asked her what troubled her.

'Tell me, mother, is it true that I am not your daughter? That father found me in a box in the river?'

Nasib felt a deep sadness enveloping her. This was the question she had been dreading all her life. Choosing her words carefully, she told Sassi the story of her infancy, how they had found her in a box and how their life changed with her. Sassi looked into her mother's eyes and memories of her childhood flashed across her mind – of returning from visits to relatives in far-flung villages, resting comfortably on her tired but joyous father's back; of difficult days, when there was little to eat and Nasib gave her all that was there. With tears springing to her eyes, Sassi asked her mother for forgiveness. That night onwards, Sassi was a new, more mature girl.

If there was one aspect of her kind, polite and considerate character that was not always admired, it was the rigidity with which she stood by what she believed to be right – nothing could shake her from it – neither censure of peers nor remonstration of elders. Similar was the stand that she took when it came to her marriage. Her beauty and character was known far and wide, proposals flowed in for her but she turned down each firmly. Considering her parents' frail health, she insisted on marrying a man who would stay in her home, with her parents after marriage. Her parents, although touched by the sentiment behind her decision, chided her gently and told her that it was a daughter's destiny to leave for her husband's house. But Sassi remained implacable in her decision.

The years slipped by and all of Sassi's friends got married and even bore children. Once in a while, she too would long for a husband and children of her own. But she never forgot that her parents were old and weak, and would be helpless without her, thus remaining firm in her resolve. Friends and relatives now mocked at her stupidity and the selfishness of her parents. She took their comments with a smile. Now in her twenty-fifth year, she still believed there would be a man who would, without any hope of inheritance, come and stay with her parents.

*

There was an old tree on the bank of the river, under which Sassi used to sit while taking a break from washing clothes. One morning, she saw someone sitting under that tree, bent over a sheet of paper and sketching something with a piece of charcoal. Going closer, she found that he had been sketching her. Angry at first, Sassi noticed that he was a middle-aged man, with an ascetic face and a radiant smile. Seeing her frown, he handed her a roll of sheets, containing many portraits painted by him.

As she went through each portrait by turn, she came across one of a handsome man, more handsome than any man she had ever seen. He wore a rich dress and adorned exquisite jewels. She looked into his eyes. She saw a sparkle, and a steely resolve behind them – something that she saw in her eyes whenever she looked into a mirror. When she looked up from the portrait, she saw the artist looking at her with a speculation in his eyes and a little smile on his lips.

Day and night Sassi was haunted by the portrait of the prince. She knew the feeling was ridiculous and tried to push it aside. But again and again she saw him in front of her eyes and by the next morning, he had become the focus of her life. When she met the artist the next day, she again looked at the prince's portrait for a long time. The artist told her that the portrait was of Punnu, the third son of Ahmad, the chief of Kach Makran. Sassi kept gazing at the picture. After a while, Sassi confessed to him that for the first time in her life, she felt she had found a man to whom she could gladly surrender her entire being, and follow wherever he chose to lead. She paused for a moment and looked into the artist's eyes, who put his hand on her head and spoke in a tender voice: 'You are possessed by a fine madness, may Allah protect you, my child!' He left, leaving the portrait with her.

Sassi knew she was in love but it was not the love she had learnt about from folklore or from her friends. There was no restlessness, no anxiety. She began to ask all those who stopped at the *serai* if they were from Kach Makran, and if they were, she would ask about Punnu. Everybody knew of her interest in him, and they soon started talking about it. Meanwhile, there came a proposal for Sassi from Ismail, her cousin, who had always harboured a secret affection for her. She turned down the proposal, and told her parents that she had made her choice, and that it had become a part of her. On being asked who he was, Sassi went into her room and returned with Punnu's portrait. Her parents looked at her and the portrait in disbelief when she added that she had never met him. Sassi sobbed and said she could do nothing about it, knowing that Punnu would forever remain unaware of her existence.

But she was wrong: Punnu was aware of her existence. When traders who had passed through Bhambhor returned home, they brought with them stories of the ethereally beautiful girl who constantly sought news of Punnu. This titillated his vanity, as well as curiosity. He too, began to feel attracted to that mysterious girl. When the artist who had seen Sassi returned to Kach Makran, Punnu summoned him. He asked him to paint a portrait of her and when the artist finished, Punnu was nothing short of being besotted by Sassi. He decided to leave for Bhambhor the next morning.

After eight days when he reached Bhambhor, he stood alone one morning under the tree the artist had told him of, watching Sassi work. When she finally saw him, she abandoned her work and ran towards him. As she cried out of excitement, he held her close, pressing her face against his chest. Afterwards, they sat by the river bank, sharing the stories of their lives so far, till dusk fell.

Sassi was now in a dilemma: she was devoted to her parents, but also obsessed with Punnu. Now that he was here, she needed to make a choice. Punnu, understanding her predicament, thought of a solution. He abandoned his rich clothes and jewels, and took on the garb of a washerman. He was clumsy in the beginning, but as he was eager to get Sassi's approval, he immersed himself in his job completely. News of his transformation spread through the town, leading at first to some jeering and then a sense of wonder. When he finally met her parents, he ate the food served to him with relish as if that was the kind of simple, frugal food he had eaten all his life. Seeing his eager transformation, her parents knew that their wait for an ideal husband for Sassi had not gone waste. Punnu asked Mahmood for his daughter's hand, while also consenting to stay with them in their hut. Mahmood asked him to speak to the maulvi, for fixing the nikah the next day.

After a simple wedding, Punnu gave all the money to his attendants, bid them an affectionate farewell and sent them back to Makran. He sent a message to his father, Ahmad, and brothers, Umar and Tumar that they should not worry about him and that he would bring his bride to visit them soon in Makran. Once back, his attendants told Ahmad of what had happened. Ahmad, amused, commented that no woman could hold Punnu for more than six months. After a general laughter, the matter was brushed aside. Back in Bhambhor, the love between Sassi and Punnu became deeper with each passing day.

*

One day, a little over a year after their marriage, Sassi saw an old man sitting under the same tree while Punnu and she washed clothes by the river. Seeing him exhausted, she requested Punnu to ask the old man if he needed help; Sassi followed and asked him where he was headed. The old man told them that he was a pundit, and that the diwan had asked him to cast a horoscope for his grandson. The old man sensed something familiar about Sassi's face; Sassi, too, felt the same about him. However, both didn't know what it was. After the couple helped him to his feet, he resumed his journey. At the diwan's place, the old man's thoughts turned to Sassi again. He told the diwan how he felt like he knew her for long, even though he hadn't met her before. The diwan, while telling him about her parents Mahmood and Nasib, told him how they found her in a box brought down by the river. The pundit, surprised yet shaken, knew that destiny had brought him face to face with his own daughter a while back. The next morning, he went to Sassi's home. Unable to hold his composure any longer, he cried aloud in deep agony, asking for Sassi's forgiveness. Sassi, gently wiping his tears said, 'You lost the right to your daughter's love but you did not lose the right to compassion and concern for your suffering.'

Meanwhile, back in Makran, Punnu had become the talk of the town. Initially, his father and his brothers ignored the gossip but things climaxed when at a conclave of chieftains one of the neighbouring chiefs referred to Punnu as 'that dhobi'. The reference evoked a ripple of laughter. Umar was enraged. Later in the night, the father and the sons sat together and devised a plan to get Punnu back. Ahmad gave the responsibility to Tumar, considering his cunningness to handle the situation with the discretion that it deserved.

Two weeks later, Tumar arrived in Bhambhor with his entourage. They stopped at the serai to wash and change their clothes, and then presented themselves at the old dhobi's house. Their manner was friendly and affectionate – they brought generous gifts for Mahmood, but not ostentatious ones that would have caused embarrassment. Then, as they all sat on string cots sipping hot milk from copper tumblers, Tumar said: 'Our tradition demands that the bridegroom's family should host a feast, a *jafat*, in celebration of the wedding. Now, when after three years, it seems that Punnu will never return to Makran, my father has asked me to come here and fulfil our obligation. Can I bid you to a feast at the serai the day after tomorrow?' With the humility with which the invitation was extended, no one could have refused.

On the appointed day, the entire community thronged the serai. Musicians, dancers and acrobats were commissioned to entertain the guests; food and wine was in abundance. The feast lasted late into the night. The guests found it difficult to refuse when the hosts pressed more wine upon them. Sassi, in this whole revelry, was given a sedative that made her drowsy, making her oblivious to the world. Punnu was drunk to the hilt. Tumar and his entourage had made their plans well, and in less than half an hour when the party began to recede, they were on their way to Makran.

In the early hours of the morning, Sassi stirred in her sleep and reached out for Punnu. She sensed he wasn't around, and woke up instantly. Her head hurt from the effects of the sedative. She rushed out of her room instantly and saw signs of Tumar and his entourage's hasty departure. A dread grew inside her. They had taken Punnu with them. She ran from the serai, out along the street and on to the road. The early morning breeze bit into her ill-clad body but she paid no heed. Soon, the sun broke over the horizon, bringing with it not only the comfort of its warmth but also some rays of hope.

She came at last to a point on a highway from where the caravans to Kach Makran had cut across the sands. Unhesitant, she too abandoned the highway and plunged into the desert. She trudged on the yielding sands, for hours on end. The hot sand burnt her feet and soon, the soles of her feet were covered with blisters, making each step an ordeal. Yet she lumbered on, ignoring her pain, because in front of her she could clearly see the wheel marks of a caravan in the sand. Night fell and the cold breeze blew strong, making her shiver. Her mind had become hazy with weariness; she feared that she had lost her way, and was heading back the way she had come.

Sassi struggled for days. The barren sand now gave way to rugged hills, but they too were bereft of any trace of vegetation, water or shelter. There was no sign of the caravan now, nothing to give her direction except the narrow path that meandered through the hills. She forced herself to go on, falling and picking herself again and again. When she looked up, she saw two vultures circling above her. 'No, not yet,' she told herself and struggled to her feet. There was no sensation left in her body now, no feelings or emotions in her heart. Finally, she fell again: Calling the name of Punnu, she lay there unconscious, with the vultures, now many in number, flying above her.

Sassi had collapsed near a little spring called Las Bela, the first oasis on the desert route. A hermit who lived nearby, saw the commotion of the vultures and Sassi lying on the ground. Clapping his hands, he shooed the vultures away, and carried Sassi in his arms into the shade of trees. There, as he put some water into her mouth, she began calling Punnu's name again. As the night drew, she lay still and he knew that she had passed away.

It took Punnu four days to realise what he was being put through. Each time he awoke from sleep and felt the dryness in his throat, he asked for water. Each time he was given a drink laced with sedative that would put him to sleep again. The next day, when he was given the drink, he threw it away and pretended to sleep again. At an opportune moment, he mounted a horse and rode back towards Bhambhor.

On his way, he met the same hermit who had tended to Sassi in her last moments. The hermit offered him his hut to rest, and in a passing moment took an earthen lamp to light next to Sassi's grave. When he asked him why he took the lamp outside, he told him that a mesmerisingly beautiful girl died there, searching for a man called Punnu. Punnu, completely broken by now, walked towards the grave and raised his hands in prayer. He kneeled down, and in the flickering light of the little lamp, the hermit could see that he was in deep mourning. Till morning, Punnu stayed still where he was. The hermit felt deeply saddened on seeing Punnu in this state. He knew that the stranger had made up his mind to join his beloved. Later that morning, the hermit had to dig another grave, next to Sassi's.

Every Thursday, the hermit would light lamps on their graves in Las Bela, near Shah Bilawal. Soon, people from nearby villages, also started doing that, praying that the lovers would at last rest in peace. On certain Thursday evenings, people would collect at the graves and they would recite *naats* (poetry in praise of Prophet Mohammad) and sing prayers. Sassi and Punnu, thus, lived and continue to live as legends to show the world the unconquerable power of love.

The most well-known version of Sassi-Punnu is the one written by Shah Abdul Latif Bhitai, a Sindhi Sufi poet. He wrote this qissa in Sufi poetry as a tale of eternal love and union with the Divine.

Kadhai Paneer

This one is my all-time favourite; it's just about paneer and I don't have to pick my paneer pieces out! Kadhai paneer derives its typical character not only from the *khada masalas* that are used, but also from the way they are sautéed in the kadhai; they lend their aroma and flavours to seep into the paneer. It's quite simple to make, so make sure you make lots of it to dig into.

Ingredients (serves 2-3)

Oil: 2 tsps
Dry red chillies, broken: 2-3 nos.
Zeera (whole): ½ tsp
Cloves: 4-5 nos.
Dhania seeds (slightly pounded to break them): ½ tsp
Cinnamon whole: 1" stick
Bay leaves: 2-3 nos.
Onion, finely chopped: 1 large
Ginger-garlic paste: 2 tbsps
Green chillies, slit: 3 nos.
Tomato, chopped: 1 large
Salt: as per taste
Haldi powder: ½ tsp
Red chilli powder: as per taste
Dhania powder: ½ tsp
Zeera powder: ½ tsp
Amchoor: ½ tsp
Paneer, cut into 1" cubes: 500 gms
Coriander leaves, chopped: a few sprigs for garnishing

Cooking

Heat oil in a kadhai. When heated, add broken red chillies, whole zeera, cloves, pounded dhania seeds, cinnamon and bay leaves. To this add the onions and sauté for two minutes. Add ginger-garlic paste and green chillies and continue to sauté till the onions turn golden brown. Then add tomatoes and sauté until they become soft.

Add salt, haldi powder, red chilli powder, dhania powder, zeera powder and amchoor and stir fry for a minute. Now add paneer cubes and mix gently to avoid them from breaking. Cook on a low flame for five minutes until the paneer is thoroughly heated and mixed with the masala.

Garnish with coriander leaves, and serve hot with phulkas or paranthas.

Assorted Barbecues

Under the starry sky, he fanned the burning wood splinters to ignite the coal. To bring the coal to burn was quite a task in that cool breeze. I covered the coal bay with the wire mesh, to cut the breeze from extinguishing the fire. But he'd rather have me stand away from the fire, because he feared I'd burn myself.

So, I made my way to the kitchen and started collecting stuff to take out to the balcony: the bowl of chicken pieces, which he had marinated even before I reached his place, the bowl of melted butter and a brush to apply it on chicken pieces while barbecuing, plates, a tissue box, green chutney, some chaat masala, some curd and yes, his beers and my breezers!

By the time I finished taking everything out, the coal pieces that refused to burn were glowing embers. He took some pieces of whole spices – cinnamon, cloves, star anise and black cardamom, and threw them on the burning coal. What a gorgeous aroma the coal emanated! I took a magazine and started fanning the coal to make it glow more. Grinning, he went inside and dragged out two bean bags.

That night, I ate beneath the twinkling sky as he cooked. The love in the air kept the embers glowing for long.

Ingredients (serves 4-5)

Thick curd: 250 gms
Besan: 2 tbsps
Ajwain: 2 tsps
Salt: as per taste
Red chilli powder: as per taste
Zeera (whole), roasted and coarsely ground: 1 tsp
Juice of 2 lemons
Ginger-garlic paste: 2 tbsps
Chicken, cut into medium pieces: 1 kg
Paneer, cut into 1" cubes: ½ kg
Assorted veggies of your choice: (broccoli, capsicum, onions, baby corn) cut into 1" pieces, as many as you like.
Salted butter: for brushing
Wooden skewers, soaked in water for an hour: 10-15 nos.
Chaat masala: to sprinkle on the barbecue skewers just before serving
Juice of 1 lemon: to squeeze just before serving

Method

Make a mixture of thick curd, besan, ajwain, salt, red chilli powder, roasted zeera powder, lemon juice and ginger-garlic paste. Add the chicken pieces, paneer cubes and vegetable pieces into the mixture and mix well. Keep aside for a couple of hours.

In the barbecue, when the coal pieces start glowing consistently, place the wire mesh/gauze on the bricks, above them. Brush the mesh with a little butter. Keep airing the coal pieces occasionally so that they keep glowing.

Take a skewer and pierce some marinated pieces of chicken, paneer or vegetables of your choice through it. Place it over the mesh and cook till done. Keep brushing some butter so that the pieces don't become dry.

Remove on to a plate, sprinkle some chaat masala and squeeze some lemon juice on the top. Serve hot with mint chutney.

TIP: Instead of using a brush for brushing butter on the mesh or the chicken, use a small bundle of fresh coriander or parsley. Dip the leafy bundle in butter and brush with quick strokes. This will give a lovely aroma to the smoke.

Rice Kheer

Rice kheer reminds me of my childhood. As a child I too was averse to drinking milk, like many of us, but I used to love it in the form of kheer. It was a splendid discovery for my mom, who made sure I had it often. She used to keep it simple – just milk, rice, sugar and elaichi (green cardamom) – because it was meant to be substituting milk in my breakfast, and was not prepared like a dessert! However, she taught me all the frills of making this delicious, classic dessert.

Ingredients (serves 3-4):

Rice: ¼ cup
Water: enough to soak the rice
Full cream milk: ½ litre
Sugar: ½ cup
Green cardamom (slightly pounded to break the pods): 6-7 nos.
Almonds, soaked, peeled and sliced: 10 nos.
Cashews, sliced: 10 nos.
Raisins: 10 nos.

Cooking:

Soak the rice in water in a cup for about twenty minutes, so that it becomes brittle. Gently crush the rice with a spoon in the same cup and keep aside.

Pour milk into an aluminium vessel and bring to boil. Add the rice and lower the flame. Cook stirring continuously, otherwise the milk will start sticking to the sides and the bottom of the vessel. When the rice is really soft and the mixture starts thickening, add sugar, green cardamom, almonds, cashews and raisins. Cook for five more minutes and adjust the sugar as per your taste.

Serve hot or cold.

Sohni Mahiwal

Sohni jahi kise preet na karni,
Uhdi preet vi pani bhardi
Vichch daryavan de
Sohni aap dubbi, rooh tardi.

(Who else could love like Sohni? Her love was divine.
While she drowned, her spirit swam across the river to meet her
beloved.)

Fazal Shah's tale of Sohni Mahiwal remains the most popular
version of this tale till date.

Mirza Izzat Baig, the merchant prince of Bokhara, had a knack
for taking risks – not because he could afford it, but because of
the peaceful detachment that he possessed, one that permeated
all aspects of his personal life. He was a dutiful husband and loved
all his four wives. He was a doting father and gave all his children
more than they desired. He was generous and took part in all social
and community activities. But amidst all this, something held him
back – a lack of fervour, an absence of intensity of emotion as if
nothing touched the core of his being – except the return of his
caravans from India.

He treated the travellers of all the returning caravans from
India lavishly, giving them generous gifts and hosting them in
comfortable apartments. But no one knew that in the night while
everybody slept, he sifted through the remnants of the long
journey till he found the pots that had been used for carrying food
and water. He looked carefully at each and carried a select few to
his apartment. After reaching the safe confines of his apartment,
he bolted the door and caressed each pot, running his fingers over
them – all detachment fell away from him and he felt such intense
happiness that it brought tears to his eyes.

Coming from a small provincial town in Gujarat, in undivided India, the pots had a finesse about them that only a seasoned potter could bring. Lately Izzat Baig had noticed a subtle change in them – a slight elongation of the neck, a delicate turning of the opening. He deduced that the potter, at last sure of himself, now wished to experiment. Long into the stillness of the night, he

caressed each pot in turn and conjured up in his mind the image of the man who had made them. Over the years, this image had changed from a young hesitant lad, to a middle-aged man, to an old man with a flowing grey beard, and a slight stoop.

Often Mirza longed to go to Gujarat and meet the potter. But he feared the potter being significantly different from the image he had framed in his mind. Therefore, even when the opportunity to go to India and meet the potter used to come his way, he hesitated. But then, as if by design, arose an opportunity which could not be brushed aside. Mirza was invited by Afzal Khan, an influential nobleman in India to discuss the grant of monopoly to Mirza over export of fine Dacca muslin to the West. There was great excitement in Bokhara over this news, and Mirza had to go himself to finalise the details.

In India, neither the lavish welcome nor the successful meeting touched Mirza. During his journey towards Gujarat – with half the caravan, since the other half had left for Dacca – he felt excited to meet the potter. Finally, when the caravan reached the doors of a serai outside Gujarat, he experienced immense restlessness. He barely touched his food and was unable to sleep. Iqbal, his attendant and confidante, sensed his unease and upon enquiring Mirza lied saying that it was due to the overwhelming excitement of the past few days. But Iqbal knew his master well. He knew that all the attention and material gain meant nothing to Mirza. He also knew that Mirza would tell him when he was ready and certainly, before anyone else.

The next morning, Mirza took a pot he had brought all the way from Bokhara and went out into the streets. Upon asking a shopkeeper, he learnt that the potter's name was Tulla. It was a small town and finding the potter posed no difficulty for him. He stood across the street and watched an old man come out of a shop and add two more pots to the display outside. He was much older than what Mirza had imagined him to be. However, he had a grey beard and the same stoop. Crossing the street, he was now looking the potter in his eyes; the latter was humbled by the presence of the merchant prince of Bokhara in his little shop.

Scanning the pots both inside and outside the shop carefully, Mirza found that they were of two kinds: one robust and strong and the other robust yet delicate in form. Upon asking, Tulla revealed that the latter set was made by his daughter, Sohni. Mirza now realised that what he had seen as a desire to experiment was actually the work of another potter. He bought some pots and insisted on seeing how they were made. Tulla led him to a small courtyard, where Sohni was busy working at the potter's wheel.

Her face was bent over her work and there was little that Mirza could see. But he saw the deft, strong fingers as they pressed in upon the wet clay and drew the formless lump into the shape she desired. When she looked up, she caught the sight of the men. Forgetting her work, she stood up, with the wheel still whirling at her feet. Mirza looked at the girl, and she took his breath away. She was beautiful beyond words; she exuded dignity and pride, yet there was a tender vulnerability to her.

At the serai, the image of Sohni standing beside her wheel kept flashing in his mind. He found himself free of all excitement, fear and restlessness. He knew that he had taken the right decision to come all the way to Gujarat – the real potter had far outshone the portrait he had painted in his mind.

Mirza declined to commence his homeward journey to Bokhara the next day. Instead, he went to Tulla's shop again to buy more pots and see Sohni again. The next day too, Mirza did the same. That very night, Sohni expressed her discomfort with the way Mirza looked at her to her mother, who in turn advised her not to appear in front of him anymore. She also told Tulla that it was not because of the pots that Mirza was coming to their shop everyday; it was because of Sohni.

Thereafter, day after day, Mirza went to Tulla's shop and returned without catching a glimpse of Sohni. The pile of pots in the courtyard of the serai grew bigger and he became restless. In the small town of Gujarat, Mirza's behaviour was noted and commented upon. Sohni stopped going out of her house to avoid the amused glances she received. Mirza's caravan also became aware that their leader tarried because of the potter's daughter. They resented this, as their leader's lust was keeping them away from their homes and families. Sensing this, Mirza called Iqbal one night and advised him to begin the return journey to Bokhara without him. He also confessed to him his longing for Sohni. Iqbal, understanding his friend's predicament, started preparing for the caravan's departure.

As days drifted into weeks and weeks into months, and Mirza did not see Sohni, he became a man possessed. He lost all desire for food and sleep. He started wandering the streets of Gujarat, at times walking down to the River Chenab and sitting on its bank staring at its waters. He would await nightfall and its darkness so that he could drown himself in wine and have the glorious visions of Sohni that came to him in his drunken stupor. As he continued to drink more, he would stagger around the streets barefoot, his clothes stained and tattered, street urchins following him. Yet each day, he went to Tulla's shop and bought more pots till Tulla had no pots to sell and he had no money to buy.

All of Gujarat now marvelled at the intensity of his love. By implication, they held Sohni responsible for this change and there was a hint of hostility in their voices when they spoke about her or met her. Sohni found it unfair because the moment she had sensed his intentions, she had quietly stepped aside. A smouldering anger built up inside her and she longed to confront him.

One night, after ensuring that her parents were fast asleep, Sohni covered her head in a shawl and left for the serai. When she found a pot and a cup made by her kept on the windowsills of one of the rooms, she knew that was Mirza's. When she saw him, she was taken aback by the transformation that love had wrought upon him. She looked at his matted hair, his wild unkempt beard, his wild eyes and the pain and misery that crowded his face. Overwhelmed by guilt, she stood beside him and wept. He drew her closer and took her in his arms. Feeling an unknown peace within her, Sohni drifted into a deep sleep, while he lay awake, not willing to believe the reality of her presence.

Thereafter, she started coming to the serai regularly in the night. As their meetings became more passionate, Mirza started paying attention to his grooming and eating habits. He discarded his wine jars and cups. One night, Mirza whispered to Sohni that he desired more than just a clandestine meeting in the night. Sohni, too, felt the same and they started meeting near a thick grove on the left bank of the river, two miles from town. They got to know each other – he learnt that there was one delicacy she could not resist – fresh Mahasher caught from the river, roasted lightly on a thin piece of slate and sprinkled delicately with salt and topped with a dash of lemon juice. He took to catching fish while waiting for her, and when she came, he cooked it for her. While watching her eat, his eyes would be flooded with love.

For a few months their meetings remained a secret. But slowly, as the lovers became careless, their comings and goings fed the gossipmongers of the town. It wasn't long before Tulla too heard about it. He and his wife, worried that no one would marry their daughter after all that was being said about her, decided to give her hand to Sheru, the son of Baba Nizam, Tulla's cousin. Sheru was a widower, much older than Sohni, ugly, indolent and a drunkard. Baba Nizam had proposed Sohni's hand for Sheru two years back, and Tulla and his wife had brushed aside the offer firmly. Baba Nizam had taken the refusal to his heart, and cut off all contacts with Tulla's family. Now, Tulla and his wife decided to keep their self respect aside and beg for Sheru's hand for Sohni.

Tulla went to Amloh, Nizam's village the next day and presented his proposal. Rukhsana, Nizam's wife, screamed a scornful refusal, calling Sohni a harlot. Tulla took off his turban and placed it at Nizam's feet. Nizam, placing it back on Tulla's head, asked for Sheru's opinion. Without waiting for a moment's thought, the lusty Sheru agreed.

The news of her impending marriage was kept secret from Sohni for as long as possible. The gold border to her bridal veil was stitched in the neighbour's house. One day, when she saw her mother keeping her bridal suit in a box under the bed, she was appalled to know that she had been promised to Sheru. Sohni cried aloud in protest, declaring her love for Mirza. Her mother, taken in by her naivety, said that if Mirza truly loved her, he would have come and asked for her hand by now. Sohni wept, and begged her mother not to speak such faithless words about Mirza. Her mother, moved by Sohni's pain promised that if Mirza came in within forty-eight hours and asked for her hand, she would marry her to him.

Sohni sprang to her feet and ran to meet Mirza. He saw the anxiety on her face and knew what was on her mind. Unable to offer her marriage, as he already had four wives, he knew it was only a matter of time that she would be wed and sent to her new home. 'Take me away then as your servant!' said Sohni. Mirza refused to perform such a demeaning act by telling her that it would be a shame upon their love.

Thus after a simple wedding, Sohni was sent off to Amloh, as Sheru's wife. In her new home, she took to taking care of all the household chores happily. She won the heart of her shrewish mother-in-law, which led to a softening in Sheru's attitude towards Sohni. She had a lot of affection for Moti, her sister-in-law. She had a malicious tongue, but having nothing to dislike in Sohni, she too found in her a confidante.

Back in the serai in Gujarat, Mirza waited to hear news of his beloved that anyone got from Amloh. As he had no money left, he decided to take upon the job of a *mahiwal*, a cowherd, for Tula Khan, a rich landlord residing on the other side of the river. The Khan always addressed Mirza as 'mahiwal' and taking cue from him, the other farm helpers too began to do the same. Like Sohni, Mahiwal too came to be loved in his little pastoral community.

*

In Bokhara, obviously, Mirza's family and business affairs were no longer the same. His business had lost its front rank. His wives were irked and irritated by his long absence. There arose increasing friction between the four of them. Ayesha, the youngest one, asked Iqbal the reason for Mirza staying back. On being told she hurried down to the maulvi, accompanied by Iqbal, wanting a *khula* so that Mirza could return with Sohni. The next day when the document was delivered, duly signed and witnessed, Iqbal was on his way to bring both of them back.

Mirza was sitting by the river bank when he heard the approaching hoof beats. He got to his feet as soon as he saw Iqbal, who jumped down from the horse, and told him that Ayesha had obtained khula and that he was now free to marry Sohni. Mirza recounted the whole chain of events – how Sohni got married, how he became the mahiwal, and how he waited for some news of his beloved – at which Iqbal lashed out at him, accusing him to cause misery to all those who loved him: Sohni, his wives, his friends and followers, and most of all Ayesha. Mirza replied that it would be a sin to destroy the happiness of Sohni's family and village, and that he had realised a part of himself there that he never did in Bokhara, and thus he refused to return.

A day later, Iqbal left, loaded with messages and advice from Mirza to all in Bokhara. Mirza sent his signet ring that belonged to his father, for Ayesha.

Life went on. Sohni and Mahiwal were happy in their respective worlds. But fate still had more in store for them. One day Mahiwal took his herd to a sand bank on the river. He was standing knee deep in water scrubbing them, when he saw a woman with pitchers balanced on her head. In an instant he recognised the familiar figure. With his heart beating wildly he swam across the river, just as she turned to go. 'Sohni!' he called out to her. The pitchers fell from her head and broke into a thousand pieces as she ran towards him. He held her close and she clung to his wet body, both unable to speak.

Sohni told him that her village was half-a-mile up the river bank. Being so near, Sohni asked him to meet again, to which Mahiwal first hesitated considering she was married, but then agreed. They decided to meet at a nearby thicket of trees on Sohni's side of the river bank.

And so the lovers began to meet again the way they had met at first, surreptitiously, like thieves in the night. Mahiwal would swim across the river after the day's work and wait for her. However, it was difficult for Sohni to meet him often; she went to meet Mahiwal only after being sure that her husband was in deep sleep and the house was still.

One evening, after a particularly tiring day, Mahiwal decided to take a short nap and then cook fish for Sohni. He was awakened by a sudden thunder, followed by a downpour and so he was unable to fish. He thought that she would probably not come that night; or even if she did, he would explain what happened – and she would understand a small thing like that. But the more he thought, the more he realised that it was a way of showing his love. As the night drew on, he thought of a way out.

A while later Sohni came. Mahiwal lit the fire and began cooking for her. Handing her the first piece, he averted his eyes from her. Sensing the difference in his behaviour, Sohni asked him the reason. She wept on realising how Mahiwal had cut his own flesh (as per Fazal Shah's version) to substitute for the fish that he could not catch that night. She advised him not to swim across the river till the wound healed, and offered to swim across to him to the sand bank where he got his cattle. She did not know how to swim through, and therefore, used an empty upturned pitcher to carry her across the river.

Moti, Sohni's sister-in-law, slept in the veranda outside her brother's room. One day she sensed somebody standing by the foot of her bed, looking down at her. She opened her eyes slightly and gasped with surprise – it was Sohni who stood there with wet clothes clinging to her body. She lay still while Sohni stole into her room. She lay awake thinking of the strange event. Why were Sohni's clothes wet when it hadn't rained? Did she go to the river? Why would she go to the river at such an unearthly hour? Night after night, Moti lay awake for almost three weeks and Sohni did not move out from the house. Then, just as she was about to dismiss the event from her mind, it happened again.

In the middle of the night, Sohni came out of her room, picked up a pitcher and left the house. Moti followed her secretly, till she reached the river, upturned her pitcher and steered herself across it with short quick movements of her arm. As she approached the bank, Moti saw a man coming down to the edge and helping her out of the water. Then together they disappeared into the shadows of the trees. Moti lay awake that night, pondering over what she had witnessed. She was sure that Sohni went to meet her lover, as she remembered the gossip she had heard about her affair with the merchant prince from Bokhara. Moti, knowing her brother's temper, resisted telling him. As days passed, she thought of various schemes to teach Sohni a lesson. Finally, one night, she replaced Sohni's pitcher with a slightly unbaked one.

It stormed the next night and Sohni knew that it heralded the monsoons, and that she would not be able to meet Mahiwal for the next two and a half months. When she went to the courtyard to take her pitcher, she understood that a trick had been played upon her, as she saw the half-baked pitcher in a flash of lightning. In another flash of lightning, she realised that all the other pitchers had been removed from the courtyard. As the lightning continued to flash, Moti saw a gamut of emotions flash through Sohni's face. Sohni was still determined to meet her lover, and this determination overwhelmed Moti. She knew she was wrong. She ran from the house to stop her and save her, but it was too late. She shouted Sohni's name. Sohni was already at the river bank, smiling at the irony of fate – she who had drawn all her strength from moulding pots would now be at her most vulnerable because of a pot of clay. Still determined to meet Mahiwal, she lowered herself into the waters with the upturned pitcher. 'Dear God, let not my Mahiwal wait in vain,' she prayed as something knocked against the pitcher – perhaps a branch of a tree. She felt the pitcher give way beneath her. She tried thrice to overcome the wild waters before she gave up her body.

Sohni's body was found late next morning tangled in a thick clump of bulrushes, two miles downstream from her village. Mahiwal's body too, was found three miles down the river, washed on to a sandbank on his side of the waters. Perhaps he had heard Sohni's cries and thrown himself into the water.

The guilt of her act constantly gnawed at Moti for years. As she aged, she told the story of Sohni-Mahiwal to youngsters with ruthless honesty, including her role. The story became a legend as it spread far and wide. She who had caused Sohni's death had also been instrumental in giving her a little measure of immortality.

Gajar ka Halwa

Also called *gajrela*, this is the only vegetable-based halwa that has made it big. During winters, almost all Punjabi families make this halwa in large quantities and store it in the fridge. Whenever required, a small amount is taken out and warmed. During my childhood when food processors were not so much in vogue, grating kilos of carrots (considering family consumption plus storage) used to be an arduous and monotonous task, and I often helped my mom by grating a few. When it comes to food, no amount of labour deters any Punjabi!

Ingredients (serves 3-4):

Red (and not orange!) carrots, peeled and grated: 1 kg
Ghee: 2 tbsps
Milk: 1 cup
Khoya/Mawa, crumbled: ½ cup (Khoya is made by reducing milk to almost a solid form. Readymade khoya is available in

the market. It would be in the form of a block that can be grated or even crumbled by hand. Once heated, khoya lends a milky-rich flavour to the dish in which it's used. The little lumps that are formed during cooking are deliciously chewy!)

Sugar: 5 tbsps

Green cardamom (slightly pounded to break the pods): 5-6 nos.

Almonds, soaked and finely sliced: 10 nos.

Cashews, sliced: 10 nos.

Cooking

Heat the kadhai on medium flame. Sauté the grated carrots without the ghee for fifteen minutes or till the water evaporates. Do not sauté the grated carrots directly in ghee, this helps in retaining the glossy red colour of the freshly grated carrots. Once the colour darkens a little, add the ghee. Sauté for five minutes, then add milk and cook for two minutes. Add the crumbled khoya, stirring continuously for two to three minutes on low flame. Then mix in sugar, cardamoms, almonds and cashews. Still stirring continuously, cook till the excess liquid evaporates. Adjust the sugar as per your taste. Do not overcook, as the halwa should be soft – you should be able to spot the succulence in each sliver of carrot!

Serve hot or warm (ambient temperature).

Moong ki Dal ka Halwa

This is one of those exotic Punjabi desserts that families reserve for very special occasions. Thus, in a traditional Punjabi wedding, you are bound to find this halwa being served as dessert. Being a lentil-based halwa, it has a very earthy and rustic feel to it. However, not many people attempt this at home, but trust me, it's not all that difficult. And even if you find it so, remember, time and effort put in cooking never goes waste.

Ingredients (serves 2)

Moong dhuli dal ('Dhuli' is used for any skinned lentil. Moong dhuli is skinned, halved green gram), soaked for five to six hours – ½ cup

Water: enough to make a paste of the dal

Kesar strands (saffron) or kesri colour: 1 pinch

Milk: ¼ cup

Ghee: ½ cup

Sugar: ½ cup

Khoya/Mawa, crumbled: ½ cup

Almonds, soaked and sliced: 10 nos.

Cashews, sliced: 10 nos.

Raisins: 10 nos.

Sliced almonds: for garnishing

Cooking

Grind the dal coarsely with very little water. Keep the paste aside. Soak the saffron strands or the kesri colour in milk. Keep aside.

In a thick-bottomed kadhai, heat ghee on medium flame. Once heated, add ground moong dhuli dal. Cook while stirring continuously over low heat till golden brown. It sticks a little, but don't worry – just stir continuously. Once the water evaporates and the mixture gets tighter and forms lumps on stirring, add sugar and saffron milk. Add a little water, if the mixture is too thick. Again, cook while stirring continuously, till well mixed and the halwa is of a semi-solid consistency. Then add khoya, almonds, cashews and raisins. Remove from flame when the khoya softens.

Serve hot, garnished with almond slices.

Badam Elaichi Phirni

The difference between phirni and kheer is that phirni is definitely rice based, whereas kheer can have variations, like vermicelli kheer or sago (sabudana) kheer. Also, in rice kheer the rice is *just* crushed, whereas in phirni rice is ground into a coarse paste, giving it a thicker consistency. Phirni is always served cold, whereas kheer can be served hot or cold, depending on the preference. Traditionally, once made, phirni is poured in individual small *mitti* (earthenware) bowls. Post cooling, they are served as individual portions only. Try and arrange for these small mitti bowls, to bring that glamour to your presentation of this classic dessert.

Ingredients (serves 3-4)

Rice: ¼ cup
Green cardamom (slightly pounded to break the pods): 8-10 nos.
Full cream milk: ½ litre
Kesar strands or kesri colour: 1 pinch
Sugar: ½ cup
Almonds, soaked and sliced: 10 nos.
Cashews, sliced: 10 nos.
Raisins: 10 nos.
Kewra essence: 1 tbsp

For setting and serving: *Mitti ke kulhad* (small earthenware bowls, if possible), else any small individual bowls.

Using the earthenware: If you are able to procure mitti ke kulhad, nothing like it! Soak them in a bucket of water for at least an hour (ideally till the time you actually use them) to allow them to soak in the water as well as lose their dust. If this is not done, the earthenware will soak excess moisture from the phirni leaving it dry.

Cooking

Soak rice for half an hour. Drain and grind it to a coarse paste, along with the cardamoms. Add a tablespoon of milk to the mixture if you find it too thick to blend. Keep aside.

Dissolve the saffron strands or the kesri colour in a tablespoon of milk and keep aside.

Pour the remaining milk in an aluminium vessel and bring to a boil. Add rice and cardamom paste and simmer the flame. Cook stirring continuously otherwise the milk will start sticking to the walls and the bottom of the vessel. When the rice is completely cooked, add saffron milk, sugar, almonds, cashews and raisins. Cook for five more minutes and adjust the sugar as per your taste. Remove from heat and leave to cool at ambient temperature.

When cooled, add the kewra essence and pour into individual earthenware or any bowls. Chill in a refrigerator for an hour or two before serving. You can give the phirni a bit of flourish by coating it with edible silver foil.

Three

Beas (Sanskrit: Vipasha)
The snacky foods; Punjabi festivals

The Vedas refer to this river as *Arijikuja* or *Vipasha*, and the ancient Greeks as *Hyphasis*. Literally, 'Vipasha' stands for 'Without a bond' (Vi ~ without, pasha ~ bondage). Etymologically, Beas is derived from 'Vyasa' the sage who wrote the *Mahabharata*, considered as the creator of this river. The waters of Beas belong to India under the Indus Waters Treaty (1960).

In ancient times, Beas has attracted many sages to its banks for meditation. Narad, Vashishta, Vishwamitra, Vyasa, Parashar, Kanav and Parshuram have on different occasions meditated on its banks, giving this river a distinct spiritual character. The temples of many such sages still exist in the Beas valley. The river is also witness to a distinct hill culture, with settlements in Himachal Pradesh like Kullu, Kangra, Bajaura, Sujanpur Tihra and Nadaun.

Amongst the many legends that surround this river, the most prominent one centres on sage Vasishtha, one of the sapt rishis (seven sages) and Vishwamitra, another sage, who was on contentious terms with Vasishtha. King Kalmashapada, a descendent of the Ikshvaku dynasty, held Vasishtha in reverence, making Vishwamitra envious.

One day, Sakti, the eldest son of Vasishtha was walking down a path in a forest when King Kalmashapada and his entourage, while on a hunting expedition, came riding towards him. The king called out to Sakti to move out of his way. But Sakti, refusing politely said, 'Oh king, I am a Brahmin, and even the king must give way to a Brahmin by law. The path is, therefore, mine.'

Seething with anger, the king lashed out at Sakti with his whip, who in turn cursed him to become a monster and an eater of human flesh.

Meanwhile, Vishwamitra, though invisible, was watching the incident. While Sakti cursed, Vishwamitra commanded a man-eating *rakshasa* (demon) called Kimkarana to enter the king's body. The rakshasa did as he commanded, and immediately the king became a man-eater. The first victim was of course, Sakti. Vishwamitra then caused the rakshasa in the king's body to kill and eat all of Vasishtha's remaining ninety-nine sons.

When Vasishtha was apprised of the death of his sons, he was overwhelmed with grief, and decided to kill himself. He threw himself from the top of Mount Meru, but the rocks turned into cotton. He plunged into a burning forest, but the fire did not even singe him. He jumped into the sea with a rock tied around his neck, but the waves lifted him and cast him upon dry land.

Vasishtha then tied his hands and feet with a sturdy rope and jumped into a mountain river, which was swollen with rain. The river refused to drown him, and, loosening his bonds, cast him, upon its banks. From that day the river was named Vipasha.

Vasishtha then threw himself into another river, flowing swift and fast and full of crocodiles…. (the story continues in Section Four.)

Like the Beas, we too have mood swings – from being calm, like the blue waters to being outrageous, like the overwhelming torrents. We rejoice the crests and deplore the troughs. Emotions are important and natural to us as no matter what we do, we are nothing but secretly vulnerable to them. Therefore, all of us submit to moods, and different moods demand different foods.

The recipes in this section liberate us from the quagmire of the mundane, and placate our mischievous and playful side. They are snacks to be enjoyed on a rainy evening, or over a game of carrom, or playing cards, or on no occasion at all. After all, it's not exactly a sin to enjoy idleness at times.

Apart from food, celebrating festivals break the cycle of banality. Festivities and celebrations are rejuvenating; they make us socialise with forgotten friends and distant relatives: they make us pull off our masks and get back to our roots. Festivals in Punjab largely celebrate harvest, and the birth and *shahidi* or martyrdom of gurus.

Punjab is a land of *melas* too. Many of them are linked to festivals, like Baisakhi. However, there is another set of melas in Punjab that are held near the tombs and shrines of *pirs*. The most famous of such melas are the Chhapar Mela, the Jarag Mela, and the Roshni Mela of Jagranvan (described later). Another popular annual mela held for four days is the one in Malerkotla at the shrine of Haider Sheikh. It is believed that if a childless woman visits the shrine and propitiates the pir, her wish for conceiving a child would be granted. Another belief is that if someone who is overpowered by a malignant spirit comes here during these four days, he would be cured if he offers sweet cakes specially cooked to be given as an offering.

There are various other small melas that are similarly held in memory of saints and sages. In Phillaur, Jalandhar, a mela is held in Dhesian Sang village in the honour of Baba Sang, at his shrine. In Nakodar, Jalandhar, a mela is held in the Kara village at the shrine of Mir Shah Hussain, who lived about five hundred years ago. In the village of Khatkar Kalan (Navanshehar district), a mela is held on the day of Baisakhi, in memory of Baba Jawahar Singh. In March, at Nathana (Ferozepur), a mela is held in honour of a Hindu saint, Kalu. He is said to have dug a large pond in one scoop and deposited the dug up earth in a closeby heap, which now forms the object of popular worship.

Festivals form a very significant part of the cultural life of Punjabis. There is seldom a month that goes without a festival. The festivals connected with the lunar days such as Ekadashi (eleventh lunar day), Pooranmashi (full moon), and Masya (new moon) occur every month. Similarly, Sankranti – when the sun enters the new zodiac sign – is celebrated on the first day of every month of the Vikrami calendar (the twelve-month solar calendar that starts from spring, i.e., 13 March, and consists of 365 days) with great gusto. Needless to say, all these days make for occasions to prepare and eat the finest of foods!

(An insider like me would also tell you that on any festive occasion, Punjabi women love to spend long hours dressing up – sifting through their best dresses and finest jewellery, before a selection on either is made. A lot of fuss is also made about selecting gifts for relatives, especially for their daughters-in-law and the daughters-in-law's families.)

Punjabis' love for socialising is not just restricted to festivals; they love to socialise in general too, making them gregarious and flamboyant by nature. Even the tandoor is a means of social gathering – getting women in rural areas together to collectively cook naans and rotis. Called *sanjha chulha* (collective tandoor), it's a social meeting point like a village well, where women bring kneaded dough and sometimes marinated meats to cook, while catching up on daily domestic affairs. The big fat Punjabi weddings are famous for their ornamental set-ups and lavish feasts. The wedding functions start a month before the wedding, including ceremonies like *chunni, mehndi, chura, sangeet,* cocktail, engagement, etc., leading to *anand karaj* (the four *pheras*, i.e., taking rounds around the *Guru Granth Sahib*, finally solemnising the marriage).

Back in your kitchen, once you submerge yourself in preparing the foods that form part of the following section, you would find yourself being liberated from the burden of the hackneyed life, that weighs all of us down at times. Try to garnish and plate these items: they should be colourful with greens of coriander, pinks of onions and the beiges of ginger juliennes.

Chet

In Punjab, where the Nanakshahi calendar is followed, the year begins with *Chet* (14 March–13 April). On the first day of this month, the arrival of the new year is celebrated by the ritual of picking the new corn, known as *ann nawan karna*. Sheafs of new corn are roasted and the parched grain is eaten. Delicacies like kheer and halwa are also prepared.

In Tehsil Pail, in the village of Jarag, the Jarag Mela is held in Chet in the honour of Goddess Seetla. It is also known as the Baheria Mela. Sweet *gurgulas* (jaggery cakes fried in oil) are prepared a day in advance and then given in offering to the goddess, and thereafter to a donkey. After propitiating the goddess, the family members eat the remaining gurgulas. This festival is observed in Malwa and Powad but the mela is held only in Jarag. The devotees of Seetla gather near a pond, scoop the earth and raise a small hillock, which is accorded the status of the goddess's shrine. Potters specially bring their donkeys decked in coloured blankets; some even put bells or conch shells and beads around their necks. In many folk songs of Punjab, there is a reference to this Jarag Mela.

Sooji ka Halwa

More than a dessert or a festive delicacy, I used to eat this halwa as a side dish with my dinner. I know it sounds strange but sometimes, the contrasting flavour works very well! You can have it hot or cold, with your meal or just like that, in the morning or at night, it's just delicious!

Ingredients (serves 2-3):

Ghee: ¼ cup
Sooji (semolina): ½ cup
Cardamoms, slightly pounded to break the pods: 2-3 nos.
Water: 1 cup
Dry fruits (cashews, almonds, raisins): as much as you like
Sugar: ½ cup

Cooking:

In a kadhai, heat ghee and add sooji. Gently roast till the colour of the sooji changes to off white. Add cardamoms to the roasted sooji, followed by one cup of water and all the nuts (you can slightly pound the nuts for a richer flavour). After the mixture comes to a boil, simmer and stir till it gets a semi-solid consistency. Add sugar towards the end, adjusting as per your taste.

Serve warm or at ambient temperature.

Aate ka Halwa

This one was my mom's curative dish for a cold and headaches. Trust me, it works. Till date, whenever I get a cold, I make this halwa, have it quickly, wrap myself up in a blanket and go off to sleep…just to wish my mom was there to take care of me.

Ingredients (serves 2-3)

Ghee: ¼ cup
Aata (wheat flour): 1 cup
Water: 3 cups
Cardamoms, slightly pounded to break the pods: 2-3 nos.
Saunf (fennel seeds): 1 tsp (optional)
Sugar: ½ cup

Cooking

In a kadhai, heat ghee and add wheat flour. Gently roast till it becomes golden brown. Don't overdo the roasting, as the wheat flour can get burnt very quickly. Add three cups of water and cardamoms (and saunf if you prefer the flavour). After it starts boiling, simmer and stir the mixture till it gets a semi-solid consistency. Add sugar towards the end, adjusting as per your taste.

Serve warm or at ambient temperature.

Baisakh

In Baisakh (14 April–14 May), the second month of the year, Sankranti is a very important day. Baisakhi also falls in this month.

Baisakhi is one of the most important festivals of Punjab. In local dialect, this festival is called *Vaisakhi*. This is the harvest festival of Punjab, celebrated on the first day of the month of Baisakh. Some farmers believe it to be a good omen to apply the sickle to the crop for the first time on this day. This is the time for the reaping of Rabi or the winter crop. Melas are held at various places during this festival too.

In Sikh culture, this day has a great religious significance as Guru Gobind Singh, the tenth guru of the Sikhs, established the *Khalsa* (the pure) on this day at Anandpur in AD 1699. The Sikhs were baptised to form the Elect, which led to the creation of the *Panj Pyare* (the Beloved Five). Each Khalsa was to adopt the *Panj Kakkas* (the Five Ks): *kesh* (unshorn hair), *kanga* (small boxwood comb in hair), *kacchera* (a pair of undershorts), *kada* (a steel bangle), and a *kirpan* (a dagger), which have become an integral part of Sikh identity ever since.

On Baisakhi, people visit gurdwaras, reflect on the Sikh values, and celebrate the birth of the Khalsa. In rural Punjab, people thank Waheguru (the Almighty) for the harvest, and celebrate by dancing to dhol beats, performing the entire process of agriculture from the tilling of the soil through harvesting. This dance is called *jhumar*, a dance that characterises itself on its story or imitations of field activities. Typically in jhumar, men perform the gait of animals, agricultural activities like ploughing, sowing and harvesting in steps. Bhangra and gidda are also inextricably linked with this festival.

Aloo Tikki Chaat

Aloo Tikki Chaat is a cult snack. Every market place in Punjab and Delhi has vendors (*tikki walas* or chaat corners), that sell aloo tikki chaat, mostly during the evenings. The pleasure of eating this chaat in the disposable plate made of dry leaves (though nowadays steel plates or Styrofoam ones are used) in a crowded marketplace, waiting for your turn to be served, asking the vendor to pour more chutney...is a different experience all together! However, by my very memory of the way this chaat looks, I have put down this recipe to the finest of details. The aloo tikki recipe per se, is from my own observation of how it's made by the vendors.

Ingredients: (Makes 6 tikkis)

For Aloo Tikki

Potatoes, boiled: 4 medium
Green chillies, chopped: 2 nos.
Zeera (whole) dry roasted: 1 tsp
Red chilli powder: as per taste
Salt: as per taste
Oil: for shallow frying

For each serving

Aloo Tikkis: 2 nos.
Thick curd, whisked: 2 tbsps
Saunth (tamarind chutney): 2 tbsps (recipe on page 255)
Mint chutney: 2 tbsps (recipe on page 253)
Onion, finely chopped: for garnishing
Spices (only for garnishing): red chilli powder, chaat masala

Chopped coriander: few sprigs

Green chillies, chopped: 1 no.

Method

For Aloo Tikki

Peel the potatoes and mash them in a bowl with clean hands. Mashing the potatoes with hands makes it easier to bind them while making the tikkis. Add chopped green chillies, roasted whole zeera, red chilli powder and salt and mix well again.

Heat a non-stick tawa or pan and brush a little oil on it. Take a little mashed potato mixture in your palm and shape it into a small ball. Flatten it gently to make a round tikki and place it on the tawa for shallow frying. Turn gently till rich golden brown on both sides. Make more tikkis following the same method.

For each serving

On a plate, place two tikkis and press them from the middle slightly. Pour whisked curd over them and both the chutneys. Then sprinkle the onions, add a dash of the red chilli powder and chaat masala. Top it with chopped coriander and green chillies. This chaat can be either eaten warm or at ambient temperature.

Nowadays, potato patties can be easily procured from the 'frozen foods' section of any store. However, the taste varies significantly for anyone who has eaten the 'real' aloo tikki chaat. Hence, even though I would encourage making your own tikkis at home, but in case of paucity of time (or laziness), the readymade frozen option can be considered too.

Jeth, Harh & Sawan

On the eleventh day of the bright half of Jeth (15 May–14 June) falls Nirjala Ekadashi, which is better known in the Punjab as Nimani Kasti. Hindus, especially women, observe a fast on this day and smear their bodies with powdered sandalwood. Charitable people put up stalls for free distribution of Kachchi Lassi (recipe on page 186). These stalls, known as *chhabils*, are a common sight on this day.

The four months beginning from Harh (15 June–15 July) are called *Chaumasa*. During this period the sky generally remains overcast, and the weather shifts between sultriness and rainfall.

Teeyan is celebrated on the third of the bright fortnight of Sawan (16 July–15 August). One day before the Teeyan, girls put henna on their hands and feet; and on the day of the festival, they wear their best attire to visit mela. The mela resounds with Teeyan songs of love and the rhythm of gidda. At homes, women make kheer, a dish specially associated with Sawan. Thus runs a saying:

'*Sawan kheer na khadia, tan kiyon jameeon apradia?*'

(If you haven't eaten kheer in sawan, why, O sinner, were you born?)

Soya Keema

This is a spicy, tastes-like-mutton dish. It's quite healthy owing to its base ingredient – soya granules. It is a lot like street food, and is generally served with a roomali roti. It tastes amazing; however, I find it difficult to indulge in it because of the copious amounts of oil that usually floats on the surface of the keema. Back in my kitchen, I tried to replicate the dish but with far less oil. You can have this with bread or kulcha. (Extremely popular in Delhi and Punjab, a kulcha is leavened bread made of *maida* or refined flour. Typically kulchas are baked in a tandoor. If you happen to visit Amritsar, make sure you experience the 'Amritsari kulchas', served with chhole and a tangy salad of pickled onions!)

Ingredients (serves 2-3)

Water: enough to boil soya granules
Soya granules: 1 cup
Oil: 2 tsps
Zeera (whole): 1 tsp
Dhania seeds (slightly pounded to break them): 1 tsp
Onion, chopped: 1 large
Green chillies, finely chopped: 2 nos.
Ginger-garlic paste: 1 tbsp
Tomato, chopped: 1 medium
Salt: as per taste
Red chilli powder: as per taste
Haldi powder: ¼ tsp
Dhania powder: ½ tsp
Meat masala: 1 tsp
Zeera powder: ½ tsp

Amchoor: ½ tsp
Coriander leaves, chopped: a few sprigs for garnishing
Ginger, julienned: a few for garnishing
Juice of 1 lemon

Cooking

Boil water and add the soya granules to it. Let it simmer for five to seven minutes. Strain and squeeze the granules, and keep aside.

Place a kadhai on medium flame. Pour oil into the kadhai. When heated, add whole zeera and broken dhania seeds. Once they sputter, add chopped onions, chopped green chillies, ginger-garlic paste and stir fry till onions become brown. Add the tomatoes and stir fry till they mash up. Now add salt, red chilli powder, haldi powder, dhania powder, meat masala, zeera powder and amchoor and stir fry for two minutes. Then add the boiled soya granules, cover the kadhai and cook for two minutes on low flame.

Garnish with coriander leaves and some julienned ginger, and add a dash of lemon juice before serving.

Kulche wale Matar

This particular variety of dried peas has become so synonymous with their accompaniment (kulche), that I've hardly seen them being made in any other way. They have been named so too – Kulche Wale Matar. Typically, this also comes under the category of street food, and is served in a *patte ki katori* (a bowl made of dried leaves), with two kulchas resting on the matar. The vendor stores the plain boiled matar in a tilted handi, so that he can easily take them out of it when needed. He dresses them as and when the orders come. I am writing down the recipe as per my own observation of this lip-smacking dish.

Ingredients (serves 2)

Dry peas, soaked for 6-7 hours: 1 cup
Onion, chopped: 1 medium
Tomato, chopped: 1 medium
Green chillies, chopped: 2 nos.
Coriander leaves, chopped: a few sprigs
Salt: as per taste
Red chilli powder: as per taste
Zeera (whole), roasted and coarsely powdered: 1 tsp
Juice of 2 lemons

Cooking

In a pressure cooker, put the soaked peas and two cups of water and seal the lid. After the first whistle, simmer and pressure cook for fifteen to twenty minutes. Once cooked, keep aside and let them cool.

In a bowl, put all the remaining ingredients and the boiled peas (ambient temperature). Mix well, without mashing up the peas.

Serve with kulchas or fresh bread.

Bhadon

In Bhadon (16 August–14 September), on the day of the full moon, Rakshabandhan (called 'Rakhdi' in Punjabi) is celebrated. Gugga Naumi, a festival in the honour of Gugga Pir, also falls in Bhadon. Gugga Pir, though a Rajput warrior king, was believed to possess a special power over all kinds of snakes. Even his shrine, 'Gugge di Marhi', has a reputation for curing snake bites: It is strongly believed that if a person is bitten by a snake, he should be taken to the shrine and laid beside it. This shrine was built in 1890. Till date, his disciples can be found all over Punjab, both among Muslims and Hindus. Legend has it that he gently descended into the earth with his steed, and never returned.

The pir's devotees paint his image on a wall in turmeric, then paint a snake in black right in front of it, and worship the image. People also pour milk and butter milk into holes burrowed by snakes. Sweet *sevian* (vermicelli) is the special dish of this festival. The Lalbagis, who are devout followers of Gugga Pir, also known as Zahir Pir, erect a long pole covered with flags, coloured cloth, coconuts, etc., and worship it just like they would worship a god. The privilege of carrying this pole from home to home by one disciple (called the pir's horse) is much coveted.

Chapar Mela is held on Anand Chaudas, the fourteenth day of the bright half of Bhadon in the honour of Gugga Pir. On the day of this mela, villagers scoop the earth seven times because they believe that in this way they invoke him, to protect them against snakes. This mela lasts for three days, and provides occasion for performance of folk songs and folk dances. Youngsters form themselves into groups and go about dancing and singing for hours.

Boiled Aloo Chaat

This is one of the simplest chaats to make as it needs minimum preparation. This chaat can be made both with large potatoes as well as baby potatoes. However, I prefer baby potatoes as they blend better with the spices – thus covering up for the rather neutral taste of a boiled potato.

Ingredients (serves 2)

Baby potatoes: 250 gms
Red chilli powder: as per taste
Zeera (whole), roasted and coarsely powdered: ½ tsp
Salt: as per taste
Chaat masala: 1 tsp
Anardana: ¼ tsp
Coriander leaves, chopped: a handful of leaves
Juice of 1 lemon

Method

Thoroughly wash and boil the baby potatoes in a pressure cooker for one whistle.

With the peels still on, cut the baby potatoes into halves, or even smaller pieces depending on your preference. Add all the spices, coriander leaves and mix well. Add lemon juice generously, and serve.

If baby potatoes are not available, then normal potatoes, boiled and cut into small cubes can be used as well.

Assu & Katak

The fifteen lunar days of the dark half of the moon in Assu (15 September–14 October) are the *Shraadh* days when one's ancestor's are propitiated. During these days nothing auspicious is celebrated. The Shraadhs are followed by *Navratras*, which are regarded auspicious for celebrations.

In Katak (15 October–13 November), on the fourth lunar day falls Karva Chauth. On this day married women observe a fast, and pray for the long life of their husbands. Sometimes even unmarried girls observe this fast and pray for their fiancés. Another festival that is celebrated with gusto is Diwali. Though this festival is not of Punjabi origin, it's still celebrated with a lot of enthusiasm. Like in other parts of India, earthen lamps and candles are lit at homes and places of worship. Houses are painted, new clothes and jewellery are purchased, and gifts are exchanged within families. The celebration at Harmandir Sahib (Golden Temple in Amritsar, Punjab) is a spectacular affair, attracting lakhs of devotees. The gurdwara is richly decked with decorations and is illuminated by millions of candle flames lit by devotees. The fireworks in the night sky create an unforgettable aura. Historically on this day in the mid-seventeenth century, Guru Hargobind Singh, the sixth guru of the Sikhs reached Amritsar after rescuing fifty-two kings from Gwalior during the reign of the Mughal Emperor Jahangir. The residents of the city welcomed him by illuminating the whole city. Therefore, Diwali is also referred to as *Bandi Chhor Diwas* (Bandi ~ Imprisonment, Chhor ~ release, Diwas ~ day).

Spicy Paneer Fingers

Lately, at one of my friend's pot luck dinners, I wanted to contribute something, which would be more of an appetiser than a main course dish. Knowing that paneer would be something everybody would like, it was a safe bet. This was an impromptu dish, but turned out to be such a delight that it became a must-have in all our future get-togethers. It's quite a simple dish – just be gentle while handling the paneer.

Ingredients (serves 2)

Paneer, cut into thick fingers: 200 gms
Red chilli powder: as per taste
Dhania powder: 1 tsp
Zeera powder: 1 tsp
Amchoor: 1 tsp
Salt: as per taste
Fresh cream: 1 tbsp
Besan: 1 tbsp
Salted butter: a little for greasing the pan
Chaat masala: to sprinkle while serving

Method

Gently place the paneer in a bowl. Add all the masalas, and fresh cream. Then sprinkle the besan over the paneer, and toss gently so that it binds the masalas and the cream on to the paneer. Sprinkle a little more besan if the mixture is too moist. Place the paneer inside the refrigerator, and let it marinate for half an hour.

Grease a heated non-stick pan with a little salted butter. This should be done on low flame. When slightly heated, gently place the paneer fingers one by one on to the pan. Turn them gently, and shallow fry till they turn into a rich golden brown. Drain excess oil on a kitchen tissue.

Sprinkle chaat masala and serve with *pudina* (mint) chutney.

Sautéed Vegetable Platter

As the name suggests, this is meant for a huge gathering. It is full of colourful, sautéed vegetables and can be teamed up with assorted dips of your choice. Ideal to go with great conversation!

Ingredients (serves 8-10)

Carrot, cut into thick fingers: 1 medium
Capsicum, cut into thick fingers: 1 small
Cauliflower, cut into medium florets: 1 small
Potato, cut into thick wedges: 1 medium
Brocolli, cut into medium florets: 1 medium
Baby corn, slit into halves: 5-6 nos.
Salted butter: 2 tbsps
Zeera (whole), roasted and crushed coarsely: 2 tsps
Salt: as per taste
Freshly ground black pepper: as per taste, though keep a little stronger
Chaat masala: as per taste

Cooking

Except for capsicum and broccoli, parboil all the other vegetables for five to seven minutes. Strain and keep aside.

In a pan, heat the butter and add all the vegetables. Add the roasted zeera, salt and black pepper, and stir fry for five minutes, till the vegetables are dry yet glossy.

Place the vegetables on a plate and sprinkle some chaat masala and serve with assorted dips like mayonnaise, thick hung curd with pepper, pudina chutney, and other dips of your choice.

Maghar & Poh

The month of Maghar (14 November–13 December) is followed by Poh (14 December–12 January). A very significant Punjabi festival, Lohri, marks the end of the cold month of Poh, and ushers in the sunny month of Magh.

I always look forward to Lohri for the bonfire. I love the romance surrounding the bonfire, below a star-studded, chilly winter night sky. Add to it some delicious snacks and food, *rewri, gajak,* friends and family, jokes, great conversations, laughter, and a little dhol and dancing – and it's always a night to remember.

During significant occasions in a family, like childbirth, marriage, etc., this festival acquires a special significance whereby the usual celebrations are replaced by a grander version. In such cases it is usually termed as *Pehli Lohri* (first lohri) of the newborn or the newly wed bride. Family and friends get together in the night, light the bonfire, and sing and dance to Punjabi folk songs. Gajak, rewri, puffed rice and popcorn are thrown into the fire as holy offerings. Needless to say, the feast to follow consists of sarson ka saag, makki ki roti and roh ki kheer (a sweet dish made of sugarcane juice and rice).

Local tales tell us that our ancestors had some secret verse or mantra that could invoke the sun god, who protected them from the winter cold. Therefore, the lohri fire was symbolic of their homage, as the flames of the fire took their message to the sun god, and the next day (the beginning of the month of Magh), the sun's rays became warm and comforted the people.

Since ancient times, communal fires have held a lot of significance with respect to protection, as well as worship. People contribute to the communal fire with pieces of firewood, which was burnt essentially to keep away wild beasts and protect hutments or dwellings. Till date, people contribute to the fire of lohri by bringing pieces of cow dung cake. Lohri, in present days, is symbolic of protection and a form of fire worship, in which couples pray to be blessed with a child and parents pray for their daughters' marriage.

The bonfire of lohri is also associated with health, regeneration, transformation and gold. Being a representative of the sun, it is believed that the fire of lohri helps fuel the growth and health of the fields, as well as bring prosperity to people. It also assures light and warmth in people's lives, therefore, making the bonfire nothing less than a deity. People surround the fire in a circle and throw peanuts, popcorn, and sweets like gajak, rewri, gur into it, as an act of its appeasement.

The folklore surrounding lohri has the central character of Dulla (Rai Abdullah Khan Bhatti), a Rajput hero, known in Indian history for leading a rebellion against Mughal Emperor Akbar. The ballad epic of *Dulle di Vaar* narrates the events of his battle. In order to build his small army (Bhatti Rajputs), he looted horses as well as other war accessories from the merchants who worked for Akbar. He distributed some of his loot to the poor as well. He also rescued the girls who were being forcibly taken as slaves to be sent to the Middle East. He arranged their marriages and gave them dowry too. He was thus looked upon as a hero. Till date in Punjab, on the morning of lohri, children go from door to door, demanding the 'loot', in the form of sweets like gajak, rewri, etc. They thank the ones who give by singing these traditional doggerels:

'*Dabba bharaya leerān da, ai ghar ameerān dā!*'

(A box full of strips of cloths, this house belongs to the prosperous!)

For those who don't contribute to the loot, the children sing:
'*Hukka bhai hukka, ai ghar bhukka!*'

(Hukka, hey hukka, this house belongs to misers!)

Roh di Kheer

Roh di Kheer is also commonly known as *ganne ki kheer*, owing to the base ingredient – sugarcane juice. This is typically a rural recipe, and is made more in the countryside than in cosmopolitan households. This kheer has no additional sugar or frills that a dessert usually does; hence, it has a very natural and earthy flavour, aroma and colour.

Ingredients (serves 2-3)

Fresh sugarcane juice: ½ litre
Rice: ½ cup

Cooking

Wash the rice, drain and keep aside.

In an aluminium vessel, pour the sugarcane juice. Bring to boil. Once it starts boiling, add the washed rice and simmer the gas. Let the mixture simmer until the rice becomes soft.

Serve cold.

Bread Rolls

This is typically canteen food. It is a deep fried snack, with an absolutely crisp bread shell on the outside, and a soft spicy potato mash inside. This is one of my favourite snacks because it reminds me of school lunch breaks.

Ingredients (makes 4-5 rolls)

Bread slices: 5 nos.
Oil: sufficient for deep frying

For filling

Potatoes, boiled: 2 large
Onion, chopped: 1 small
Ginger, chopped or grated: 1" piece
Coriander leaves, chopped: as preferred
Green chillies, finely chopped: 2 nos.
Red chilli powder: as per taste
Anardana: ½ tsp
Zeera (whole), roasted: ½ tsp
Amchoor: ½ tsp
Zeera powder: ½ tsp
Dhania powder: ½ tsp
Salt: as per taste

Cooking

Mash the boiled potatoes with your hand. Mix all the ingredients together and mash again so that the spices are mixed evenly.

Soak a bread slice in water and press it gently in between your palms to squeeze out the water. Take a spoonful of the potato mixture and place it in the centre of the soaked bread. Turning the slice around, make it into a roll, sealing the top and bottom gently by pressing.

Heat oil sufficient for deep frying in a kadhai. Slide in the bread rolls one by one, frying a maximum of three at a time. Fry till rich golden brown evenly. Remove excess oil on a kitchen tissue. Serve hot with ketchup.

Magh

After Lohri comes the month of Magh (13 January –11 February), which hosts Makar Sankranti (entry of the sun in the sign of Capricorn).

Basant Panchami (basant ~ spring, panchami ~ from panch, meaning five) falls on the fifth day of the bright half of Magh (latter half of January). Before Partition, the main mela of Basant Panchami used to be celebrated in Lahore at the samadhi of Hakeekat Rai, who at a young age chose martyrdom at the hands of the Mughals, to any deviation from his chosen path of duty. Though in most parts of India this festival is celebrated to honour Saraswati, the goddess of learning, in Punjab this festival marks the commencement of spring, as mustard fields bloom all over. The air is laden with enthusiasm over the flourishing crop, the fields are yellow and the sky is dotted with colourful kites on this day. A special yellow preparation of rice, sweetened and coloured by saffron, called Mitthe Chawal, is made on this day.

In Punjab, many melas are held at places associated with the lives of some Sikh gurus, such as the Masya Mela in Taran Taran, and the Muktsar Mela in Ferozepur. In Phagun, a mela in memory of Guru Nanak is held on full moon night at Dera Baba Nanak. However, the Muktsar Mela remains to be one of the largest Sikh melas held in Punjab.

This mela is also called Mela Maghi (Maghi ~ Magh), owing to the period under which it falls. Held on 14 January in Muktsar in Punjab (earlier known as Khidrānā), this mela pays tribute to the forty Sikhs who achieved shahidi while fighting for Guru Gobind Singh against the Mughal army in 1705. The forty Sikhs are known in Sikh history as *Chalis Mukte* (forty immortals) and the gurdwara erected to commemorate their martyrdom is called Shahidiganj. The *Ferozepur Gazetteer*, describes this mela in detail:

The fair is held in the middle of January on the Makar Sankranti day. It is one of the biggest Sikh festivals, and lasts for three days. On the first day, the worshippers bathe in the sacred tank. On the second day, the people go in a procession (mohalla) to the three holy mounds which lie to the north west of the town, namely, Rikab Sahib, Tibbi Sahib, and Mukhwanjana Sahib. The Rikab Sahib, a mound formed out of the handfuls of earth taken from the tank by the faithful and thrown there, commemorates the spot where the Guru's stirrup broke. The procession goes up the slope to the Tibbi Sahib which, crowned with a Gurdwara, is the mound where Guru Gobind Sahib stood and aimed his arrows at the imperial forces. The devotees then proceed to the Mukhwanjana Sahib where the Guru is said to have cleaned his teeth with a tooth stick. Prayers are offered here and the devotees then return. This mound has been built in the same way as the Rikab Sahib. On their return journey, people visit the Tambu Sahib where the Guru's tent was pitched before the fight started, the Shahid Ganj, which is the samadhi of the forty martyrs, and the Darbar Sahib, where the Guru held his darbar after the cremation of the slain.

Harmeet

The Slim Punjabi

The festival is in commemoration of the battle fought in 1705-06 by Guru Gobind Singh against the pursuing imperial forces which overtook him here and cut his followers to pieces. The Guru himself escaped and had the bodies of his followers disposed of with the usual rites. He declared that they had all obtained *mukti* and promised the same blessing to all his followers, who should thereafter, on the anniversary of that day, bathe in the Holy Pool which had been filled by rain from heaven in answer to his prayer for water. On this spot, a fine tank was afterwards dug by Maharaja Ranjit Singh and called Muktsar (the pool of salvation).

Mitthe Chawal

Mitthe chawal is one dish most of the Punjabi households would make on the day of Basant Panchami. What fascinates me about this sweet rice is the usage of various khada masalas, instead of essences to impart flavour.

Ingredients (serves 2-3)

Rice: 1 cup
Ghee: 1 tbsp
Zeera (whole): ½ tsp
Cloves: 5-6 nos.
Cinnamon: 2" stick
Water: 2 cups
Saffron: a pinch (if not available then a pinch of *kesri* or yellow edible colour can be used)
Green cardamom, slightly pounded to break the pods: 6-7 nos.
Cashews, halved: 10 nos.
Almonds, soaked, peeled and halved: 10 nos.
Raisins: 10 nos.
Sugar: 2 tbsps

Cooking

Wash and drain the rice. Keep aside.

Heat the ghee in an aluminium vessel. Add whole zeera, cloves and cinnamon. After the zeera begins to sputter, add water in double the quantity of rice (so here, 2 cups), saffron or the *kesri* colour and add the drained rice into it. Once the water boils, simmer the gas, cover the vessel partially and allow the rice to cook for five minutes. Then add the green cardamom, cashews, almonds and raisins, and mix gently; be careful not to break the rice. Again cover the lid partially, and let it cook for five minutes.

Take off the lid and check if the rice is almost done. Add sugar only towards the end, else the rice will stick to the bottom of the pan. Mix the sugar gently, cover the vessel and turn off the gas after a minute. Let it stand for ten minutes. Serve hot.

Phagun

On the full moon day of Phagun (12 February–13 March), Holi is celebrated and the very next day, Hola Mohalla is concluded.

The first time I saw someone playing *gatka*, I was speechless – teenage boys performing martial arts with such bravery, finesse and vigour! I was an excited spectator, proud of being a Punjabi.

This festival, chiefly celebrated at Gurdwara Anandpur Sahib, is thrilling to say the least. It is held annually about the same time as the Holi festival in March-April. It lasts for three days, starting a day earlier and finishing a day later than the Holi festival. The first Hola Mohalla was celebrated in AD 1700, the year after the formation of Khalsa. (Literally meaning 'Pure', Khalsa collectively refers to the body of 'Singhs' and 'Kaurs' represented by the five beloved ones, i.e., the *panj pyare* elected by the people. The Khalsa was constituted on the day of Baisakhi, AD 1699, by Guru Gobind Singh, initiating every Sikh into the commitment and philosophy of Sikhism, as well as the adoption of the five 'K's'. These are described in detail in Section Five.)

The Hola Mohalla celebrations are reminiscent of the great plans of Guru Gobind Singh, who wanted to infuse martial spirit in the masses to face the tyrannical Mughal rulers of his day. The guru gave the festival the masculine name Hola Mohalla and transformed it into an arena for training in warfare.

In this festival, Sikhs demonstrate their martial skills in simulated battles. Processions are carried out in war-like formations with drum beating. Martial arts like archery, sword fencing, skillful horse-riding and tent-pegging are displayed by the Nihangs (the militaristic sect of Sikhs, visibly differentiated by their blue, lofty conical turbans decorated by quoits or chakras of steel. Known for their alligator-like ferocity and bravery in the battlefield, the

Nihangs once formed the guerrilla squads in Maharaja Ranjit Singh's army during his reign from 1801-39). The most famous of them is gatka, the dangerous and deft art of handling martial contraptions, so thrilling that the air reverberates with bravery.

The festival is marked by religious congregations, political conferences, recitation of the *Guru Granth Sahib*, pilgrimage of various shrines, fresh attiring of Nishan Sahib (Nishan ~ symbol. Nishan Sahib is a tall pole outside every gurdwara that hoists the Sikh holy triangular flag with the Sikh emblem. The flag is typically saffron in colour with the emblem in blue; however, in the gurdwaras managed by Nihangs, the flag is blue with the emblem in saffron. The pole is draped in fabric of the flag's colour. The emblem is known as 'Khanda Sahib', and depicts a double-edged sword called a *khanda* in the centre with a *chakkar* or circle behind it, and flanked by two single-edged swords, or *kirpans*. The Nishan Sahib can be seen from far away, therefore signifying the presence of Khalsa in the neighbourhood), morning and evening prayers, and congregation prayers, Guru da Langar (the practice of a common kitchen where food is served to all visitors for free), administration of baptism and Mohalla procession. More than two lakh people attend this festival every year.

Dahi Bhalle

This curd-based dish is served as an accompaniment at buffets, sold as a chaat in markets and made at home as an evening snack. The softness of the bhallas compliment the spiciness of the masalas in the curd. I like to add a little papri (crisp fried wafers made from maida) to it, as the crispiness makes the dish so much more interesting. The recipe is a result of my observation while having it at a chaat corner in a market near my house in New Delhi.

Ingredients (serves 3-4)

For the bhallas

White urad dal, soaked for 2-3 hours: 1 cup
Water: enough to make a paste of the dal
Ginger, finely chopped: 1" piece
Green chillies, finely chopped: 2 nos.
Salt: as per taste
Oil: sufficient to deep fry

For each serving:

Bhallas, soaked and freshly squeezed: 2 nos.
Papri: 2 nos.
Thick curd, whisked to a smooth consistency: 4 tbsps
Saunth (tamarind chutney): 1 tbsp
Green mint chutney: 1 tbsp

For garnishing:

Red chilli powder
Chaat masala
Chopped coriander

Chopped green chillies

Ginger, julienned

Cooking the bhallas

Grind the urad dal to a fine paste using very little water. Put the paste into a bowl, add chopped ginger, chopped green chillies and salt.

Heat oil, sufficient for deep frying in a kadhai. With a service spoon, drop dumplings of the urad dal mixture into the oil, to make voluminous bhallas. Fry till rich golden. Put the bhallas into lightly salted, lukewarm water. Soak for ten minutes, then take out and squeeze the water.

Assembling the snack (per serving)

In a plate, place freshly squeezed bhallas. Crush the papris a bit over the bhallas. Pour thick curd and add tamarind and green mint chutney. Then add a dash of chilli powder and chaat masala. Top it with chopped coriander, green chillies and julienned ginger.

Papris can be easily procured from any local grocery shop. While buying, try to buy papris that have been baked and not fried.

Shakarkandi ki Chaat

Shakarkandi or sweet potato tastes brilliant when roasted: It's sweet, smoky and the texture is fibrous yet silky. In a typical marketplace, the vendor places the shakarkandi over smoldering coal on his cart and as orders come, he prepares and serves the chaat. At home, I found the roasting slightly time consuming – I roasted the sweet potato on a tawa, on an absolutely low flame, by placing a pressure cooker (upside down) over it to create more heat. However, in case of paucity of time, you can pressure cook the shakarkandi for one whistle, and proceed as follows.

Ingredients (serves 2)

Shakarkandi, boiled or roasted: 250 gms
Salt: as per taste
Kala namak (black salt): as per taste
Red chilli powder: as per taste
Chaat masala: as per taste
Zeera (whole), dry roasted and coarsely powdered: ½ tsp
Juice of 2 lemons

Method

In a bowl, cut shakarkandi into medium cubes. Add all the remaining ingredients and mix well, vigorously. Serve immediately.

Gurpurabs

No matter where I am travelling, my mom always reminds me to visit a gurdwara on a gurpurab. Gurpurabs celebrate the births, and honour the martyrdom of Sikh gurus. They are well spread throughout the year, and though all gurpurabs are equally revered, the four most notable ones are the birth anniversaries of Guru Nanak and Guru Gobind Singh, and the shahidi of Guru Arjan Dev and Guru Tegh Bahadur.

Proceedings

Akhand Path (non-stop reading of the *Guru Granth Sahib*, lasting for forty-eight hours) is held two days before the day of Gurpurab, with *bhog* (completion of the reading) on the day of Gurpurab. Religious congregations are held, and *shabads* (hymns from the Guru Granth Sahib) are sung. Traditionally, though this part of the culture has now become very selective, large processions of people singing and offering prayers march through the towns, typically called a *Nagar Kirtan*. At night homes and gurdwaras are illuminated.

Day

The birth anniversary of Guru Nanak

The birth anniversary of Guru Nanak is celebrated by devotees with great ardour on *puranmasi*. Though his actual birthday is on 15 April 1469, the date of celebration varies according to the lunar calendar. The biggest celebrations happen in Gurdwara Janam Asthan (the gurdwara of birth), which represents the home of Baba Kalu (father) and Mata Tripta (mother), situated at Rai-Bhoi-di-Talwandi in the present district of Sheikhupura (Nanakana Sahib) in Pakistan.

The birth anniversary of Guru Gobind

Guru Gobind Singh was born on 22 December 1666 to Guru Tegh Bahadur (the ninth Sikh guru) and Mata Gujri. Though this gurpurab is usually celebrated on the same date every year, the dates keep varying with respect to the lunar calendar. It generally falls in December or January, or sometimes biannually as it is calculated according to the lunar calendar.

The martyrdom anniversary of Guru Teg Bahadur

This gurpurab falls on 24 November, as on this day in the year 1675 Guru Teg Bahadur, the ninth guru was beheaded at Chandni Chowk in Delhi, because he refused to convert to Islam under the orders of Mughal Emperor Aurangzeb. The gurdwara is named after his shahidi as Gurdwara Sisganj Sahib.

The martyrdom anniversary of Guru Arjan Dev

This gurpurab falls typically in June, as Guru Arjan Dev achieved martyrdom on 30 May 1606, after being tortured for days under the orders of Mughal Emperor Jahangir in Lahore. Since it is the period of peak summers in India, voluntary stalls called *Chhabeel* are set up at almost all gurdwaras or/and in their vicinity in the cities of Delhi and Punjab. These stalls freely distribute *kachchi lassi*, a sweet cooling drink made of milk, water, sugar and some essence, to all passer-bys, irrespective of their religion or social status.

Kachchi Lassi

Kachchi lassi is said to have a tremendous cooling effect on the body, so much so that as kids we were given this drink after we ate mangoes in summers, in order to counter the warm effect of the mangoes.

Ingredients (makes 4 glasses)

Chilled water: 3 glasses
Sugar: 2 tbsps
Milk: 1 glass
Rooh Afza (rose syrup can also be used): 1½ tbsps
Ice cubes: as desired

Method

In a jug, dissolve the sugar in the chilled water. Add the milk, Rooh Afza and the ice cubes. If Rooh Afza is not available, then alternatively you can use rose syrup, or any other syrup that would give a pinkish colour. Make sure you don't make it too pink – it should be just the right baby pink colour!

Assorted Pakode

The big daddy of all *desi* snacks, pakodas are delicious and quick to make. The most popular pakodas are those of bread, aloo (potato), pyaaz (onion), gobhi (cauliflower), baigan (aubergine) and paneer (cottage cheese). I have had pakodas at street *thelas* (carts), dhabas, as well as at home. The following recipes are the best of the lot.

Ingredients

Respective pakoda base, i.e., bread, paneer, etc.
Oil: sufficient for deep frying
Chaat masala: to sprinkle just before serving

For the besan batter: Mix all the ingredients below and make into a thick batter by adding water. It should be thick enough to coat the pakoda item.

Besan: 2 cups
Salt: as per taste
Red chilli powder: as per taste
Ajwain: 1 tsp
Water: enough to make the batter

For the pakoda masala: Mix all the masalas mentioned below in a katori. To make more, repeat in the same ratio.
Red chilli powder: ½ tsp
Zeera (whole), roasted and coarsely powdered: 1 tsp
Amchoor: 1 tsp

Cooking

Bread pakodas: Cut a bread slice diagonally to make two triangles. Dip them one by one into the besan batter and deep fry till golden yellow on both sides. Drain excess oil on a kitchen tissue, sprinkle chaat masala and serve hot.

Aloo pakodas: Cut a potato into thin round slices; dip them one by one into the besan batter and deep fry till golden yellow on both sides. Drain excess oil on a kitchen tissue, sprinkle chaat masala and serve hot.

Pyaaz pakodas: Chop onions coarsely and mix with the besan batter. The mixture should be thick enough to form dumplings. In the heated oil, drop little dumplings of the mixure with the help of a serving spoon. Fry till golden brown. Drain excess oil on a kitchen tissue, sprinkle chaat masala and serve hot.

Gobhi pakodas: Cut gobhi into small/medium florets. Fill the pakoda masala into the empty spaces, sprinkling the masala from below the stalk. Let it rest for half an hour. Then, dip them one by one into the batter and deep fry till golden brown. Keep the batter a little thick in this case; else the masalas will drip down the vegetables. Drain excess oil on a kitchen tissue, sprinkle chaat masala and serve hot.

Baigan pakodas: Cut baigan into thin semi circles. Toss them in a generous amount of pakoda masala and let them rest for half an hour. Then, dip each piece in the batter, and deep fry till golden brown. Keep the batter a little thick in this case; else the masalas will drip down the vegetables. Drain excess oil on a kitchen tissue, sprinkle chaat masala and serve hot.

Paneer pakodas: Cut paneer into thin, flat one-inch squares. Further, slit each square horizontally from the middle and sandwich in the pakoda masala. Don't 'cut' the square – just a slit to spread the masala inside. Let it rest for half an hour. Then, gently dip one by one into the batter and deep fry till golden brown. Keep the batter thick in this case. Drain excess oil on a kitchen tissue, sprinkle chaat masala and serve hot.

Shaheedi Jor Divas

Shaheedi Divas (martyrdom day) occupies a very sentimental place in Sikh history as it pays homage to the two young *sahibzadas* (princes) of Guru Gobind Singh – Zorawar Singh (nine years old) and Fateh Singh (six years old). This mela is held at district Fatehgarh Sahib, located north of Patiala in Punjab. Its name is derived from Fateh Singh, the younger of the two martyrs, and literally means the fort of victory (Fateh ~ Victory, Garh ~ Fort).

In 1701, the Mughal Emperor Aurangzeb's forces attacked Guru Gobind Singh and besieged the fort of Anandpur Sahib, a city in Rupnagar district of Punjab where the guru and his family were encamping. The siege continued for three years. The enemy made an offer to the guru that if he left the fort the siege would be lifted and he would not be attacked on the way. The guru accepted the offer and left the fort, but the enemy did not keep his word and attacked the guru, caught Mata Gujri (his mother) and bricked alive his two sons. Mata Gujri died on hearing the tragic death of her grandsons. The cremation rites of the three were performed by Diwan Todar Mal of Sirhind, who purchased a piece of land for the purpose from the ruling fanatics after paying a heavy price in gold mohars. There are five gurdwaras at Fatehgarh Sahib to which the visitors throng during the *divas*; Gurdwara Shri Fatehgarh Sahib, Burj of Mata Gujri, Gurdwara Bibangarh Sahib, Gurdwara Joti Saroop and Gurdwara Shahid Ganj.

Usually, the proceedings for Shahidi Divas begin on 24 December with the akhand path of *Guru Granth Sahib* at Gurdwara Jyoti Saroop, and conclude on 26 December with a Nagar kirtan from Gurdwara Fatehgarh Sahib to Gurdwara Jyoti Saroop.

Most Punjabis have a sweet tooth. They love mithais, and halwas with a lot of ghee. Whenever there is some good news in the family, which can be as simple as kids clearing exams to someone getting engaged, a halwa is quickly made by the lady of the family. A Punjabi day and a Punjabi meal is incomplete without something sweet, therefore, let me end this section not with a halwa, but with the sweetness (and spicyness) of a very unique dessert!

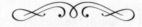

Masala Gur

Punjabis love *gur* (jaggery). This is their simple sweet dish after every meal. Usually, gur is broken into smaller pieces and stored in a box at home, and is a must-have after every meal. Masala gur, specifically, is a winter food, because it contains certain spices that prevent common cold and cough.

Ingredients

Ghee: 2 tsps
Gur, crushed to a *choora*: 250 gm
Sonth (dry ginger powder): ¾ tsp
Almonds, coarsely pounded: 15 nos.
Ajwain: ½ tsp
Zeera, dry roasted: ½ tsp

Cooking

Heat the ghee in a kadhai. When heated add gur, sonth, almonds, ajwain and zeera. Keep stirring continuously till gur melts into a fine paste. Keep for half a minute and remove from the flame.

Immediately, pour this mixture while still hot on a greased thali. Let it cool for a minute; then cut into smaller pieces. When it cools completely, store in a jar.

Enjoy a little piece after your meal.

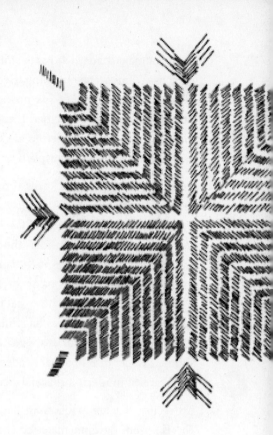

Four

Sutlej (Sanskrit: Śutudri)

The quick foods; Punjabi fashion and dressing

… Vasishtha then threw himself into another river, flowing swift and fast and full of crocodiles.

But the river refused to kill him and instead bifurcated into hundred small streams. The river was thenceforth called Shatadru – the one with hundred arms. Today this river is known as Sutlej.

At last, after trying all means to kill himself, Vasishtha returned to his ashram in the forest. There he ran into the unfortunate

King Kalmashapada, who was still possessed by the man-eating rakshasa, Kimkarana. The king tried to eat Vasishtha, but the sage, through the strength of his powers, chased away the rakshasa from his body, and redeemed the king from his curse. Vasishtha then ordered him to return to his kingdom, to rule wisely and to pay Brahmins their due respect.

Known as Śutudri in the Vedic times, Sutlej is also called the Red River. It is also referred to as *Haimavati*, and the Greeks named it *Hupanis*. This is the longest of the five rivers, the waters of which are allocated to India under the Indus Waters Treaty (1960). Sutlej has irrigated acres of Indian lands through its diversified irrigation canals, and boasts of many hydroelectric projects. Geographical evidences show that the high rate of erosion caused by the modern Sutlej river has influenced the local faulting, and has rapidly exhumed rocks above Rampur, a small township in the Shimla district of Himachal Pradesh, India. Ludhiana, in Punjab, is the largest modern industrial city on its banks.

The recipes that are to follow are like the Red River: rapid fire foods. This is serious deadline material. These dishes can be quickly made, without much ado. This doesn't reduce their health quotient; they are still healthier than any junk substitute you might be indulging in.

Punjabi fashion, too, has a very active sentiment about it: extremely colourful, comfortable, yet tasteful. The attire of the people makes up most of the visual culture of any place, and that's why the zest of Punjabi culture: colours like red, yellow, pink, and saffron dominate its palette. Women's accessories like the *chunni* (dupatta or a stole), parandi, jutti, etc., are extremely colourful, giving a cheerful and energetic vibe to the entire outfit.

Appearance wise, Sikhs look significantly distinct from many people because of their unshorn hair. Men are differentiated by their beards and *pagris* (turbans). Apart from this, a distinct accessory which every Sikh dons is a kada (in the right hand).

It is said that because a Sikh is so distinct in his appearance, he cannot hide behind any cowardice. It's only a matter of belief in the culture that we live in, that we uphold its values and take pride in them. Sikhism laid out certain mandates as far as appearance was concerned, and it has been able to survive for hundreds of years because Sikhs took glory in upholding and living as per those mandates. The turban, as a garment, would have lost its way, like it did in many other cultures, if a Sikh did not believe in it and made it his fashion statement.

Sikh women love flamboyance. They like to dress up, and pay due attention to their long hair, which is their characteristic. The way a cosmopolitan Punjabi woman dresses up may be ostentatious to a certain extent, but that's just an extension of her elaborate self. She likes to enjoy each day of her life, she likes the colours, and she likes the small pleasures that come her way through her dressing, that make her life queen size.

Coming back to the kitchen, a bad day at work might discourage you to cook, and tempt you to call up the nearest fast food chain for a quick delivery at your house. Or, tiredness might mar your enthusiasm, dissuading you from even entering your kitchen. Don't consider cooking to be a chore, it is, in fact, an experience. The kitchen is always a few steps away and with the recipes to follow, a steaming hot dish a few minutes away.

Khichdi

Staying in Bengaluru for a considerable duration now, I am happily surprised to see the prominence of khichdi's South Indian variant, called *pongal*, and its presence especially on ceremonial occasions and festivals. However, in most Punjabi homes, khichdi is rather low on its likeability quotient, maybe due to its blandness – but that's exactly why I like it – it's quick, easy to make, and you can always temper it the way you want to suit your mood.

Ingredients (serves 2)

Oil: 1 tsp
Zeera (whole): ½ tsp
Dhania seeds, slightly pounded to split them: ½ tsp
Ginger, chopped or pounded: 1" piece
Garlic, chopped or pounded: 4-5 flakes
Green chillies, slit: 2 nos.
Rice, soaked: ½ cup
Toor (arhar) dal, soaked: ½ cup
Water: 4 cups
Salt: as per taste
Red chilli powder: as per taste
Haldi powder: a pinch, only for colour
Zeera powder: ¼ tsp
Dhania powder: ¼ tsp

Cooking

Heat oil in a pressure cooker. When heated, add whole zeera and dhania seeds. Once they sputter, add ginger, garlic and green chillies. After a minute, add rice and dal along with four cups of water, followed by salt, red chilli powder, haldi powder, zeera powder and dhania powder. Close the lid, and after the first whistle simmer for five minutes.

After removing from the flame, mix the khichdi well. You can add some water if you find the consistency too thick. If you like, you can top your khichdi with a teaspoon of ghee.

Serve hot with a pickle of your choice.

Mixed Vegetables

This one is a result of my experiments with the colours of vegetables – you can practically use any vegetable lying in your refrigerator and quickly toss this dish. I used to be innovative with this one – often due to lack of time, I would lightly sauté the vegetables in the same set of condiments and spices, and have it as a side dish or as a snack.

Ingredients (serves 2):

Potato, cut in thick batons: 1 medium
Beans, cut in 1" pieces: 10 nos.
Carrot, cut in batons: 1 medium
Peas: ½ cup
Oil: 2 tsps
Bay leaf: 1 no.
Zeera (whole): 1 tsp
Dhania seeds, slightly pounded to break them: 1 tsp
Ginger, julienned: 1" piece
Garlic, pounded: 5 pods
Green chillies, slit: 2 nos.
Onion, sliced: 1 medium

Tomato puree: 4 tbsps
Capsicum, cut in batons: 1 medium
Salt: as per taste
Red chilli powder: as per taste
Dhania powder: ½ tsp
Zeera powder: ½ tsp
Amchoor: ½ tsp
Coriander leaves, chopped: a few sprigs for garnish
Lemon juice

Cooking

Parboil the potatoes, beans, carrots and peas for five minutes. Drain and keep aside.

Heat oil in a kadhai. Add bay leaf, whole zeera and dhania seeds. To that add ginger, garlic and green chillies and stir fry for a minute. Put onions, and stir fry till translucent. Add the tomato puree, stir fry for five minutes till it boils. Then add the boiled vegetables and capsicum, as well as salt, red chilli powder, dhania powder, zeera powder and amchoor. Stir fry for ten minutes.

Garnish with coriander, add a dash of lemon juice. Serve hot with phulkas or paranthas.

Pagri (turban)

The pagri (or *pág*, as Sikhs usually call it), as an element of dressing is not of Punjabi origin; rather it dates back to an era when Sikhism as a religion was not even born. Historically, kings and other prominent social figures used to don a turban to signify their power. In certain cultures, the masses used to wear a turban as a climatic defence. The size, style and material of the turban portrayed the social status of the wearer. It carried more of an accessorising character than a compulsive one, until unshorn hair was defined as a mandate for a Khalsa. Thenceforth, turbans became an imperative part of a Sikh's lifestyle, giving them an ease of maintaining their hair. In the *Rehatnāmā* (code of conduct) of Guru Gobind Singh, it is mentioned that a Sikh should not wear a cap/hat/*topi*, and it is forbidden to take off the turban while eating.

Many cultures have evolved and given up on this part of dressing, but for a Sikh, it is a matter of glory and respect to wear a turban every day – that's what sets him apart. The present turban is the development of the ones worn by the princes at Maharaja Ranjit Singh's (the first maharaja of the Sikh Empire; r. 1801–39) court. Its function is both religious and that of imparting a social identity. An insult to the turban is regarded as an insult to the Sikh faith because the turban covers the *kesh* or hair, one of the five emblems of the Khalsa code of conduct.

Pags are usually of a soft fabric like voile or *mulmul*, and are two-and-a-half to five metres in length, depending on an individual's style of tying. The art of folding a pag in a length-wise, fan-fold manner before tying is called *puni*. Young Sikhs nowadays experiment with colours, prints and even ornamentations like *mokaish* (small pieces of metal inserted in the fabric, so tiny that they almost look like crystals) on their turbans. Elder men still stick to starched fabric (and usually neutral colours like maroon, black and navy blue) for tying theirs, which gives a more defined shape.

Various sects of Sikhs have adopted a typical turban style of their own over time. For example, the Nihangs (the militaristic sect of Sikhs) tie blue (sometimes yellow) turbans that are almost forty yards long. They wear iron rings around their turbans. These rings are called *chakkars*, and as a Nihang advances on the spiritual life, the chakkars are placed higher, symbolising his enlightenment. The Akali Dal members wear deep blue coloured turbans. The Namdharis (also called Kukas, another sect of Sikhs) wear white turbans, tied in a flat, coif-like style. A Sikh army soldier wears a military green turban, tied with crisp and neat folds.

Pag Vatauna

Pag vatauna means 'exchanging of turbans'. Exchange of turbans is a symbol of respect, honour and commitment. When two men or families exchange turbans, they forge a bond that binds their friendship or loyalty towards each other for life – a highly respectful gesture. Every Sikh marriage has this ritual.

second

Dal-Chawal

Dal-Chawal is one of the most wholesome and preferred foods in a Punjabi kitchen. Rice being the constant accompaniment, the dals can be different, depending on your mood and availability of ingredients. I am listing the recipes for four most easy-to-make made dals – arhar, moong dhuli, moong sabut and chane ki dal. My favourite amongst all is arhar (toor) dal and chawal, accompanied by onions and mango pickle.

ARHAR DAL

Ingredients (serves 2)

Arhar (toor) dal, soaked for 2-3 hours: ½ cup
Water: 2 cups
Oil: 2 tsps
Zeera (whole): ½ tsp
Dhania seeds, slightly pounded to break them: ½ tsp
Onion, chopped: 1 medium
Green chillies, slit: 2 nos.
Ginger-garlic paste: 1 tbsp
Tomato, chopped: 1 medium
Salt: as per taste
Red chilli powder: as per taste
Haldi powder: ½ tsp
Zeera powder: ½ tsp
Dhania powder: ½ tsp
Coriander leaves, chopped: a few springs for garnishing

Cooking

Boil the dal in two cups of water in a pressure cooker for ten minutes. Keep aside.

In a kadhai, heat oil and add whole zeera and dhania seeds. Once they sputter, add onions, green chillies and ginger-garlic paste. Stir fry till the onions turn golden brown. Then add tomatoes and stir fry till they mash a little. Add salt, red chilli powder, haldi powder, zeera powder and dhania powder and stir fry for a minute. Then add the boiled dal. After it comes to a boil, simmer for five minutes.

Garnish with coriander, and serve piping hot with steamed or zeera rice.

TWIST: If raw mangoes (*ambi*) are in season, then add a few pieces into the dal while boiling. They would give a distinct tanginess to the dish.

MOONG DHULI DAL

Ingredients (serves 2)

Oil: 2 tsps
Zeera (whole): ½ tsp
Dhania seeds, slightly pounded to break them: ½ tsp
Green chillies, slit: 2 nos.
Moong Dhuli Dal: ½ cup
Salt: as per taste
Red chilli powder: as per taste
Haldi powder: ¼ tsp
Zeera powder: ½ tsp
Dhania powder: ½ tsp
Water: ½ cup
Coriander leaves, chopped: a few sprigs for garnishing

Cooking

In a pressure cooker, heat oil and add whole zeera and dhania seeds. To this add green chillies. Stir fry for a minute. Then add dal, salt, red chilli powder, haldi powder, zeera powder, dhania powder and one-and-a-half cups of water. Fasten the lid of the pressure cooker, and turn off the gas after one whistle. Don't overcook the dal.

Garnish with chopped coriander.

MOONG SABUT (GREEN) DAL

Ingredients (serves 2)

Oil: 2 tsps
Zeera (whole): ½ tsp
Dhania seeds, slightly pounded to break them: ½ tsp
Onion, chopped: 1 medium
Green chillies, slit: 2 nos.
Ginger-garlic paste: 1 tbsp
Tomato, chopped: 1 medium
Moong sabut dal, soaked for 2-3 hours: ½ cup
Salt: as per taste
Red chilli powder: as per taste
Haldi powder: ½ tsp
Zeera powder: ½ tsp
Dhania powder: ½ tsp
Water: 2 ½ cups

Cooking

In a pressure cooker, heat oil and add whole zeera and dhania seeds. Once they sputter, add onions, green chillies and ginger-garlic paste. Stir fry till the onions turn golden brown. Then add tomatoes and stir fry till they mash a little. Add the dal, along with salt, red chilli powder, haldi powder, zeera powder, dhania powder and two-and-a-half cups of water. After the first whistle, simmer for ten minutes and remove from flame.

Serve hot with phulkas or steamed rice.

CHANE KI DAL

Ingredients (serves 2)

Oil: 2 tsps
Zeera (whole): ½ tsp
Dhania seeds, slightly pounded to break them: ½ tsp
Green chillies, slit: 2 nos.
Ginger, julienned: 1" piece
Chane ki dal, soaked for two to three hours: ½ cup
Salt: as per taste
Red chilli powder: as per taste
Haldi: ½ tsp
Zeera powder: ½ tsp
Dhania powder: ½ tsp
Water: 2½ cups

Cooking

In a pressure cooker, heat oil and add whole zeera and dhania seeds. To this add green chillies and julienned ginger. Stir fry for a minute. Then add the dal, along with salt, red chilli powder, haldi powder, zeera powder, dhania powder and two-and-a-half cups of water and then fasten the lid of the pressure cooker. After the first whistle, simmer for ten minutes and remove from flame.

Serve hot with phulkas or steamed rice or zeera rice.

Sookhi Urad ki Dal

This dal is slightly pasty in nature, hence, best made dry. A very quick-to-make dal.

Ingredients (serves 2)

Urad dal: 1 cup
Water: enough to soak the dal
Oil: 2 tsps
Zeera (whole): ½ tsp
Dhania seeds, slightly pounded to break them: ½ tsp
Onion, chopped: 1 large
Green chillies, chopped: 2 nos.
Tomato, chopped: 1 large
Salt: as per taste
Red chilli powder: as per taste
Haldi: ½ tsp
Zeera powder: ½ tsp
Dhania powder: ½ tsp
Amchoor: ½ tsp

Cooking

In a pressure cooker, put the washed dal and add little water, just enough to soak the dal (water should be just a couple of millimetres above the surface of dal). Pressure cook only for one whistle.

In a kadhai, heat oil and add whole zeera and dhania seeds. To this add chopped onions and green chillies. Stir fry till onions become translucent. Then add chopped tomatoes and stir fry till they mash up. Now add salt, red chilli powder, haldi powder, zeera powder, dhania powder and amchoor. Stir fry for a minute.

Now add the boiled dal and mix gently. When it is evenly coated with the masala, cover with a lid and remove from flame.

Serve hot with phulkas or paranthas.

Phulkari and Bagh

According to an ancient tradition, observed in certain Punjabi families to this day, the moment a daughter is born in a family, the mother conceives the idea of embroidering a phulkari to be presented to her daughter at the time of her wedding. Regardless of the time, energy and care she would have to contribute, she works towards making the prospective wedding gift a genuine piece of art, year in and year out, which will be an embodiment of her love.

Phulkari is probably the most significant contribution of Punjab to fashion. It is a style of embroidery done in darn stitch, involving floral patterns, as the name suggests (phul ~ flower, kari ~ work/art). Over time, the name phulkari has become generic to the garment on which it is done. Originated as a folk art around the fifteenth century, there are references to phulkari in many Punjabi folk songs, as well as the *Guru Granth Sahib*, the *Mahabharata* and the Vedas. The sheer colours of the art can be attributed to the desire of the women *karigars* (workers, usually housewives) to break away from the mundane.

The base of traditional phulkari embroidery is coarse khaddar-like cloth, of red or blue colour. The design is worked out on the reverse side of the cloth with medium strands of untwisted silk, which gives it an effect of tapestry with a silken sheen. Yellow, white, green and red are the four colours invariably preferred

in selecting silk floss for phulkari work, although the shades of any particular colour are not always the same. It is a motif-styled artwork, where the motif (usually a diamond-tilted square divided into four of its constituent triangles; each square has two triangles, each of two different colours) repeats itself over the entire length of the fabric on which it's being embroidered. With skilful manipulation of the darn stitch, intricate designs are made through horizontal, vertical and diagonal stitches, covering the base fabric with embroidery completely.

Bagh is a similar embroidery style, but more elaborate and picturesque. It is done in a manner so dense that the fabric beneath is hardly seen (bagh ~ garden). It has several varieties known by different names, such as shalimar bagh, kakri bagh, mircha bagh and dhunia bagh, each name being derived from the motifs, and the motifs being suggested by objects with which the embroiderers are familiar. Phulkari is usually done on dupattas and scarves, and bagh on more elaborate garments like shawls. If only the sides of the fabric are embroidered, like the ends of a dupatta, it is called a *chope*.

During marriages and ceremonial occasions, phulkaris and baghs are a significant part of the ladies' wardrobe; they make an imperative part of the bride's trousseau as well. Red is the most preferred colour for baghs, whereas elderly women prefer colourful phulkaris on an off white base.

Phulkari work is labourious and slow, and the art is acquired and perfected over time and with practice. There are different formulae for the various patterns, and these have been handed down through generations. Lahore, before the partition of Punjab, was a well-known market for phulkari chaddars that were produced in other neighbouring towns. In Amritsar and Ferozepur, phulkari work of magnificent quality is done but it is rather disheartening that this art is slowly fading away.

Pyaaz-Tamatar ki Sabzi

The name of this dish is suggestive of its basic ingredients – however, the dish is so delicious that I love eating it spread on a toast or even with a plain slice of bread. You can literally make this in five minutes.

Ingredients (serves 2)

Oil: 2 tsps
Zeera (whole): ½ tsp
Green chillies, chopped: 2 nos.
Onions, sliced: 2 medium
Ginger-garlic paste: 1 tsp
Salt: as per taste
Red chilli powder: as per taste
Haldi powder: a pinch, only for a hint of colour
Zeera powder: ½ tsp
Dhania powder: ½ tsp
Amchoor: ½ tsp
Tomatoes, cut lengthwise: 2 medium
Coriander leaves, chopped: a few sprigs for garnishing

Cooking

In a kadhai, heat oil and add whole zeera. To this add chopped green chillies, sliced onions and ginger-garlic paste. Stir fry till the onions become translucent. Then add salt, red chilli powder, haldi powder, zeera powder, dhania powder, amchoor and tomatoes. Stir fry till the tomatoes mash up slightly.

Garnish with coriander and serve hot with phulkas or paranthas or even bread.

Paneer Bhurji

This one is another quick fix: the only critical ingredient being cottage cheese, you can throw in practically any vegetable that you have in your kitchen (even if it means just onions and tomatoes), and get the bhurji ready in literally ten minutes! I love to make this bhurji colourful with vegetables. And in the mornings, I eat the leftover bhurji with bread and enjoy a delicious breakfast with chilled fruit juice.

Ingredients (serves 2)

Fresh paneer: 200 gms
Oil: 2 tsps
Zeera (whole): 1 tsp
Dhania seeds (slightly pounded to break them): 1 tsp
Onion, chopped: 1 large
Green chillies, finely chopped: 2 nos.
Ginger-garlic paste: 1 tbsp
A few diced pieces of vegetables of your choice: capsicum, carrot, beans, peas or mushrooms.
Tomato, chopped: 1 medium
Salt: as per taste
Red chilli powder: as per taste
Haldi powder: ¼ tsp
Dhania powder: ½ tsp
Zeera powder: ½ tsp
Coriander leaves, chopped: a few sprigs for garnishing
Ginger, julienned: a few for garnishing

Cooking

Crumble paneer with your hand and keep aside. Avoid grating it, as crumbled paneer tastes better due to its coarse and chunky texture.

On medium flame, heat oil in a kadhai. When heated, add whole zeera and broken dhania seeds. To this add chopped onions, chopped green chillies, ginger-garlic paste and stir fry till onions become brown. Add diced vegetables and stir fry for two minutes. Then add crumbled paneer and chopped tomatoes together. Add salt, red chilli powder, haldi powder, dhania powder and zeera powder and stir fry the whole mixture for five minutes or till the water from the paneer subsides. Cover the kadhai and cook for two minutes, the flame being simmered. Leave it covered till the time you eat or serve.

Garnish with coriander leaves and some julienned ginger, and serve with phulkas or paranthas.

Aloo ka Bharta

This dish is an outcome of one of those packed-with-work-office days, when I couldn't stock my groceries over the weekend and ultimately, one night, I had nothing substantial in my kitchen except for two potatoes. Well, as good as a blessing in disguise, in just ten minutes I was savouring the chunky, mashed potatoes loaded with flavours. This bharta can be toasted in bread for a lip-smacking breakfast as well!

Ingredients (serves 2)

Potatoes: 2 large

Oil: 2 tsps
Zeera (whole): 1 tsp
Hing: a pinch
Onion, finely chopped: 1 large
Green chillies, chopped: 2 nos.
Ginger, pounded: 1" piece
Garlic, pounded: 4 to 5 pods
Tomato, finely chopped: 1 large
Salt: as per taste
Red chilli powder: as per taste
Zeera powder: ½ tsp
Dhania powder: ½ tsp
Amchoor: ½ tsp
Coriander leaves, chopped: a few sprigs for garnishing
Lemon juice: to squeeze in while serving

Cooking

Boil the potatoes, peel and mash them with clean hands and keep aside. Do not over boil them as that would make peeling the potatoes a messy affair.

On medium flame, heat oil in a kadhai. When heated, add whole zeera and hing. To this add chopped onions, chopped green chillies, pounded ginger and garlic, and stir fry till onions become brown. Add chopped tomatoes and stir fry the mixture till they are mashed. Now add mashed potatoes and salt, red chilli powder, zeera powder, dhania powder and amchoor. Mix well, then cover the kadhai and cook for two minutes on low flame. Leave it covered till the time you eat or serve.

Garnish with coriander leaves, add a dash of lemon juice and serve hot with phulkas or paranthas.

Paranda

Well, I am a proud owner of one! Another traditional handicraft of Punjab, *paranda* or parandi is considered quite a sensuous accessory. It is a tri-parted group of black cotton threads, at the ends of which are intricately woven, silken thread tassels. Punjabi women tie parandas at the end of their long plaits, to enhance their look; the tassels typically reach the hips, adding to the appeal of their gait.

Available in innumerable colours and intricate designs, it forms an integral part of weddings and other ceremonial occasions. A rage in international markets as well, its colourfulness represents the vivaciousness and flamboyance of the Punjabi women. Paranda, as an accessory, has inspired many artists and musicians, and many songs have been composed complimenting women, a very popular one beginning as follows:

Kaali teri gut te paranda tera laal ni,
Rup di o rani tu parande nu sambhal ni.

(Mind the red paranda, braided in your black plait, O beautiful princess!)

Districts of Hoshiarpur, Ludhiana, Amritsar, Jalandhar and Nikodar are centres of paranda-making, handful of skilled craftsmen make them for women all over the country, as well as abroad.

Masala Bread

Well, this is not exactly a Punjabi dish but definitely a quick-fix solution using the simplest of ingredients. The base ingredient, i.e., bread for this recipe is accredited to my office canteen's cook, who makes something called as a bread *upma*. By default, I ended up making a Punjabi version in my kitchen, and here it goes:

Ingredients (serves 2)

Bread slices: 4 nos.
Oil: 2 tsps
Zeera (whole): ½ tsp
Green chillies, slit: 2 nos.
Onion, chopped: 1 medium
Ginger-garlic paste: ½ tsp
Tomato, chopped: 1 medium
Salt: as per taste
Red chilli powder: as per taste
Haldi: ½ tsp
Zeera powder: ½ tsp
Dhania powder: ½ tsp
Water: ½ cup

Cooking

Cut the bread slices into nine pieces each (3 rows x 3 columns). Keep aside.

In a kadhai, heat the oil and add whole zeera. Once the zeera sputters, add green chillies, onions and ginger-garlic paste. Stir fry till onions become translucent. Then add tomatoes. Stir fry till the tomatoes mash up slightly. Add salt, red chilli powder, haldi powder, zeera powder and dhania powder. Stir fry for a minute, and then add half a cup of water. When the water comes to a boil, add the bread pieces and mix gently. You can add a little more water literally by tablespoons, if the masala is not mixing well.

Stir fry for just a couple of minutes, till the bread is soft and the masala is evenly distributed.

Serve hot with mint chutney.

Ghiye ki Sabzi

Not many people are fond of *ghiya* (bottle gourd). Honestly, even I am not too fond of it. But ever since I have read that it's extremely good for the skin, it has become my staple diet – even though initially I had to force myself (they aren't completely wrong when they say that vanity rules a girl's life!). This recipe is quite tangy and flavourful, to counter the blandness of the vegetable.

Ingredients (serves 2-3):

Oil: 2 tsps
Zeera (whole): 1 tsp
Onion, chopped: 1 large
Green chilli, finely chopped: 1 nos.
Ginger-garlic paste: 1 tsp
Tomato, chopped: 1 medium
Curd, whisked: 2 tbsps (optional)
Ghiya or lauki (bottle gourd), diced: 1 medium
Salt: as per taste
Red chilli powder: as per taste

Haldi powder: ¼ tsp
Dhania powder: ½ tsp
Zeera powder: ½ tsp
Coriander leaves, chopped: a few sprigs for garnish
Water: just a little
Juice of 1 lemon: to squeeze in just before serving

Cooking

In a pressure cooker, heat oil and add whole zeera. Once the sputtering gets over, add onions, chopped green chilli and ginger-garlic paste. Stir fry till the onions turn golden. Add chopped tomatoes and stir fry for a minute. Add two tablespoons of whisked curd. Now add ghiya, salt, red chilli powder, haldi powder, dhania powder and zeera powder and mix well.

Add a little water, close the lid and pressure cook for five minutes (five minutes after the first whistle, flame simmered).

Garnish with coriander, add a dash of lemon juice and serve hot with phulkas or paranthas or rice.

Vegetable Pulao

I get very creative with my pulao. I have added soya chunks, shredded chicken (you can make a non-vegetarian version of pulao with chicken), imli pieces, something my mom sends – *wadiyan* (a Punjabi speciality consisting of sun-dried, spicy dry chunks of moong dal paste), and even mushrooms. Mentioned below is my recipe for the vegetable pulao, with beautiful specs of natural maroon colour of beetroot – however, feel free to experiment and splash your own colours and flavours on to the white canvas of rice!

Ingredients (serves 2)

Oil: 2 tsps
Hing: a pinch
Zeera (whole): 1 tsp
Dhania seeds (slightly pounded to break them): 1 tsp
Cloves: 5-6 nos.
Cinnamon (dalchini): 2" stick
Bay leaves: 2-3 nos.
Onion, sliced: 1 large
Green chillies, slit: 2 nos.
Ginger-garlic paste: 1 tbsp
Diced pieces of vegetables of your choice: capsicum, carrot, beans, peas
Salt: as per taste
Red chilli powder: as per taste
Dhania powder: ½ tsp
Zeera powder: ½ tsp
Water: 2 cups
Rice, soaked for an hour: 1 cup
Beetroot, chopped finely: 1" piece

Cooking

Heat oil in an aluminium patila (boiling vessel) on medium flame. When heated, add hing, whole zeera, broken dhania seeds, cloves, cinnamon and bay leaves. To this add sliced onions, slit green chillies, ginger-garlic paste and stir fry till onions become translucent. Add chopped vegetables and salt, red chilli powder, dhania powder and zeera powder and stir fry for two minutes. Keeping the flame high, add two cups of water and bring to a boil. Add soaked rice, simmer the flame, and cover it partially. Let it cook till the rice is done.

Once done, sprinkle finely chopped beetroot and toss gently (just once or twice) to give beautiful specs of maroon.

Leave it covered till the time you are ready to eat or serve. This will help maintain the fragrance of the spices. Raita is a good accompaniment.

Patiala Salwar

As the name suggests, this pleated salwar for women has its roots in Patiala. This type of salwar is very loose, and stitched with a lot of pleats (hence the name *pattian wali salwar*), therefore making it a very comfortable outfit. In olden days, *Patiala salwar* was worn mostly by the ladies of the royal families, (hence the name Patiala 'Shahi' [royal] salwar) owing to the amount of fabric required to make it (a typical salwar could be made out of 2.25 metres, but a Patiala salwar uses more than 4.5 metres of cloth). The royal ladies could easily wear the salwar because it was made of *chhalle wala resham*, i.e., silk so fine that it could pass through a ring.

I fondly remember a discussion I had with my tailor in Delhi, while I had gone to him to get a Patiala salwar stitched. He is an old man named Mahinder, and for traditional clothes I prefer him over fancy boutiques because he stitches a classic garment, like a classic: with no additional frills. Recounting the history of the garment, Mahinder told me that originally the Patiala salwars that were stitched for the royal ladies did not have a belt for holding the pleats together. Instead, the salwar had a huge *ghera* (round) of fabric, which was tied up together with the *nada* or drawstring, thus leading to a lot of pleats. Once, Sardar Santokh Singh, master tailor for the maharanis, while accompanying the royal family to Shimla saw some British women wearing pleated skirts and decided to use the pleats and the belt for Patiala salwars. He re-engineered the construction of the garment by attaching a belt at the top, which held all the pleats together.

He told me about another famous tailor of the royal family, Pritam Singh, who began working with a tailor in Delhi's Connaught Place stitching clothes for the royal family of Gwalior. Later, he joined the service of Maharaja Bhupinder Singh (1891–1938, ruled Patiala from 1900–38) as the royal tailor on a salary of fifteen rupees a month. Mahinder, suddenly emotional, recollected his days when he used to work in his little shop in *Darjiyan wali Gali* (Lane of Tailors) in Patiala. He claimed that the modern-day design of the Patiala shahi salwar may differ but its popularity remains unchallenged.

It's true ... the ladies of the royal families may have moved on to their favourite designers and boutiques now, but the Darjiyan wali Gali in Patiala would remain synonymous with the stitching of these salwars. The master tailors, who used to stitch for the maharanis, Santokh Singh and Pritam Singh, are still held as institutions in those lanes for not just having stitched for royalty but also for giving the Patiala salwar its contemporary look.

Over years, this garment has made its place in a Punjabi woman's wardrobe almost imperative. In recent times, it has been a fusion dresser's delight, as it can be teamed both with a kurti, as well as a T-shirt. Usually, the edges of the kurti are rounded from the side slits when worn with this salwar. Since a Patiala salwar has a beautiful draping effect due to the pleats that meet at the end, the more fluid the fabric used for making it, the more beautiful the draping is. Typically, it is accessorised with *juttis* and a phulkari dupatta.

Zeera Aloo

This dish is a potato lover's delight. It's a perfect example to prove that you need not be 'elaborate' to achieve a delicious dish in under a few minutes. One of the signature dishes of Punjabi cuisine, this one takes me back to my school days when my mom used to pack it for my tiffin, with two chapattis and some cucumber.

Ingredients (serves 2)

Potatoes: 3 medium
Oil: 2 tsps
Green chillies, chopped: 2 nos.
Zeera (whole), roasted and ground to a coarse powder: 2 tsps
Freshly ground black pepper: as per taste
Salt: as per taste
Red chilli powder: as per taste
Dhania powder: ½ tsp
Amchoor: ½ tsp
Coriander leaves, chopped: a few sprigs for garnish
Juice of 1 lemon: to squeeze in just before serving

Cooking

Cut the potatoes into thick wedges and parboil them for five minutes. Keep aside.

In a kadhai, heat oil and add parboiled potatoes. If you are not using a non-stick kadhai, then make sure the oil is well heated, to prevent sticking of potatoes, and while it heats, just spread it around the walls of the kadhai using a flat wooden spoon. Stir fry the potatoes for five minutes, and then add the chopped green chillies, roasted zeera powder, fresh black pepper, salt, red chilli powder, dhania powder, and amchoor. Stir fry for two minutes till the masalas are well mixed.

Garnish with chopped coriander leaves and add a dash of lemon juice while serving. Serve hot with phulkas or paranthas. Thick curd is a good accompaniment.

Choori

'Choori' is actually a derivative of 'Choora', suggesting the very build of the dish. This was my grandmother's favourite recipe for us when we were kids. It can be made both *namkeen* (salty) and *meethi* (sweet), and is an extremely satisfying dish… and yes, slightly fattening too – owing to the fact that mothers go really generous on the ghee while preparing food for kids! But you can control the amount of ghee to suit your liking and eating habits. Having said that, I won't hide or deny the fact that the real taste of this classic preparation does lie in the generous use of ghee. I guess once in a while, it's okay!

MEETHI (SWEET) CHOORI

Ingredients (serves 1)

Wheat flour chapattis (even leftover ones would do): 2 nos.
Ghee: 1 tbsp
Sugar to sprinkle: as per taste
Saunf (fennel seeds): 1 tsp

Method

Heat the chapattis a little, and break them into tiny pieces in a bowl. Heat ghee, and pour over the broken chapatti bits. Sprinkle sugar and saunf on the mixture, and mix well. Serve hot.

NAMKEEN (SALTY) CHOORI

Ingredients (serves 1)

Wheat flour chapattis (even leftover ones would do): 2 nos.
Ghee: 2 tbsps
Salt: as per taste
Freshly ground black pepper: ¼ tsp

Method

Heat the chapattis a little, and break them into tiny pieces in
a bowl. Heat ghee, and pour over the broken chapatti bits.
Sprinkle salt and pepper on the mixture, and mix well. Serve
hot.

Jutti

Not just in Bollywood movies, but in real life too, the trend of
wearing juttis has undergone a lot of change over the years: one can
see so many students wearing them with jeans as well. However,
even in contemporary times, when spoken of tradition, juttis
form an integral part of the Punjabi attire. It is a quintessential
accessory for all Punjabi weddings.

Juttis as a type of footwear, have a huge unisexual appeal. Men and
women both don it on various occassions – men, typically with
kurta-pyjamas and women, with Patiala salwars. Juttis leave the
top of the foot nearly bare, as they support the foot by covering
the toes at the front and the Achilles' tendon at the back. The part
where it covers the toes is usually round shaped or M-shaped, and
is heavily embroidered. Punjabi juttis have always been in vogue
due to their intricate craftsmanship, varied colours and elaborate

embroidery. Traditionally, they are crafted with fine leather and are delicately embroidered with threads or beads. These juttis were specially hand-crafted for the royal families, with Mughal-period-inspired embroideries done with threads of real gold and silver. Lately, due to an increase in both domestic and international demand for juttis, they are now mass manufactured with rubber soles too.

Elsewhere in India, the jutti is commonly known as *mojari*. In Pakistan, they are often known by its variant *khussa* – leather juttis with the end at the toes curled upwards, with rich golden threads and colourful beads that are used to craft exquisite motifs on them. Like juttis, they have been traditionally handed over by generations with each generation contributing some variation to it.

Typical Punjabi Rotis

Mind you, these are *rotis*, and not paranthas: the difference between the two being that in a roti, all the items are *kneaded* in the dough, rather than *stuffing* it in later. This method, obviously, would take lesser time than making a stuffed parantha. These can be a main course in themselves, when accompanied with thick curd and some pickle.

A key point to note while making these rotis is to chop the ingredients very finely; else the roti will break from parts where the bits are chunkier. The cooking method for all the rotis remain the same. Hence, I would describe the cooking method first and then list the ingredients of various types of rotis.

Cooking method for all

Knead the atta with all the respective ingredients of a roti, gradually add water to make a firm yet soft dough. Heat the tawa and grease it with a little oil. Take a little portion of the dough and make a medium-sized ball. Flatten it to form a thick roti. Cook the roti on the tawa, till rich golden on both sides. You can also tawa fry the roti using a little salted butter towards the end for more crispiness.

PYAAZ KI ROTI

Ingredients (makes 4 rotis):

Wheat flour: 2 cups
Onions, finely chopped: 2 small
Coriander leaves, chopped: a few sprigs
Green chillies, finely chopped: 2

Salt: as per taste
Red chilli powder: as per taste
Zeera powder: ½ tsp
Dhania powder: ½ tsp
Anardana: ¼ tsp
Amchoor: ¼ tsp
Ajwain: ½ tsp
Water: enough to make a dough

DAL KI ROTI

Ingredients (makes 4 rotis)

Wheat flour: 2 cups
Any left over dal: 1 cup
Ginger, finely chopped or grated: 1" piece
Garlic, finely chopped or grated: 4-5 flakes
Coriander leaves, chopped: a few sprigs
Green chillies, finely chopped: 2 nos.
Salt: as per taste
Red chilli powder: as per taste
Zeera powder: ½ tsp
Dhania powder: ½ tsp
Ajwain: ½ tsp
Water: enough to make a dough

METHI KI ROTI

Ingredients (makes 4 rotis):

Wheat flour: 2 cups
Methi leaves, washed and chopped: 1 small bundle
Green chillies, finely chopped: 2 nos.
Salt: as per taste
Red chilli powder: as per taste
Zeera powder: ½ tsp

Ajwain: ¼ tsp
Water: enough to make a dough

Tip: Preferably, methi should be chopped, and not blended into a paste, as the leaves give a better flavour.

MISSI ROTI (A signature roti, usually had as brunch)

Ingredients (makes 4 rotis)

Besan: 1 cup
Atta: 1 cup
Onion, chopped: 1 small
Zeera (whole): ½ tsp
Dhania seeds, slightly pounded to break them: ½ tsp
Coriander leaves, chopped: a few sprigs
Green chillies, finely chopped: 2 nos.
Hing: a pinch
Ghee: 1 tsp
Red chilli powder: as per taste
Haldi powder: a pinch, only for colour
Zeera powder: ½ tsp
Dhania powder: ½ tsp
Ajwain: ½ tsp
Anardana: ¼ tsp
Salt: as per taste
Water: enough to make a dough

Elements of a traditional Punjabi dance dress

Every dance form has a typical dress, and so do bhangra and gidda. The dress meant for a dance enhances the art visually, by means of props. Therefore, the attire is significantly dictated by the dance moves. The more delicate the dance form, the more elaborate the dress (like classical dances – pleats, jewellery, make-up), and the more active the dance, the more fluid and loose the dress.

Bhangra and gidda, being active dance forms, therefore, have quite comfortable outfits. Following are the typical elements for a man's outfit:

Pagri – A well-pleated turban, sometimes adorned with *gota* (a broad golden lace).

Turla – A fan-like adornment on the pagri, usually made with the starched end of the same.

Kaintha – A necklace, usually of big beads, though some men also wear earrings.

Rumal – Scarves knotted on the fingers. When the hands move during the course of bhangra performance, these colourful scarves look very striking.

Kurta – A loose, long shirt with at least four buttons. Usually embroidered, this is white in colour, though in recent times, colours like yellow, green and red have also been in vogue.

Lungi or *Chadar* – This is a loose-fitting rectangular fabric tied around the dancer's waist, which is usually decorated or embroidered.

Jugi – A waistcoat, with no buttons. The jugi, pagri and the lungi are typically of the same colour.

Jutti – Traditional footwear, but mostly the men dance barefoot.

The women, apart from the outfit, are more elaborately adorned with jewellery and accessories. Following are the main elements for a woman's outfit:

Dupatta – This is a 2.5-metre long heavily embroidered scarf, also called *chunni*.

Kameez – A long shirt, usually a little above the knees, well-fitted yet comfortable.

Patiala salwar – Pleated trousers.

Tikka – An ornate piece of jewellery worn on the forehead.

Jhumka – Long dangling earrings.

Paranda – Silky long tassels braided in the hair.

Raani-Haar – A long necklace made of solid gold.

Baazu-Band – Tight band worn around the upper-arm.

Pazaibs – Anklets.

Jutti – Traditional footwear, but mostly the women too, dance barefoot.

Ande ki Bhurji

What we read as scrambled eggs in English menus are ubiquitously eaten in Punjabi homes as *ande ki bhurji*. Usually a quick breakfast for me, I often carry egg bhurji with two slices of bread as a quick working lunch.

Ingredients (serves 2)

Oil: 2 tsps
Zeera (whole): ½ tsp
Green chillies, chopped: 2 nos.
Onion, chopped: 1 medium
Salt: as per taste
Red chilli powder: as per taste
Haldi powder: ½ tsp
Zeera powder: ½ tsp
Dhania powder: ½ tsp
Tomato, chopped: 1 medium
Eggs: 3 nos.
Coriander leaves, chopped: a few sprigs for garnishing

Cooking

In a kadhai, heat oil and add whole zeera. To this add chopped green chillies and chopped onions. Stir fry till onions become translucent. Then add the spices and the tomatoes. Stir fry till tomatoes mash up slightly. Then on low flame, break the eggs and add to the mixture, stirring vigorously, so that the eggs clot in small chunks and not big ones. Cook stirring continuously, till the eggs are cooked.

Serve hot with phulkas or paranthas.

Panjeeri

This particular preparation lay forgotten in the backyard of my mind until I had it at a friend's place. The differentiating ingredient was fresh banana slices, which is not used in the Punjabi version. I am not sure about the origin of *panjeeri*, but it's considered to be an energy food in Punjabi homes. Mentioned below is the recipe for the simplest and quickest of panjeeris. However, I have skipped many ingredients – watermelon and muskmelon seeds (*magaz*), *cheed* (a type of resin), black pepper, sonth – which are added to make it a desired food for ladies in the post-natal phase. You can add them too (during the roasting), on the basis of your energy needs.

Ingredients (serves 2)

Ghee: 2 tbsps
Wheat flour: 1 cup
Almonds, coarsely pounded: 15-20 nos.
Sugar: ½ cup

Cooking

Heat ghee in a kadhai and roast wheat flour, until it turns rich golden brown. Add almonds and mix well. Remove from flame and add sugar. Don't heat after adding sugar else it will melt.

An extremely energetic and quick food.

Five

Ravi (Sanskrit: *Purushni*)

Accompaniments; Sikh traditions

On 31 December 1929 slogans of *Inquilab Zindabad* filled the midnight air. The Tricolour had been unfurled on the banks of River Ravi. Historically called Iravati, the waters of Ravi belong to India under the Indus Waters Treaty (1960).

Historically, Iravati was dug as a strategic warring move to displace and destroy King Sudas of the Bharata tribe. This great legendary battle was called *Dasarajana*, the Battle of the Ten

Kings, and the ten chiefs, or kings, who fought against Sudas were instigated by Sage Vishwamitra. Under the mentorship of Sage Vasishtha, Sudas – even though unprepared for this sudden attack and greatly outnumbered by the forces of the ten kings – managed a magnificent victory with his small yet strong army.

According to legend, Indra (God of Thunder) supported Sudas in the Battle of the Ten Kings, due to the moral superiority of the latter. The *devas* were witness to this battle that took place on a stormy night by the banks of Ravi, when both the river and the storm came to the aide of Sudas. The rival soldiers were either drowned in the flood, or massacred by Sudas's army.

The swift waters of Ravi are used to carry timber. The river is fordable for almost eight months of a year, and the deposits made by it are extremely fertile.

The items to follow are not 'dishes' per se, but they play a critical role in Punjabi cuisine. These accompaniments give the cuisine a consciousness, a character that it is famous for. Just like these preparations, the religion under which we are born, doesn't completely define our existence, unless we absorb the values and principles it rests on. Unconsciously, many of us are secret agnostics. We follow certain rituals and customs because they have been followed for ages, without knowing the reasons ourselves.

The beauty of religion lies in the magnanimous pool of knowledge it has to offer through scriptures, recitations or chants that have been handed down to us from generations. There is a reason behind a baby getting its name in a particular religion, how a wedding is conducted, which god is worshipped, and why or what makes a place so holy that it becomes a shrine. Most of these reasons maybe irrational, but that's purely of personal belief.

There are certain aspects of Sikhism that are very deep-rooted in the pursuit for equality and oneness. A classic example is *langar*, common kitchen for all. The practice of langar was instituted by Guru Nanak, in an attempt to get people of all castes and creeds to eat together. Anybody eating a langar, irrespective of social status has to sit on the floor and eat it.

Just like the little aspects of religion – which we follow every day, which make us feel secure, which give us some power to fall back on, some power to blame, some power to thank – these little food items will play a critical role in giving soul to even the most common of foods. Some of these dishes have a longer shelf life; they can be made once over a weekend, stored in the fridge, and consumed for almost a week. I have mentioned the shelf life against the preparations that can be stored.

Breads

Phulka

Knead the wheat flour in cold water, adding the water bit by bit. After kneading, let it rest for ten minutes. Make small balls, flatten them with a rolling pin and cook them on a tawa (preferably iron). Don't worry if they aren't exactly round! When taken off the tawa, you can top it up with some ghee/salted butter.

TWIST: You can also try to knead the dough in milk. Add half a teaspoon of ajwain as well. The phulkas will be extremely soft and nutritious.

Parantha

Knead the dough as above, and make medium-sized balls. Flatten a ball into a roti. Spread some ghee on the surface, and fold the sides (one fold each), to make a square packet. Now again roll this square packet, to make into a square roti. This step makes the parantha more *khasta*, i.e., short in bite and texture. Cook on a heated tawa, shallow frying in the end.

TWIST: Before folding the sides, you can sprinkle some red chilli powder and ajwain over the ghee. It would make the parantha spicy and more delicious.

Mūl Mantra

Mūl mantra, literally means the root verse. It is a summation of the fundamental belief of Sikhism, regarding oneness of God. The *Guru Granth Sahib* begins with the mūl mantra:

Ik Onkar	There exists only one God
Sat Naam	Whose name is the eternal Truth
Karta Purakh	Who is the creator of everything
Nirbhau	Who is fearless
Nirvair	Who doesn't have any enmity with anyone
Akal Murat	Who is timeless and immortal
Ajooni	Who is beyond birth and death
Saibhang	Who is self-existent
Gur Parsad	Who is known and realised by the Guru's Grace.

These words of the mūl mantra represent a Weltanschauung that centres on an absolute, yet all-pervading, sole creative force without fear or favour, immanent in creation and transcending it at the same time.

Rice

Though Punjabis are not much of rice eaters, but considering that some of the dals and gravies go really well with rice, it is a critical element of the cuisine. Rice is effortless to make, just make sure you add water that is equal to double the quantity of rice.

PLAIN RICE

Ingredients (serves 2)

Rice: 1 cup
Water: 2 cups
Salt (optional): as per taste
Oil: 1 tsp

Cooking

Wash the rice and keep aside.

In an aluminium vessel, pour double the water (here, two cups) and add washed rice into it. Add salt and oil. Bring to a boil. Simmer and partially cover with a lid, to let the steam escape. Let it cook till the water evaporates. Serve hot.

ZEERA RICE

Ingredients (serves 2)

Rice: 1 cup
Oil: 1 tsp
Zeera (whole): 2 tsps
Water: 2 cups
Salt: as per taste

Cooking

Wash the rice and keep aside.

In an aluminium vessel, heat oil. Add whole zeera, and once the sputtering is over, pour double the water (here, two cups) and add washed rice into it. Add salt and bring to a boil.

After the boil, simmer the flame and partially cover with a lid, to let the steam escape. Let it cook till the water evaporates. Serve hot.

TWIST: You can also golden fry some onion slices after the zeera sputters for enhanced taste. Proceed similarly as above.

Langar

Langar or free kitchen is the gurus' way of combining worship with food. From the time of Guru Nanak Dev the practice of a common kitchen for the whole congregation has been almost a rule. The gurdwara is both the temple for prayer and the temple of bread. The community mess – refectory – is a practical institution to demonstrate the principle of sharing our earnings with others. Guru Amar Das made the langar an integral part of the Sikh temple by providing accommodation for the kitchen, dining hall and a pantry. Langar is the joint responsibility of the Sikh community and does not depend on charities from outside. Guru Gobind Singh directed his followers to maintain langar in their own homes too.

Langar is a place of training in voluntary service and the practice of philanthropy and equality. Service is involved in the collection of fuel and rations, cutting of vegetables, cooking of food, distribution of meals, serving of drinking water, washing of utensils and dishes, and the cleaning of dining halls. Doing service for langar (*langar sewa*), is considered pious and a lot of men, women and even children volunteer for sewa by making chapattis, cooking dal, serving plates and food to the *sangat* or congregation, etc. The plates, too, are washed by the *sewadars* or volunteers. No paid help or caterers are ever employed to prepare langar or maintain the langar hall in a gurdwara.

Apart from this, the langar ensures social equality and integration. It is the most effective step for removing caste prejudice and exclusiveness. It is a free kitchen for Sikhs and non-Sikhs alike. It is a means for a better treatment of the poor and the underprivileged. Based on equality of men and women, it proclaims the dignity of an ordinary human being.

The Sikh community is under an obligation to maintain langar in the gurdwara. Therefore, langar as a practice has been followed wherever Sikhs have established themselves, in India as well as abroad. Voluntary donations or *daswant* support the langar. Maharaja Ranjit Singh (1780–1839) made endowments of land and properties to many gurdwaras to enable them to discharge their services to the community. In such case of a land being allocated to a gurdwara, it yields enough grains and vegetables on its own, or if the land is given on lease, it can yield income sufficient to meet the requirements of food purchased from the market. Only vegetarian food is provided in the langar. On certain occasions like Gurpurabs, the langar feeds more than one hundred thousand people at the same time.

Many people who arrange kirtan programmes or *paath* in their homes serve langar at the end of the function.

Langar wali Dal

There is something about this dal that makes it unforgettable; and you can never replicate it at home. This dal is prepared by mixing several dals and it is then left to simmer for many hours. The key dals, however, remain Mah ki Dal (black whole lentil) and Chane ki Dal (split Bengal gram). In an attempt to replicate this dal at home, it has almost been renamed as 'kali peeli dal' by many families.

Ingredients (serves 3-4)

Mah ki Dal, soaked for 5-6 hours: 1 cup
Chane ki Dal, soaked for 5-6 hours: ½ cup
Water: 5 cups
Salt: as per taste
Haldi powder: ½ tsp
Oil: 2 tsps
Zeera (whole): 1 tsp
Dhania seeds, slightly pounded to break them: 1 tsp
Onion, chopped: 1 large
Green chillies, slit: 3 nos.
Ginger, pounded: 1" piece
Garlic, pounded: 6-7 flakes
Tomato, chopped: 1 large
Red chilli powder: as per taste
Zeera powder: ½ tsp
Dhania powder: ½ tsp

Cooking

In a pressure cooker, add five cups of water to the dal; add salt and haldi powder. Seal the lid and after the first whistle, simmer and cook for thirty minutes. Keep aside.

In a kadhai, heat oil. Once heated, add whole zeera and dhania seeds. Once they sputter, add chopped onions, slit green chillies and pounded ginger and garlic. Stir fry till the onions turn golden brown. Then add chopped tomatoes and stir fry till they mash a little. Then add red chilli powder, zeera powder and dhania powder and stir fry for a minute. Now add the boiled dal and mix well. After it comes to a boil, simmer for ten minutes, mashing the dal gently against the base of the kadhai. Adjust the seasoning and thickness as per your preference.

Serve hot with phulkas.

Beverages

LASSI

In a typical dhaba, lassi is served in a tall, almost an eight-inch copper glass. Lassi is essentially a curd-based beverage blended with sugar or spices. The thicker the dahi (curd), the richer and heavier the lassi becomes.

MITTHI (SWEET) LASSI

Ingredients (serves 1)

Dahi (curd): 1½ cups
Sugar: as per taste
Water/milk: as required

Method

In a blender, pour dahi and sugar, and blend it. Add water or milk, to a consistency of your choice, and blend again. Pour into glasses over ice cubes and serve.

Typically, sweet lassi is of a thick consistency; therefore it makes a satisfying breakfast item.

NAMKEEN (SALTY) LASSI

Ingredients (serves 1)

Dahi (curd): 1½ cups
Salt: as per taste
Zeera (whole), roasted and ground to a coarse powder: ¼ tsp
Water/milk: as required

Method

In a blender, pour dahi, salt, a pinch of zeera powder, and blend it. Add water or milk, to a consistency of your choice, and blend again. Pour into glasses over ice cubes and serve.

Typically, salty lassi is comparatively thinner in consistency; therefore it makes a good accompaniment with meals.

TWIST: You can also add mint leaves and chopped ginger while blending the salty lassi to make it more refreshing and healthy.

PANNA

Panna is a summer drink and is made with ambi (raw mangoes). It is very refreshing and is both sweet and tangy in taste. Raw mangoes have a cooling effect, and the spices make up for the lost salts in summer. You can make this panna paste (concentrate), and put one tablespoon in a glass of cold water, add some ice cubes and drink instantly. Stored in the refrigerator, it can last for a week.

Ingredients

Ambi (raw mangoes), peeled: 4 nos.
Water: just a little to create steam

Sugar: as per taste

Mint leaves: 10-15 nos.

Cloves: 4 nos.

Zeera (whole): 1 tsp

Kala namak (black salt): ½ tsp

Black pepper: ½ tsp

Method

Cut the raw mangoes into big slices and put in a pressure cooker, along with a little water. Boil for one whistle. Keep it aside with the water in which it was boiled.

In a pan, dry roast cloves and whole zeera, till they sputter. Keep aside.

In a blender, put the boiled ambi, sugar, mint leaves, dry roasted cloves and zeera, black salt and black pepper. Blend it into a paste. Add the water of boiled ambi if needed. Store this paste in the refrigerator, and mix one tablespoon in a glass of chilled water to enjoy a healthy drink.

CHAI

The teas to follow are the ones that I had at a dhaba some years ago. Strong teas are a hit with truck drivers, as it keeps them awake and alert while they drive through the night. These teas are spiced up with condiments, which make them extremely refreshing and tasty. Their names are as tantalising as their flavours!

TANATAN CHAI

Ingredients (serves 2-3)

Ginger, grated or pounded: ½" piece

Water: 1½ cups

Sugar: as per taste

Tea leaves: 1 tsp
Black pepper: one pinch
Green cardamom, slightly pounded: 2 nos.
Milk: 1 cup

Preparation

In a heavy bottom pan, put ginger along with one-and-a-half cups of water, sugar, tea leaves, black pepper and green cardamoms. Bring to a boil, cover the pan and let the mixture simmer for ten minutes to extract the flavour from the spices. Add milk, bring to a boil, and simmer for two minutes. Strain and serve.

MARDON WALI CHAI

Ingredients (serves 2-3)

Ginger, grated or pounded: ½" piece
Water: 1 cup
Sugar: as per taste
Cloves: 2 nos.
Cinnamon: 1 cm piece
Green Cardamom, slightly pounded: 2 nos.
Black pepper: one pinch
Tea leaves: 1 tsp
Milk: 1½ cup

Preparation

In a heavy bottom pan, put ginger, one cup of water, sugar, cloves, cinnamon, green cardamoms, black pepper and tea leaves. Bring to a boil, cover the pan and let the mixture simmer for five minutes, to extract the flavour from the spices. Add milk, bring to a boil and simmer for five minutes. Strain and serve.

FRESH JALJEERA

Ingredients (serves 2):

Mint leaves: 1 small bunch
Coriander leaves: equal to mint leaves
Ginger: ½" piece
Zeera (whole), roasted: 1 tsp
Lemon juice: 1 tbsp
Kala namak (black salt): as per taste
Chaat masala: ½ tsp
Sugar: 4 tsps
Water, chilled: 2 glasses
Ice cubes: just a few
Boondi (fried, spiced little balls of gram flour, available readymade at grocery stores): for garnishing

Preparation

Wash mint and coriander leaves thoroughly. Blend both the leaves along with ginger and roasted zeera into a fine paste. Use some water if required. Keep aside. If refrigerated, this paste has a shelf life of two to three days. Whenever needed, you can take out the required quantity and prepare as explained below.

In a jug, add three tablespoons of this paste, lemon juice, kala namak, chaat masala, sugar and two glasses of chilled water. Mix well till the sugar dissolves. Add some ice cubes.

Strain into tall glasses and serve chilled. Add a little boondi before serving. It looks beautiful when it floats on the surface!

MATTHA

Ingredients (serves 2-3)

Thick curd: 1½ cups
Hing: 1 pinch

Ginger: ½" piece
Green chillies: 1-2 nos.
Coriander leaves: a few sprigs
Water, chilled: 2 glasses
Salt: as per taste

Preparation

Blend curd, hing, ginger, green chillies and half the coriander leaves in a blender. Gradually add two glasses of chilled water. Once again, blend thoroughly. Adjust salt as per your taste. Finely chop the remaining coriander leaves and stir them in the glasses while serving. Serve chilled.

NIMBU SHIKANJVI

Ingredients (serves 2)

Sugar: 4 tsps
Kala namak: ½ tsp
Lemon juice: 4 tbsps
Water, chilled: 2 glasses
Ice cubes: just a few

Preparation

Dissolve sugar and black salt in a glass of water. In a jug, add this sugar-and-salt syrup and lemon juice. Add another glass of water and lots of ice cubes.

Check for salt and sugar as per your taste. Serve chilled.

GAJAR KANJI

Ingredients

Black carrots (cut into batons): 2 large
Beetroot (cut into batons): 1 medium
Salt: 1½ tbsps

Mustard seeds (ground gently to get a coarse powder): 2 tbsps
Water: 10 cups
Red chilli powder: as per taste

Preparation

Take the carrot and beetroot batons in a non-metallic bowl. Add salt and coarse mustard powder. Mix well. Add ten cups of water to this spiced mixture and stir. Cover the bowl with a clean muslin cloth. Tie it around the rim to hold it in place.

Keep this bowl in the sun for three to four days. Check if ready by tasting it (it should be tangy, not pungent) and smelling it (it will have a slightly fermented smell). When ready, put it in the refrigerator. Serve chilled, adding a little red chilli powder as per taste. It can be stored for two to three days in the refrigerator.

CHHUARE WALA DHOODH

This is a Punjabi drink for festivities. Usually made in winters, this is a rich milk-based drink. The first time I had it was at a *prabhat pheri* (early morning nagar kirtan), when the congregation stopped at a house for ardas.

Ingredients (serves 3-4)

Chhuaras (dried dates), soaked: 10-15 nos.
Milk: 1 litre
Nutmeg powder: a pinch
Green cardamoms, coarsely grounded into a powder: 8 nos.
Sugar: 3 tbsps

Preparation

Finely chop the soaked chhuaras and keep aside.

In an aluminium vessel, bring milk to a boil. Once boiled, add chopped chhuaras, nutmeg powder and green cardamom powder. Keep stirring continuously else the milk will start sticking to the walls and the bottom of the vessel. Simmer for fifteen to twenty minutes. Add sugar in the end. Mix for two minutes, check for sugar as per your taste and remove from the flame.

Serve hot in glasses. Do not strain. The chewy chhuaras are delightful!

BADAM THANDAI

The traditional thandai is a very elaborate beverage, and uses exotic ingredients like saffron and dried rose petals. However, below is a slightly simplified version of the same (but still elaborate compared to the other beverages) to make sure the availability of ingredients doesn't deter us from enjoying this drink on a sunny day!

Ingredients (serves 3-4)

Almonds, soaked and peeled: 20 nos.
Cashews, soaked: 10 nos.
Pistachios, soaked and peeled: 15 nos.
Melon seeds (*kharbuze ke beej* or magaz): 1½ tbsps
Green cardamoms: 8 nos.
Cinnamon: 1" piece
Peppercorns: 8 nos.
Poppy seeds (khus khus), soaked: 1 ½ tbsps
Milk: 1 litre
Sugar: ½ cup

Preparation

In a blender, put almonds, cashews, pistachios, melon seeds, green cardamoms, cinnamon, peppercorns and poppy seeds. Add a little milk and make a fine paste. Keep aside.

In an aluminium vessel, bring milk to a boil. Once it boils, simmer the flame and add sugar. Keep stirring continuously else the milk will start sticking to the walls and bottom of the vessel. Add the paste to the milk and mix well. Simmer for another five minutes. Check for sugar as per your taste.

Let it cool a little before placing it in the refrigerator. Serve chilled without straining.

Kadah Prasad

Kadah Prasad (kadah ~ large iron pan; prasad ~ offering) is a sweet gruel made of flour (at times, even broken wheat or sooji) and ghee; it is offered to the sangat at a gurdwara, or after a religious ceremony conducted at home. Before being served, it is touched with the tip of the *kirpan* to sanctify it symbolically. It is served in equal quantities to everybody in the sangat by a sewadar.

The kadah prasad is considered very sacred, and is received in a particular manner; the person must join both his hands (right palm on top of the left) and form a cup-like shape; he/she must then transfer the prasad to the left palm and eat with the help of the right hand. The prasad should never be refused or thrown.

In late 1990s when Bangla Sahib Gurdwara in Delhi did not look the way it does today (it got renovated some years ago), the kadah prasad was served outside the prayer hall throughout the day. There used to be a disciplined queue to receive it. The kadah prasad used to be piping hot; but the sewadar would dig his hand, with that sturdy kada into it and distribute it to everybody without a frown. The kadah prasad would have so much of ghee that, it would drip down my hands while eating. This memory of my teenage years flashes in my mind whenever I am served kadah prasad on various occasions.

Kadah Prasad

Ingredients

Ghee: 1 cup
Wheat flour: 1 cup
Water: 2 cups
Sugar: 1 cup

Cooking

In a kadhai, heat ghee. Add flour, and roast while stirring continuously till it becomes a lovely golden brown colour. This would take around eight to ten minutes. Then add two cups of water and cook for five minutes, stirring continuosly. When the mixture starts becoming thick, add sugar. Add some more water if the mixture becomes too tight and stirring is difficult. Cook for five more minutes or till it leaves the sides of the pan. Serve hot.

Chutneys

PUDINE KI CHUTNEY

Green chutney made with mint or coriander (or both) is an accompaniment to almost all Punjabi dishes. It is my desi sandwich spread as well. It can last for almost a week, if stored in the refrigerator. Though, if the chutney is mixed in yoghurt to make a dip for snacks, it should be consumed within a day.

Ingredients

Pudina (mint leaves): one bunch
Dhania (coriander leaves): one bunch
Green chillies: 4 (or as per your taste, since no additional red chilli powder needs to be added)
Onion: 1 small
Garlic flakes: 2
Ambi (raw mango), coarsely chopped: ½ no., (optional)
Salt: as per your taste
Amchoor: ¼ tsp, (only if raw mango is not used)

Method

Pick the leaves off the stems and wash thoroughly under running water. Put all the ingredients in a blender and mix well. If the paste is too thick, add a few drops of water. Store in the refrigerator, and enjoy with meals.

TWIST: A little bit of this chutney mixed with thick yoghurt is an excellent dip for snacks like chicken tikkas, French fries, chips, etc.

You can also try mixing half or one spoonful of the masala (not the pieces) of mango pickle while blending, to add an extra zing.

This chutney tastes best when 'pounded': so if you have time, pound the mixture with a pestle.

AAM KI CHUTNEY

Ingredients

Ambi (raw mangoes), peeled: 3 nos.
Water: ½ cup
Oil: 2 tsps
Sugar: 2 tbsps
Cloves, dry roasted: 4
Zeera (whole), dry roasted: 1 tsp
Salt: as per taste
Kala namak (black salt): ½ tsp
Black pepper: ½ tsp
Red chilli powder: as per taste
Water: just enough to enhance the texture

Method

Grate the ambi (the gratings should not be too fine) and put in the pressure cooker with half-a-cup of water (only to create steam). Pressure cook for one whistle and keep aside.

Heat oil in a kadhai. Cook the parboiled mangoes, stirring continuously, till the mixture becomes glossy and firm. If the mixture is too tight to stir then add a little water. Add sugar and all the spices. Adjust the seasoning as per your preference. Cool, and store in the fridge. This chutney can last for a week under refrigeration.

TWIST: In the same recipe, you can slice the mango, rather than grating it. It uses a little more water and the final product looks like mango slices in tangy sugary syrup.

SAUNTH

Ingredients

Water: 1½ cups
Imli (tamarind), soaked in a cup of water for two hours: 100 gms
Gur: 2 tbsps
Muskmelon seeds: 1 tsp
Zeera (whole), dry roasted: ½ tsp
Kala namak (black salt): as per taste

Cooking

Boil the imli with gur, in a cup-and-a-half of water. Simmer
and cook till it gains a sauce-like consistency. Sieve and keep
aside. Add muskmelon seeds, roasted whole zeera and black
salt and mix well while it is still warm. Saunth can last for
three to four days under refrigeration.

AMLE KI CHUTNEY

Ingredients

Amla (Indian gooseberry): 250 gms
Water: ½ cup
Oil: 2 tsps
Sugar: 2 tbsps
Zeera (whole), dry roasted: 1 tsp
Salt: as per taste
Kala namak (black salt): ½ tsp
Black pepper: ½ tsp
Red chilli powder: as per taste

Method

Put the amlas in a pressure cooker with half-a-cup of water
(only to create steam). Pressure cook for one whistle. When
cooled, press the amla vertically from top and bottom – it

would easily break into five crescent shaped pieces. Keep the parts aside.

Heat oil in a kadhai. Put in the amla pieces, sugar and all the spices. Adjust the seasoning as per your preference. Cool, and store in the refrigerator; it can last for a week.

DHANIA TAMATAR KI CHUTNEY

Ingredients

Coriander leaves: 1 bunch
Tomato: 1 medium
Garlic: 8-10 flakes
Green chillies: 2 nos.
Salt: as per taste

Method

Grind all the ingredients coarsely in a blender. Adjust the seasoning.

Singh and Kaur

Some people are amazed when they know of a girl and a boy both named Harmeet. They are even more flummoxed to know that all the surnames of typical Sikh names are the same: either a Singh or a Kaur.

The custom of using Singh and Kaur as surnames was introduced by Guru Gobind Singh in 1699. Singh (from Sanskrit's 'Simha'), literally means 'lion' and Kaur (from Sanskrit's 'Kumari') means 'princess'. The main intention of giving a common surname to both Sikh men and women was to remove any inequality based on the family lineage and caste. It gives an equal status to women after marriage, by making them continue with their maiden names, and not requiring to adopt their husband's surname.

Amongst the Sikhs, Lord Indra's name (God of thunder, a personification of the sky, the chief of devtas) has become very popular, e.g., Inder Singh, Rajinder, Ravinder, Balvinder, Dharmendra, Narinder, and so on. The name 'Inder' is used more as a suffix, indicating the martial qualities of Lord Indra. The attributes of Indra correspond to those of Jupiter Pluvius and Jupiter Tonans of the Greeks and Romans, and Thor of Scandinavia, and as such he is the impersonation of the skies.

There are many suffixes like the above that are used traditionally while naming a child. One of them is 'Jeet', which means victory. Hence, we have Inderjeet, Manjeet, Kuljeet, etc. And then we have 'Meet', which means friend – Manmeet, Parmeet, Harmeet, etc. For example, my name means God's own friend. ('Har' ~ derived from 'Hari', meaning God and 'Meet', meaning friend)

Almost all traditional Sikh names are interchangeable between men and women, the only differentiating factor towards gender being the surname Singh or Kaur, like Harmeet Singh/Harmeet Kaur, Baljit Singh/Baljit Kaur, Surinder Singh/Surinder Kaur, etc.

Raitas

Raita is essentially curd (dahi) to which chopped vegetables, spices, or *boondi* are added. They are a quintessential accompaniment to Punjabi meals. All raitas should be consumed fresh.

BOONDI RAITA

Ingredients (serves 2-3)

Thick curd: 2 cups
Boondi: a handful
Salt: to taste
Red chilli: a pinch
Roasted zeera powder: 1 tsp
Freshly ground black pepper: to taste
Coriander leaves, chopped: a few sprigs
Water: just enough to reduce the thickness of the raita

Method

Whisk the curd to remove any lumps. Mix a handful of boondi to the smoothened curd. Add salt, red chilli, zeera powder, black pepper, and chopped coriander leaves. Add a little water if you like it less thick. Keep aside for ten minutes, till the boondis absorb some of the water and become soft. Serve cold.

VEGETABLE RAITA

Ingredients

Thick curd: 2 cups
Onion, chopped: 1 small
Tomato, chopped: 1 small
Cucumber, chopped: 2" piece
Salt: to taste

Red chilli: a pinch
Roasted zeera powder: 1 tsp
Freshly ground black pepper: to taste
Coriander leaves, chopped: a few sprigs

Method

Whisk the curd to remove any lumps. Mix chopped onions, tomatoes and cucumber in the smoothened curd. Add salt, red chilli powder, zeera powder, black pepper, and chopped coriander leaves. It tastes best when kept thick. Serve cold.

KHEERE KA RAITA

An excellent raita that keeps you cool in summers.

Ingredients (serves 2-3)

Thick curd: 2 cups
Cucumber, grated: 1 medium
Salt: to taste
Freshly ground black pepper: to taste
Roasted zeera powder: 1 tsp

Preparation

In a bowl, whisk the curd to remove any lumps. Add grated cucumber, salt, black pepper and roasted zeera powder. Mix well. This raita should be kept thick. Serve cold.

LAUKI KA RAITA

Ingredients (serves 3-4)

Lauki (Bottle gourd): 1 small (or ½ of medium-sized)
Water: 2-3 tbsps
Thick curd: 2 cups
Salt: to taste
Freshly ground black pepper: to taste
Roasted zeera powder: 1 tsp
Red chilli powder: for garnish

Preparation

Peel the lauki, wash and grate it. In a pressure cooker, add a little water, add the grated lauki and boil for one whistle. Let it cool and keep aside. Do not throw away the water.

In a bowl, whisk the curd to remove any lumps. Add the boiled lauki (along with the water), salt, black pepper and roasted zeera powder. Mix well. Sprinkle a little red chilli powder on the top for garnish. Serve cold.

ALOO KA RAITA

Ingredients (serves 3-4)

Boiled potato, peeled: 1 medium
Thick curd: 2 cups
Salt: to taste
Roasted zeera powder: 1 tsp
Red chilli powder: to taste
Chaat masala: ½ tsp
Coriander leaves, chopped: a few sprigs
Water: Just enough to reduce the thickness of the raita

Preparation

Cut the boiled potato into small (half centimetre) cubes. Keep aside.

In a bowl, whisk the curd to remove any lumps. Add salt, roasted zeera powder, red chilli powder, chaat masala and mix well. Add the boiled potatoes and coriander leaves and mix gently, not to break or mash the potatoes. Add a little water if the raita is too thick. Serve cold.

Dastaarbandi

Dastaarbandi is a ceremony in a Sikh family where the young boys are initiated into tying the turban (dastaar ~ turban; bandi ~ tying). Usually, it is a private ceremony where kirtan is conducted and an elder member of the family, usually the grandfather, ties the turban on the young boy. After this ceremony, wearing the turban becomes mandatory for the boy; it becomes a part of his life that demands complete respect and commitment.

Salads

Salads in Punjabi cuisine are tangy and spicy, almost pickle-like.

KACHOOMBAR SALAD

Ingredients

Onions, coarsely chopped: 1 small
Tomatoes, coarsely chopped: 1 small
Cabbage, coarsely chopped: 2" block
Cucumber, coarsely chopped: 2" block
Coriander leaves, chopped: a few sprigs
Salt: as per taste
Chaat masala: 1 tsp
Red chilli powder: as per taste
Juice of 2 lemons

Method

Put coarsely chopped onions, tomatoes, cabbage, cucumbers and coriander leaves (and other vegetables of your choice like capsicum, carrots) in a bowl and add salt, chaat masala, red chilli powder and lots of lemon juice. Mix well, and keep aside for fifteen minutes in the refrigerator, so that the vegetables get marinated in the lemon juice. This salad is for immediate consumption.

PICKLE SALAD

Ingredients

Onion, sliced lengthwise: 2 medium
Radish, cut into thin 1" long batons: 2" block
Salt: 1 tsp
Salad vegetables of your choice (cucumbers, carrots, capsicums): a few pieces, cut into thin 1" long batons
Mango pickle: 2 tbsps

Method

Put sliced onions and radish in a bowl, add some salt and keep aside for ten minutes. Then, wash to remove the pungency of the vegetables. Add other vegetables of your choice like cucumber, capsicum, carrots, etc., and add a spoon of mango pickle (more masala than pieces). Let it stand for twenty minutes before you consume, so that the vegetables soak the flavour of the pickle.

TIPS: This salad, if marinated for a longer time, say two to three hours, tastes better as the pickle marinates all the vegetables. However, make sure you consume this salad on the same day.

SIRKE WAALE PYAAZ

Sirke wale Pyaaz or vinegar onions, as they are often called, are imperative to Punjabi dishes. These are baby or Madras onions that are soaked overnight in white vinegar with a pinch of salt, giving them a very crunchy, sour taste. They are soft pinkish in colour.

MASALA PAPADS

Ingredients

Papads: 4 nos.
Onions, finely chopped: 1 medium
Tomatoes, finely chopped: 1 small
Green chillies, chopped: as per taste
Coriander leaves, chopped: a few sprigs
Salt: as per taste
Red chilli powder: as per taste
Chaat masala: ½ tsp
Juice of 1-2 lemons

Method

Roast the papads. Make a mixture of finely chopped onions, tomatoes, green chillies and chopped coriander leaves. Add salt, red chilli powder and chaat masala. Mix well with a dash of lemon juice. Top the papads with this mixture and serve immediately. If kept for long, the papad will become soggy.

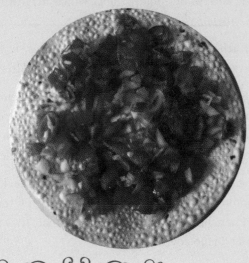

Panj Kakkas

Guru Gobind Singh modified the Sikh baptism ceremony when he created the Khalsa in 1699. This ceremony was called Amrit or the baptism by nectar, stirred by the double-edged sword (Khande de Pahul). Five Sikhs offered themselves for the first amrit ceremony. The recipients were asked to take certain vows and abide by the code of discipline (Rehatmaryada) and keep the *Panj Kakkas* (five Ks), as following:

1 **Kes** (unshorn hair): Kes is considered to be a symbol of living in harmony with the will of God.

2 **Kanga** (comb): Kanga is considered necessary to keep the hair neat and tidy. The hair should be covered neatly with a turban, which promotes social identity and cohesion.

3 **Kada** (steel bangle): Kada symbolised restraint from evil action. Its click or knock reminds the Sikh of his vows and that he should not do anything, which may bring him disgrace or shame.

4 **Kachh** (underpants): Kachh symbolises control over passion or sex. It also ensures briskness of action and freedom of movement.

5 **Kirpan** (steel dagger): Kirpan is an emblem of courage, and is meant both for protection of the weak and the poor and also for self-defence. It promotes a martial spirit and willingness to sacrifice oneself for the defence of truth, justice and moral values.

The five Ks along with the turban are the Khalsa uniform for promoting the solidarity and identity of the community. For women, however, the turban is optional. They may wear a chunni or a scarf to cover the head.

The five Ks are not meant to foster an air of exclusivity. They keep the Sikhs united in the pursuit of ideals and vows made to the guru. The value of the five Ks in character formation is obvious: the Khalsa can be identified among a large group, and any unworthy behaviour on his part would make people point fingers at him as an unworthy or an irresponsible Sikh. The five Ks demonstrate the Khalsa obedience to the commands of Guru Gobind Singh.

Pickles

GAJAR-GOBHI-SHALGAM KA ACHAR

This achar is so addictive that you would end up digging into it and almost munching it like a snack. This is a widely made pickle in Punjabi homes, usually in winters when the constituent vegetables (carrots, cauliflower and turnip) are seasonal, for best taste. This achar has a shelf life of four to five weeks.

Ingredients

Mustard oil: 3 tbsps
Ginger, grated: 2 tbsps
Garlic, grated: 1 tbsp
Red chilli powder: 1½ tsps
Mustard seeds, coarsely ground: 1½ tsps
Salt: 2 tsps
Shalgam (turnip), halved and sliced in semi circles: 1 medium
Gajar (carrot), cut into roundels: 1 large
Gobhi (cauliflower), cut into florets: 1 small
Vinegar: 2½ tsps
Jaggery, grated: 2 tbsps

Preparation

In a kadhai, heat mustard oil. Add grated ginger and garlic, and sauté till golden. Then add red chilli powder, powdered mustard seeds, and salt. Mix well and sauté for half a minute. Add shalgam, gajar and gobhi. Mix well in the masala and cook for one minute. Then add vinegar and jaggery. Mix and cook for two more minutes.

Remove from flame and allow it to cool completely. Transfer into a sterilised bottle. This achaar will be ready to eat after seven to eight days. No need to place the bottle under the sun.

ADRAK NIMBU MIRCHI KA ACHAR

If you love green chillies, then this achar is for you. Of the three key ingredients (ginger, lemon and chillies), the chillies taste the best. This pickle has a shelf life of three to four weeks.

Ingredients

Ginger, scraped: 100 gms
Lemons: 6-7 nos.
Long green chillies: 15 nos.
Salt: 2½ tsps
Sugar: ½ tsp
Red chilli powder: ½ tsp (or as per taste)

Preparation

Cut ginger into medium, around 1" long batons. Cut lemons into halves and squeeze out the juice. Keep the juice aside. Cut each half of the lemon rind further into four pieces. De-stem the green chillies and slit lengthwise into halves.

Now mix the lemon rind, green chillies and ginger in a glass container. Add the lemon juice (about five tablespoons), salt, sugar and red chilli powder. Seal the glass container and shake lightly to mix all the ingredients. Keep the container under the sun for three to four days and the pickle would be ready.

KACHCHE AAM AUR MIRCHI KA ACHAR

You won't find an achar simpler than this. This is my all-time favourite. Usually made in summers when raw mangoes are available easily, I love its texture, soft due to marination in basic spices… and the immediate bite of its sturdy peel… just brilliant!

Ingredients

Ambi (raw mango): 1 large
Long green chillies: 5 nos.
Haldi: a pinch
Salt: to taste
Red chilli powder: to taste
Lemon juice: 1 tsp

Preparation

Cut the raw mango into thin wedges. Do not peel it. Slit the green chillies lengthwise into halves.

Mix all the ingredients together in a non-metallic container and keep inside the refrigerator for two to three hours. The pickle is ready to be consumed. This pickle should be consumed the same day, so make sure you don't make it in a large quantity!

Anand Karaj

A Sikh marriage is called an Anand Karaj. It differs from a Hindu marriage as instead of circumambulating (*pheras*) the holy fire seven times, the couple walks around the *Guru Granth Sahib* four times. The 'lavan phere', which are a counterpart of the pheras (going around the holy fire by the Hindus) but known to Sikhs as parikramas, constitute the binding part of the ceremony.

The Sikh marriage ceremony initiated by Guru Amardas for the Sikh community consists of the recitation of Anand Sahib (therefore called Anand Karaj). Later, Guru Ramdas added the lavan (wedding song) for recitation and singing.

A Sikh wedding takes place in the presence of the *Guru Granth Sahib*, which is placed on an altar under a canopy. All guests take their shoes off and cover their heads before entering the hall where the ceremony takes place. Everyone proceeds towards the altar and bows to the scripture, touching the ground with the forehead. Everyone sits cross-legged on the floor. The bride and the groom publicly assent to the marriage by bowing down to the *Guru Granth Sahib*. When they sit down, the bride's father comes forward and places one end of the scarf that hangs from the groom's shoulder in the hand of his daughter. After a short hymn is sung, the officiant opens the Sikh scripture and begins to read the lavan of Guru Ramdas (*Guru Granth Sahib* – page 773).

Lavan is the name of a composition of four verses in the *Guru Granth Sahib*, of Guru Ramdas in Raga Suhi. It was composed as a wedding song for the Sikhs. These verses are recited twice, first by the granthi, and then sung when the couple goes around the holy granth. The purpose of repetition is to stress upon the couple to relate their married life to the spiritual goal of the life mentioned in the lavan.

The first verse of the Lavan mentions the performance of duties in married life. The couple is enjoined to maintain the household and family life, and discharge its duties and obligations. The second verse emphasises the need to follow the Sikh way of life – *rehatmaryada* – and the guru's teachings. The husband and wife must derive from gurbani the moral strength to avoid sin and to feel the presence of God in his manifold creation. The third verse emphasises non-attachment and consequent joy in the midst of wordly temptations, encouraging both to cultivate the virtue of detachment and egolessness, leading the couple to ultimate enlightenment. The fourth verse describes the stage of peace and bliss, where one will cease to be disturbed by joy or sorrow. These verses, thus, sum up the values and virtues of the ideal married life, as a journey towards perfection and salvation.

Each of the four verses of the lavan is read and then sung as the couple walks slowly around the *Guru Granth Sahib* in a clockwise direction, the groom leading. They return to their places and sit down. Three more verses are sung and the circling is repeated in the same fashion. The service concludes with the singing of the first five and last verses from the Anand Sahib (composed in Raga Ramkali) followed by the ardas. The congregation is served with kadah parsad, which is usually followed by a lunch.

Appendix

Setting up the Bachelor's Kitchen

(Exclude/ignore items you 'hate'!)

Setting up a kitchen can be confusing, tedious and in worst cases a daunting job. Its elaborate nature discourages many, making them survive on a *dabba* (delivery of home-cooked food) system or a neighbourhood mess. Yet, it's the first step towards a de-stressing activity called cooking. So here is a checklist, which can be used to buy all the raw material from a neighbouring store at one go. But again, setting up the kitchen is a one-time task, and maintaining, replenishing, and improving it is up to oneself. The more you fall in love with cooking, the more you would pay attention and the more you would innovate.

Spices and Condiments

Powder spices: Salt, red chilli powder, red chilli flakes, black pepper (kali mirch), turmeric (haldi), coriander powder (dhania powder), cumin powder (zeera powder), asafoetida (hing), garam masala, chaat masala, mango powder (amchoor).

Whole spices: Cumin seeds (zeera), coriander seeds (dhania), cloves (laung), cinnamon (dalchini), carom seeds (ajwain), bay leaves (tej patta), mustard seeds (rai), fennel seeds (saunf), green cardamom (chhoti elaichi), black cardamom (moti elaichi), dried red chillies, fenugreek seeds (methi), pomegranate seeds (anardana).

Pastes and Sauces: Ginger-garlic paste, tomato puree, ketchup, mayonnaise, soya sauce, a sandwich spread of your choice.

Cooking Mediums: Table butter, oil (I prefer sesame seed oil, called *til ka tel* or *gingelly oil*, but refined vegetable oil can be picked up, or whatever oil suits your palette), clarified butter (ghee).

Utensils

Cooking Utensils: Pressure cooker, kadhai (ideally, kadhai for frying should be kept separate from the one used for cooking), patila (both aluminium and steel – rice cooks best in an aluminium vessel), tawa, mixing bowls, wooden flat spoons, karchchi, rolling pin (chakla-belna), scissors, cutting board and a big knife, small knife for peeling/cutting, peeler, grater, pan for stir frying, a pair of tongs, small sieve for tea, soup strainer, lemon squeezer, a handled vessel (thick bottomed) for tea.

Serving Crockery: Plates, small bowls, big bowls, spoons, forks, mugs, glasses. Be as colourful and imaginative as you can in buying crockery – like square plates, colourful spoons, kitschy or graffiti merchandise. Also, if you are a romantic person, please keep a set of special crockery, you can buy as less as two pieces each of something elegant like black plates, or tall clear glasses, tall candles for evenings when you would cook for him/her at your home.

Staples

Perishables: Onions, tomatoes, potatoes, green chillies, paneer (cottage cheese), eggs, bread, milk, curd, fruits and vegetables of your choice, a pack of tissues as well.

Non-Perishables: Lentils (dals); Arhar or Toor (yellow), Moong Sabut (green), Moong Dhuli (yellow), Chane Ki Dal (gram, yellow), Malka Masoor (pink), Urad (white), Mah Ki Dal (black), Rajma (kidney beans), Lobia, Black Chhole, White Chhole (chick peas).

Instant noodles, sugar, tea leaves, coffee, rice, gram flour (besan), wheat flour (atta), corn flour, hard wheat semolina (sooji), vermicelli, macaroni, cornflakes, porridge (daliya), beaten rice flakes (chidwa or poha), dry druits, jaggery.

Foods for Common Ailments

COLD AND FEVER

Adrak Wali Chai: Grate or pound half-an-inch of ginger. In a heavy bottom pan, put grated ginger, one-and-a-half cups of water, sugar (as per taste) and one teaspoon of tea leaves. Let the mixture boil and simmer for five minutes. Then add half-a-cup of milk, and bring to a boil. Simmer for a minute, strain, and serve.

Very effective to combat fever arising from sore throat and cold.

UPSET STOMACH

Make khichdi, and have it with dahi. Best thing to have during an upset tummy. It's light, yet filling.

STOMACH ACHE

Take half-a-teaspoon of ajwain and a pinch of salt, and chew it. If you can't chew it for long, then swallow it with water. This will remove any pain due to indigestion or infections in the stomach.

SORE THROAT

Grate one inch of ginger and squeeze out the juice. Mix one tablespoon of honey into it, with a pinch of black pepper. Have a little of this mixture several times during the day. This home remedy is absolutely non-sedative, yet extremely effective.

NAUSEA

Take a pinch of black salt. It offers immediate relief from nausea and general feeling of vomiting/sickness.

Some Observations and Tips:

- If time permits, grate fresh ginger and garlic and use it instead of the readymade paste. The flavour of the dish would be much more intense and exotic.

- Ginger-garlic paste is more flavourful when added as a second ingredient, i.e., not directly into oil as it is conventionally done, but after or with the first ingredient, usually onions.

- Gingelly oil (sesame oil) is healthier than many other alternatives, try using it. It is rich in anti-oxidants, and is also known to reduce blood pressure and cholesterol levels.

- Chopped green chillies give the same spiciness to the dish as red chilli powder would do, but with a more delicate and distinct flavour. Therefore, use freshly chopped green chillies instead of red chilli powder as much as you can.

- Gravy made of chopped onions, tomatoes and chillies is tastier than that made with purees/pastes, because of its chunky texture. But again, under time constraints, pastes can be used.

- All sabut (with outer covering) dals/lentils should be well soaked, preferably overnight or in the morning, before you leave for office.

Bibliography

An Advanced History of India (R.C. Majumdar, H.C. Raychaudhuri, Kalikinkar Datta)

A History of the Sikhs Vol. I and II (Khushwant Singh)

The Sikh World (Ramesh Chander Dogra and Urmila Dogra)

Sohni Mahiwal (Fazal Shah)

Heer (Waris Shah)

The Adventures of Hir and Ranjha (Waris Shah's translation by Charles Frederick Usborne)

Love Stories from Punjab (Harish Dhillon)

Simple Guide to Sikhism (Sewa Singh Kalsi)

All about Sikhism – The Guru's teachings (Kamal Singh)

Folklore of Punjab (Sohinder Singh Bedi)

Food trails of Punjab (Yashbir Sharma)

Indus Waters Treaty (1960)

Tuzk-e-Jehangiri

The Ferozepur Gazetteer

Bulleh Shah (Dr Harbhajan and Dr Shoaib Nadvi)

Index

Harmeet

The Slim Punjabi